M000219195

"*The Obligation* is an e
who and what we a
makes me very prou.. wonc snows tnat we are indeed
capable of greatness."
—**William E. Burrows**, author of *This New Ocean*
and *The Survival Imperative*

"If you care about a better world and if you want to be part
of the change and improvement process contributing to a
better world, I strongly suggest *The Obligation* as your first
stopping off point on what will be an incredible, productive,
and rewarding journey for you."
—**Dr. David Livingston**, Host of *The Space Show*

"[It] is our goal, our duty, our "Obligation" to open the
frontier of space to human settlement and the expansion of
life beyond the Earth. There is no grander cause, no more
worthy goal than this. BUY [*The Obligation*]. READ IT. AND
TELL YOUR FRIENDS."
—**Rick Tumlinson**, Chairman, Deep Space Industries and
Co-Founder, Space Frontier Foundation

"*The Obligation* will take you to a new level of thinking. If you
want to know "why space?" or even to think about humanity's
place in the universe, then read *The Obligation*."
—**Charles Miller**, President, NexGen Space LLC

"*The Obligation* reminds us of the big picture and why we need a
philosophical approach to settling the solar system."
—**Bart Leahy** for the National Space Society *Book Reviews*

"*The Obligation* was an engrossing read that I finished in one sitting. I am eagerly looking forward to a sequel and more from Steven Wolfe as the struggle to achieve space settlement enters a particularly difficult and perhaps decisive phase."

— **Vidvuds Beldavs** for *The Space Review*

"Steven Wolfe does a brilliant job intertwining the mystery behind the human compulsion to explore the universe with the tale of a young congressional aide caught up in a romance and the political maneuvering inside the Beltway."

—**Walter Putnam,** Author and journalist

"*The Obligation* transports the reader on a creative and comprehensive voyage through the dialectics that define our nature as a space-faring species. A most inspiring narrative that I would highly recommend to anyone who is curious about the raison d'être of humankind."

—**Jim Crisafulli**, Director of the Hawaii Office of Aerospace Development

THE OBLIGATION

A Journey to Discover Human Purpose on Earth and in the Cosmos

A Novel

BY

Steven Wolfe

For Stacey, Zoe and Bram

Copyright © 2015 Steven Wolfe
All rights reserved.

Vauxhall Publishing
New York, NY
www.theobligationbook.com

Cover designed by Mitch Mondello

ISBN-10: 0-6924-4307-X
ISBN-13: 978-0-6924-4307-1

CONTENTS

ACKNOWLEDGMENTS

I owe a debt of gratitude to Frank White for his generous assistance in reviewing my manuscript and helping me to greatly improve the final product. I thank William E. (Bill) Burrows for his insightful notes on the text. I thank my brother Christopher Wolfe who is the real writer in the family. His help and encouragement were essential to bringing my manuscript to satisfactory completion. I thank my editor, Erin Medlicott, who did an excellent job cleaning up the text and making useful suggestions. I also thank other reviewers who came to my aid with corrections after the novel was initially available in eBook form, including Rand Simberg, John Walker, Jeffrey Kramer and one of my oldest friends in the space movement, Gary Oleson. I thank my brother Richard Wolfe for his honest and accurate critique, and his wife Pamela Wolfe for her creative work on an early cover design. Charlie Huettner gets credit for convincing me to finally publish a print version of the book, which you now hold in your hands. I thank Shelley Souza whose acute editing and comments on early draft chapters inspired me to redirect the structure of the story, which made for a stronger narrative. And most of all, I thank my wife Stacey who has always been both my biggest critic and biggest supporter.

THE PLAQUE

While I waited for Mr. Grant to finish editing the remarks I had written for him, my eyes wandered once again to the plaque that occupied a minor spot on the wall behind his mahogany desk. The small object was easily lost among an impressive display of photographs, awards and other mementos that chronicled a long career in politics. Its smooth surface was covered in a thick lacquer. The maple wood grain was prominent but did not obscure the engraved lettering.

In simple bold font, the plaque read: "*The colonization of space will be the fulfillment of humankind's Obligation to the Earth.*"

Mr. Grant looked up unexpectedly and caught the direction of my gaze. He paused for an instant as our eyes met. He grunted a weak smile and returned to his editing.

I was on the job a week or so when I first noticed the plaque. I didn't think much of it or the inscribed words, but I soon found myself preoccupied about its meaning and what relevance it had to Mr. Grant. When I asked other staffers they had nothing particular to say about it. I could find no one who shared my curiosity for the object.

I made up my mind that I would take the opportunity to ask Mr. Grant about the plaque during that meeting. What harm could it do? If nothing else, it was a chance to bond with the congressman on a personal level, which I'd been wanting to do anyway for some time.

I sat silently in the straight back armchair next to his desk as he read through the draft statement I had written for him to read during an appropriations subcommittee hearing on the 1992 NASA budget. The draft offered praise and support for the President's proposed agenda for NASA, and suggested some modest changes that Mr. Grant felt would help NASA better fulfill its mission.

I thought about the statement and how it compared to the inscription on the plaque. Both had to do with outer space. That much was true. Yet, the distance between the capabilities of the American space program at that time and the fanciful vision of space colonies engraved on the plaque were eons apart.

Congressman Harrison B. Grant, a Democrat from the 38st District of California, was a bear of a man. His massive hands swallowed the fountain pen he used to edit my draft. Though his suit was of quality wool and well-tailored it rumpled quickly under the stress of his brawny frame. Despite his thirty years in public office, he still looked more suited to pitching bales of hay on the Inland Empire family farm where he grew up than crafting national space policy.

I had come to work for Mr. Grant four months earlier, just out of grad school. My plan was to accrue a few years of practical Washington experience before applying to law school. National space policy was one of five broad issue areas that I staffed for the congressman though I had no particular background in the subject other than a degree in political science. I also covered health care, taxation, energy and agriculture. I was eager to learn as much as I could and welcomed the heavy workload that came with the Hill job.

When he finished his task he handed me the marked pages, "Not bad. Make these changes and we'll be all set."

As I gathered my materials, I prepared to casually ask about the plaque, but he spoke first. "Are you up to speed on the Weinstein amendment?"

"Yes," I answered after taking a moment to recall the topic. "Mr. Weinstein wants to zero out funding for the space station. I understand he's tried that before without getting much traction. Committee staff says he's not expected to be any more successful this year."

"Really? I've heard otherwise. In fact, I hear he has a damn good chance of success this time around." I squirmed, knowing my own information was probably a week old.

"A larger effort is building this year to cancel the space station altogether and I'm already feeling pressure to take sides. Weinstein and his coalition think they have a real shot this time. With NASA having already spent, or 'wasted' as they say, $10 billion on the program with little to show for it so far, they certainly have a point. Let's keep on top of that, alright?"

"Yes, of course."

Instead getting up to leave, I took the moment as planned and ask, "That plaque, Mr. Grant? I've been wondering for a while now…" I froze in mid-sentence as his face shifted from a flat expression to one of intense interest.

After a beat I continued, "…I've been wondering, what is the meaning of the saying on that small wood plaque in the corner there?" He did not turn to see where I pointed, but merely stared at me for an agonizing ten seconds without saying a word. I wanted to fill the silence, but had no facility to speak. He studied me as if he never before noticed my existence. I panicked that I had made a major blunder.

Then with a shrug he turned to another folder on his desk and sniffing dismissively said, "It's a gift I received once." He seemed to be about to add something, but only said, "I'll need those edits as soon as you can get them to me."

I should have obediently gotten up and gone about the task of updating the paper, but something held me back. Something in the way Mr. Grant stared at me for so long, as though he was sizing me up in some way. I almost felt he was deciding whether or not I was worthy to receive an explanation about the plaque, and had decided I wasn't.

Despite my better judgment, I pressed him again. "I'll get right to that, Mr. Grant. But, about the plaque. There's something very unusual about it. What is it referencing?"

With uncharacteristic intensity he glared at me. "And, why does it matter to you? It's just another quotation like thousands you see everywhere." He was impatient with me, but not angry. "Does this speak to you in some way?"

I was taken by his challenge. I stammered as he waited for my reply. "I...It doesn't particularly speak to me, but...at the same time I can't help feeling there is something familiar about the quote. I think I must have heard it before somewhere."

He studied me again as he did a moment before. "Well, forget it. It's nothing worth your remembering." He was less gruff, but still wanted to end the conversation.

I wanted to press him further, but he wouldn't allow it, saying only, "Can you have those remarks back to me in an hour?"

I assured him I would and left. Rather than satisfying my curiosity, Mr. Grant's reaction only heightened my interest in the plaque.

The amendment to cancel the space station proved to be a serious challenge. It was only two days later that a delegation of about a dozen members from the Coalition for Responsible Federal Spending, the CRFS, crowded into Mr. Grant's office to make their case. There were not enough seats for everyone to sit, so a few of the junior lobbyists and I stood along the wall.

"Every year the VA benefits get cut more and more. Brave men and women give everything for this country, and instead of taking care of their medical needs when they come home, we are spending billions on joy rides into space."

Bill Hogan, a wheelchair-bound Vietnam War veteran, got right to the point. He leaned forward with a white-knuckle hold on the arms of his chair, his face flush with emotion. Mr. Grant told Bill about his own military service and how he fought in the Battle of the Bulge in WWII. Bill respected that, and his grip relaxed.

In the eight years since Ronald Reagan had announced the space-station project, it had become what many considered an albatross around NASA's neck as costs rose and schedules slipped. It was an easy target for critics of all stripes. The best organized of the groups calling for an end to the space station was the CRFS.

"I have to tell these poor people there is no place for you. And it breaks your heart. And all we get from Washington is more cuts. How are these folks supposed to get their life back together if we can't give them a helping hand up?" Janet Bennett, a social worker from a public housing agency pleaded her cause. Mr. Grant reassured her that he would always be a strong advocate for affordable housing as he always had been.

Mr. Grant was an eager and empathetic listener as each citizen activist said their piece. The CRFS was a collection of unlikely allies united in the notion that the money the U.S. government had committed to the space station could be much better spent supporting their respective programs and agencies. The delegation was mostly grassroots activists who lived in, worked in, or had close connections to Mr. Grant's congressional district. In other words, they had real influence on his voting constituency.

"What will become of this country if we don't invest in education?" argued a fifth-grade school teacher. Two scientists from University of California at Riverside in Mr. Grant's district, a neurobiologist and a geologist, explained big budget projects like the space station were actually causing the U.S. to fall behind in basic research. There were also a conservationist and an environmental-hazard activist.

And then there was Tara Bingham, a young legislative affairs staffer with the World Conservancy Alliance. She stood out among the lobbyists as much for her attractive looks as for her intelligent input. "EPA has already reported that its current budget can only support a third of its pending investigations, delaying indefinitely many environmental cleanup operations that should be going on *right now*." She offered me a quick smile when our eyes met.

It was CRFS's Executive Director Kyle McAllister, in a pale blue seersucker suit and bow tie over his skinny frame, who summed up the issue. Tara Bingham handed a CRFS folder to Mr. Grant and one to me as McAllister spoke. "Mr. Grant, in the packet is a copy of the amendment Congressman Weinstein will offer to the HUD-IA Appropriations bill when it comes to the floor in a few weeks. We already have more than two dozen members who have co-signed this initiative. Senator Miller is preparing a similar measure in the Senate."

Mr. Grant was a statue of focused attention. HUD-IA was shorthand for Veteran Administration, Housing and Urban Development and Independent Agencies Appropriations Act. It was the catchall spending bill that Congress must pass each year in order for a range of agencies to receive funding in the coming fiscal year. The measure included funding for the National Science Foundation, the Environmental Protection Agency, as well as NASA.

McAllister continued, "With so many priorities facing our nation, many of your colleagues agree that it is time to call it quits on the space station." The assembled murmured their agreement. "We have spent over ten billion dollars on the space station and NASA does not have a single piece of flight-ready hardware to show for it. By any calculation, if we follow through with this program, we will be committing taxpayers to spending over a hundred billion dollars before this project is done. Let's be honest, this project represents a cash cow for the military-industrial complex. It's time to recognize the folly of this expense, and put the resources where they can do the most good for this country. That's what the Weinstein amendment would do, and we need your support." The group was energized by McAllister's words. "Mr. Grant, we have an obligation to spend taxpayers' money as responsibly as possible."

Obligation. My eyes went to the plaque that hung on the wall in plain sight, and for a few moments the dialogue in the room faded as people chimed in to reinforce McAllister's statement.

"*The colonization of space will be the fulfillment of humankind's Obligation to the Earth.*"

I wondered if anyone had noticed the inscribed message whose stated goal was in such contrast to the purpose of the CRFS. The obligation McAllister spoke of was an obligation that government had to its people, or on a more basic level, it was an obligation people had to each other. That kind of obligation I could understand. The plaque had certainly become an annoying fascination, and one whose meaning I was eager to comprehend.

When I broke my gaze from the plaque I saw Mr. Grant looking directly at me. His expression showed no disapproval at my lapse of attention. I felt he knew where my mind had wandered to.

Kyle's forceful voice brought Mr. Grant's and my full attention back to the moment. "Federal support for the constituencies we represent have been eroding shamelessly. Your voting record has been very positive on these issues over the years. That's why it would be an enormous help to our respective causes if you would join us and oppose continuation of this wasteful program."

Mr. Grant rubbed his chin and cheek, "Well, Kyle, as you know, I am and will continue to be an aggressive advocate for your causes." At this he scanned the room making eye contact with each person, his searching sincerity defusing any tension.

"This is one of those decisions that I dread making, but it is the very reason I am here in Washington. As much as I will support full funding in each of your priorities, and as much as I agree that the space station project has been poorly managed up this point, this is an important vote. I will need to spend more time discussing this amendment with other Members in the House and Senate, as well as other constituents, before I can commit one way or the other. And I must add that you have all done a marvelous job of making your case, and for that I am very thankful."

He paused, looked at me and said, "And now I am being signaled that I am already late for my next appointment." I had given no such signal.

Kyle attempted to keep the conversation going, but all Mr. Grant did was nod politely as he excused himself from the room, saying before he walked out the door, "John is my lead staff on space policy. Please direct any questions or comments to him for his very capable response." As the gathering turned and blinked in my direction, Mr. Grant slipped from the room through the side door.

It was after seven that evening when I went into Mr. Grant's empty office to leave a memo brief on his desk for his review. It had gotten to a point where I could not enter his office without being drawn to the plaque. On that evening however, the plaque was not there. It had been removed from the wall. A quick scan of the area revealed that the plaque sat face down on the short cabinet. After depositing the brief into Mr. Grant's in-box, I slipped behind his desk and carefully lifted the wooden object of my curiosity for a closer examination. There was nothing particularly remarkable about it. I was certain that over the years Mr. Grant had received enough awards and plaques to fill the wall behind his desk ten times over. So why, I wondered, did he select this particular item to showcase? And why now did he choose to take it down?

Without warning, the door that led directly to the corridor opened with a loud clatter. Mr. Grant stood there startled by my presence behind his desk with plaque in hand. He relaxed once he sized up the moment while I remained in a state of mortification. I fumbled to quickly replace the object to its position on the cabinet where I found it. He just chuckled.

"I'm sorry, Mr. Grant. I was just…"

"Don't worry about it, John. Have a seat. Let's chat for a moment." I wanted only to leave for all my embarrassment, but dutifully sat down.

While he studied me, I tried to explain myself. "I'm sorry. I'm just curious what the quote is referencing. Maybe if I knew the author…"

"The author… yes. I suppose that would help. I am not sure who that is, unfortunately. The plaque was a gift from a friend. I've always found it… inspiring."

"Yes, I agree." In truth, I was neither inspired nor uninspired. Just unusually curious. "But, I don't quite understand what the quote is trying to convey. In what way is space colonization an *obligation* that humanity owes to Earth? It doesn't make sense to me."

"Hmm. I can see where that notion would be confusing. And I don't know if I can give you a meaningful answer at the moment, particularly with it being so late."

Another surge of embarrassment ran through me. "Yes, of course. I wasn't expecting a lengthy explanation… Maybe another time. It's not important. I was just curious, is all…"

I started to get up, but he stopped me. "Now just a minute. Don't rush off. Believe it or not, this actually *is* important—*very important*. I'm impressed that you have taken an interest in the plaque, but I can't quite tell if giving you a full answer would be worth the effort." He leaned forward.

"The question is: how much do you care to know its full meaning?...Would you say that you *need* to know the answer?"

Maybe it was the way he asked the question, but in that moment, I felt something shift inside, and became a bit light headed. I sensed a strange combination of exhilaration and dread in this question. I opened my mouth slightly in preparation of forming a response, but he cut me off.

"Don't answer now. Think about it. If you're still interested, ask me again and we'll see where we go from there." He smiled broadly as I puzzled for a response.

"Now, if you don't mind, John, I have a few calls to make."

"Yes, Mr. Grant."

It was always the same. I felt myself falling from an extremely high altitude though there was no sensation of rushing air. Only silence. The topography spread out far below. I looked to the horizon at the pronounced curvature. The sun blazed just above the horizon, but otherwise the sky was black. I could make out stars and the moon that looked so close I could almost touch them.

It was only after I awoke that I could consciously tell myself that I had dreamt about flying in orbit around the Earth. In the dream, however, there were no such labels, only the experience and the sheer wonderment of it. It was so peaceful. I regretted in those first few moments after waking that it was only a dream. I was ten years old the first time the dream invaded my sleep.

The dream was always the same until the night Mr. Grant asked if I needed to know about the plaque. That night I was once again immersed in the bliss of orbiting the Earth. Sun shining. Moon in full view. Then the words came, like a strong breeze in my mind, *"The colonization of space will be the fulfillment of humankind's obligation to the Earth."* The words acted like a catapult, propelling me higher and higher. I was moving with increasing speed away from the Earth and past the moon. Speeding out of the solar system and among the rushing stars which became denser in number until I finally came to rest, as odd as it sounds, enmeshed in the very fabric of the galaxy itself. I could see the stars sparkling on and in my translucent hands and arms. My body was just an indistinct outline, seeming at the same time to be part of the galaxy and the galaxy itself.

I sat up in bed for a long while recalling the details and vividness. I had heard those words in other orbital dreams, many times long before I ever saw the plaque.

THE NEED TO KNOW

Tara Bingham, the World Conservancy Alliance lobbyist, had long dark hair and an athletic body, judging from the toned arms exposed by her sleeveless dress. I was certainly attracted to her at the meeting with the CRFS delegation, but didn't give her much thought until I ran into her the next day outside the Natural Resources Committee Hearing room. She seemed as glad to see me as I was to see her again. We joked a little about the size of the group that packed into Mr. Grant's office and Bill Hogan's overly impassioned appeal.

"I'm glad I ran into you. The Alliance just decided to invite your boss to speak at our global climate change conference in Tucson next month. It would be a great chance for him to share his views on how to best ensure the long-term health of the environment. That sort of thing." Though global climate change was a minor policy issue at the time, Mr. Grant was already a strong supporter of more research into the veracity of global warming trends data, as well as the long-term implications.

I told her it sounded like a great opportunity, and explained our office policy that all speaking invitations needed to be in writing. She agreed to get something over to me in a day or so.

In those few minutes, I became completely taken with her. The attraction was certainly physical. The clean lines of her face and body were easy to look at. But, it was the humor mixed with an intensity of purpose I found even more appealing. Seizing the moment, I found myself sputtering an invitation to lunch. "Say, how about, uh, I mean, do you have any plans for lunch? I thought maybe if you weren't..."

"Lunch? Sure. Why don't we meet in the Rayburn Cafeteria in at 12:30?" She gave me a smile and slipped back into the hearing room.

We picked up some sandwiches in the cafeteria in the Rayburn Building, and decided to picnic on a bench in the small park across 'C' Street adjacent to the south side of the building. She got a crab cake sandwich and I had turkey and tomato on a roll. I would have been satisfied to sit in the cafeteria, but Tara insisted we get outside. It was a beautiful spring day.

"Everything is really blooming now," she said. I looked around at the manicured park space, with a stone fountain at the center. It was quiet oasis from the chaos on the Hill. Though I had passed that park many times, I had never stopped to take it in. I was feeling at ease with Tara. She identified for me the trees and flowers that were close by. I was perfectly content to listen to the sound of her voice as she lectured on the park's botany. The sun danced in her hair, as it swayed with her expressive movements. Her lips frequently stretched to expose her irresistible smile.

"How did you get stuck working on the NASA budget anyway?" She asked the question playfully as the conversation ambled back to issues of the Hill. "NASA is *not* the hot issue at the moment."

"Yeah, I suppose you're right. Being the new guy on staff I didn't have much to say about it. Still, I have to admit, I'm finding the topic fascinating." I didn't tell her that it was the chance to work on space policy that attracted me to the job.

"Don't tell me you're one of those space geeks," she poked.

"Hey, if you play your cards right, I might let you see my Spock ears," I replied, as I turned my head to one side striking a pose, which got her to let out a delicious laugh.

Swallowing another bite of her sandwich, Tara said, more seriously, "I have to say, though, I never cease to be amazed at the amount of money we're spending on the space program? It's something like $13 billion a year."

"$14.2 billion, actually. And that's not counting how much DOD spends on space projects."

"You see!" She jabbed me in the arm. "That's *a lot* of money that could do so much good in other areas. All the Weinstein amendment is asking for is to transfer just a couple billion from that budget."

"I hear you, but it's not my call. The Coalition has a good argument. The space station could wait until other priorities are met. Or perhaps we should encourage the private sector to invest in a space station and run it for profit. Then NASA could just pay for the space services it needs." I stopped short of saying that I agreed with that logic. "But, of course, it's Mr. Grant's decision. I have to support whatever he decides."

She reached over and put her hand on my arm. "You probably have more influence than you think. But sure, you wouldn't want to do anything to compromise your integrity. I completely respect that. I just feel a sense of obligation to those in need and to future generations, and that maybe a space station is a luxury we can't afford right now."

"Yes, of course. It is an *obligation*," I repeated. The strange conversations I had with Mr. Grant about the plaque came back to me, and his cryptic response about the plaque's meaning. Did I *need* to know its meaning, as he asked? Of course, I didn't *need* to know. That was a nonsense question.

"Hey, are you still with me?" I had lingered on the thought a little too long and Tara noticed.

I was looking at a distant flower bed, feeling very relaxed. "Sure, never left."

She laughed. "Funny, you look like...Have you ever meditated before?"

This pulled me back to the moment, "Uh, no. Why?"

"It's just the way you look... It's that look people get when they are in a meditative state."

"Don't know what to say to that. I don't think I would go for saying 'Om' if that's what you mean."

"Well, you could meditate that way if you want. But...here, let me show you a really simple way to do it." Without waiting for my agreement, she began to instruct me. "Just sit in a relaxed position."

"Don't I have to sit cross legged or something?" She assured me it wasn't necessary. If the park hadn't been nearly empty, I'm sure I would have been more reluctant to follow her lead.

"Now close your eyes. Take a deep breath." Her voice became soft as she guided me. "Put your attention on your breath. Be aware of each in-breath. Now the out-breath. That's it...Now imagine you are lying on a beach and there is an ocean of relaxation, and the tide is coming in. First it washes over your feet. Your feet feel deeply relaxed. Feel the relaxation. Now it washes over your ankles." As I followed Tara's visualization instruction, my body responded with wave after wave of relaxation until the imagined ocean reached the top of my head. I had never felt so relaxed.

She went silent, and the space she drew me into felt expansive. For a few moments there was deep comfort and tranquility. Then, in the absence of Tara's soothing voice, my own thoughts began to intrude and dissect the experience, dissipating the sense of wholeness. After a few minutes, she said, "Okay, when you're ready, you can open your eyes."

When I fluttered my eyes open, the scene in the park looked a little more vibrant than it had earlier. I turned my head to Tara, who was laughing at me. She seemed to glow as well, looking more beautiful. I laughed along with her, and felt a little embarrassed.

"Man, you're an easy one. You sure you never did this before?"

"What did I do?"

That short meditation made me feel a bit lighter and more comfortable with Tara. And somehow, the response to Mr. Grant's challenge seemed quite obvious.

"You'll need to write a floor speech for the Weinstein amendment," Mr. Grant announced after summoning me to his office.

"Then you'll be supporting the amendment?" He hadn't previously given me a clear indication either way on the issue, but had dropped hints that he would likely give in to pressure to vote in favor of the measure to cancel the space station.

"What? Support the amendment? Of course not." The irritation in his voice sent my adrenaline flowing. "We have too many allies in California and around the country who are counting on my 'No' vote. There may not be much NASA money spent in my district, but overall twenty-five percent of all NASA's budget is spent in California, so we need to be supportive of our state delegation. You should know that." My face went red with this reprimand.

"And, you never know," he added impishly, "the space station just might turn out to be a worthwhile investment." We shared a smile, which put me at ease again.

"We need a balanced message," he continued, "that won't set me apart from the intentions of the CRFS members. I want to express my deep support for their respective programs. At the same time, we must outline the three main reasons why keeping the space station program going is so important to the country and the world. Got that?"

"Yes. But, so I'm clear. Just what are the three main reasons to keep the space station going...in your opinion?"

"Well, John... that's your job, isn't it?" His mouth curled in a mischievous smile. "I'm sure you'll come up with a very compelling argument."

That would have been the end of the meeting had the plaque not caught my eye.

I stood to leave, but turned back to Mr. Grant. "And regarding the plaque, my answer is yes. I mean… I do need to know."

I had wanted to be casual. But the awkwardness left Mr. Grant momentarily confused. I stammered a fuller explanation. When he realized what I was getting at, he frowned and leaned back in his chair.

"Ah, yes. The plaque!" He sounded slightly annoyed that I had bothered him again with the topic. He turned his body toward the object, and then looked at me with a worried expression on his face. My anxiety heightened.

"Few people even notice it. Most people who do don't give it a second thought. But every once in a while, it gets its hooks into someone." He paused to look at the plaque again for a long few moments.

Finally, with melancholy in his voice, he continued, "For thousands of years men have been captivated by the idea of space travel. Today, we squabble like idiots over whether or not to build a space station, when we should stand in awe that we are even capable of such a feat. For millennia, before Apollo and Vostok, humankind wondered what secrets the heavens held for us. In the twentieth century some folks began to view space as not only an intriguing place to travel, but also as a place where humanity might start new civilizations." There was a low intensity in his voice that disarmed me in a similar way Tara had done on the park bench. Mr. Grant smiled at me and continued, "I think a lot about our world. How the Apollo astronauts took the first pictures of the whole planet in one frame, showing how very small the Earth is in the vast ocean of space. In the last hundred years we've pulled back the veil on the solar system, replacing a mystery with an amazing reality. We've calculated the physical composition of the solar system and the resources that it holds. With that information, the idea that we could use those resources to develop large bases and eventually colonies on the moon and Mars and other places became a reasonable goal…and, well, it has become a fascination of mine."

I was taken by the grand attributes he assigned the words on the plaque and how intrigued he was by the idea of space colonization. But, there was still something I didn't understand.

"Wow… I see the possibilities too. I've always wondered where we would be today if we didn't cancel the Apollo program… Still, I keep coming back to the part of the plaque that says that space colonies will be the fulfillment of an *Obligation*. I still don't get just what that means."

He had a smile on his face. "Well, that's the whole point of this conversation, isn't it? That's the essence of the meaning that you've decided that you *need* to know. Unfortunately getting to that understanding is a much longer process, and you'll have to be clear with me that you are willing to put in the effort to make that discovery."

I was confused. I was looking for a short answer, or perhaps a book title I could go get from the library. What real effort could there be? Mr. Grant seemed to recognize my bafflement and stared at me again for a long time. He must have seen the doubt on my face because he finally concluded, "No, John. My recommendation is that you leave it alone. It's best to think about space colonization, if you think of it at all, as just a really cool thing that humankind will one day achieve. Enjoy the sci-fi novels and movies about space travel for now, and leave it at that."

Something boiled up in me in response to Mr. Grant's dismissal. It was part anger at some judgment he seemed to be making about my character or sincerity. It was also a feeling that something very important was slipping through my fingers that if I didn't grasp for it firmly right then and there I might lose it forever.

"I'm willing to put in the effort, Mr. Grant. Whatever is required. I don't understand what that will involve, but if you want a commitment from me to put in some effort in order to understand the meaning of the plaque, I'm willing to do what it takes." This all came out in a desperate rush that took both Mr. Grant and me by surprise.

"And why is that?" he demanded in a low tone.

"I…I…I've heard those words before. In my dreams. Many times. At least I'm pretty sure I have. Even before I came to work here."

He studied me again, wide eyed. "I see. All right then. I suppose we have no choice then. The choiceless choice is always the best kind. You have no idea what you're getting yourself in for, but let's give it a try. There is a lot of information you must absorb. In order for it to make sense, you must be completely open and receptive to whatever is presented to you. Can you do that?" I nodded my agreement to the condition.

"Whatever is required is strictly between you and me. No one else needs to know. And, of course, you must not let your regular work here suffer in any way. Is that understood?" Again, I eagerly assured him it was, even as a sharp twinge of apprehension twisted in my gut.

"Now, let's see," he asked himself aloud. After searching a corner of the room for an idea, his eyebrows went up as he came to a decision, "Chip Johnson. That's it. That's who you should see first."

"Chip Johnson? The astronaut?"

He shifted in his chair and leaned toward me, "If you are interested in knowing the full meaning of the plaque and the Obligation, you'll have to first understand why some people are so passionate about space travel. Talk to Chip and ask him about the source of his passion for spaceflight, and listen carefully to his reply. But—and this is important—do not ask him about the plaque. That will come later. After you speak to Chip, let me know and we can talk more at greater length. Does that sound okay to you?"

Bewildered, I nodded in agreement.

"Good!" And just as abruptly, he said no more on the subject and waved me out of his office.

I sat at my desk for a long while not quite sure what I had just committed myself to.

I woke in the dim predawn hour in my room. Tara's form lay next to me motionless in a deep sleep. It was four AM, and the street lamps cast just enough light to illuminate Tara's tranquil features. The simple but attractive lines of her face reflected her inner strength. Her straight black hair swept across her chin. The sheet carelessly covered her naked body from the waist down, allowing me to admire once more the wonderfully taut curves of her torso. She twitched, adjusted herself and became motionless again.

Things had moved much more quickly between us than I had expected. There was certainly a mutual physical attraction. But, the ease we had with each other made all the difference.

I had called her the previous afternoon on a whim to grab a few minutes of small talk. Without expecting much, I asked her to dinner that night and she agreed. I wasn't really pushing for anything to happen. I was perfectly happy to settle into a leisurely courtship that could eventually, I hoped, lead to something more intimate. I don't think either of us thought things would progress so quickly on the first date.

We shared a pizza and a pitcher of sangria at Machiavelli's Restaurant on Pennsylvania Ave, SE, a few blocks from the Hill. It was late. We both had worked past eight PM, and in some unspoken way decided to relieve the stress of our demanding jobs by indulging in pure silliness.

"Open up. Come on, open up." Holding up a chunk of sangria-soaked apple I coaxed her to open her mouth so I could take a shot. I was proud of my ability to toss bits of food into peoples' mouths at a distance, and wanted to demonstrate. She would only open her mouth into a narrow circle and with her eyes wide she swayed her head back and forth. She was not making it easy for me to make the shot. "Curse you!" I cried in mock frustration. Laughing uncontrollably, I tossed the piece of fruit and bopped her on the left nostril. The rebounding morsel landed onto the pizza at the table next to ours. It hit the edge of the pie and skittered across the mushroom and black olive toppings before coming to rest on the red and white checkered tablecloth between our co-patrons. Tara and I apologized while vainly trying to suppress our laughter. Our fellow diners were not amused and asked to be moved to another table, and demanded a fresh pie. This only made us laugh harder. We were eighth graders in trouble. And it was wonderfully delinquent.

We left the restaurant still amused with ourselves. About three blocks away, on the first quiet street we came to, we embraced for the first time. We kissed and joked and pressed our bodies into one another. Finally, Tara announced that she just *had* to walk me home to make sure I got there safely, Captain's orders. I dutifully obeyed.

As much as I liked the playful side of Tara, I was even more taken by the intensity of her passion for what she believed. After love making, we sat up for a long while talking about issues that were important to us. She talked about biodiversity and the destruction of the rain forests and the changing climate. I did my best to hold up my end of these conversations, and she patiently explained aspects of the issues not familiar to me. I was humbled by her depth of knowledge and commitment.

In turn, she wanted to know what I cared about, and

what I really thought of the space program. This question brought me back to Mr. Grant's plaque and odd instructions to speak with an Apollo astronaut.

I sat up and scratched my head, and decided to confide my true feelings on the topic. "I guess space travel has always been a strong interest."

Her head cocked at my admission. Sleepily, she said "You really are a space geek. I knew it."

"I'm just old enough to remember the Apollo missions. Even at that age I was captivated. My favorite toy was Billy Blastoff, you know. He was a little guy in a space suit. And the batteries in the backpack powered his different vehicles, like a mini space shuttle, a moon rover and a jet pack." She listened to me reminisce, snuggling close.

"Even then I was into space infrastructure." She smiled with eyes fading, and I went on. "I remember when I heard the Apollo program was being canceled. It seemed strange and painful to me. I didn't understand why everyone wasn't as disappointed as I was." Her eyes were closed, but I continued just the same. Her eyelashes tickled the hair on my forearm. "I wanted to be an astronaut. I applied for the Air Force Academy. I didn't get in. I could have joined Air Force ROTC, but that held less interest for me. Law made more sense. I was better at writing papers than doing physics labs anyway. But, through it all there has always been something about space travel that really interested me."

She stirred, and looked up. "I want to fly in space. Especially with you!" She grinned. Then her voice took on a serious tone. "Promise me something. Let's make a deal that we don't let what you're doing for NASA and what I'm doing for the environment come between us." The thought hadn't even occurred to me that such a divide were possible. Perhaps it should have.

"I can agree with that. But, you had me worried for a second. I thought you were going to ask me to stop wearing my Spock ears. And that I will never agree to." With that I leaned in for another caress. As I kissed her neck, she chuckled, "Billy Blastoff? For real?"

As I waited for her to awake, I considered again the compact I had made with Mr. Grant. It all seemed harmless enough, but all so strange. What would an Apollo astronaut have to tell me? I wanted to share the story with Tara, but decided to wait and see what actually happened.

THE WANDERER

It was two days after Mr. Grant had instructed me to speak with Chip Johnson, and I had made no attempt to reach out to the famous astronaut. Tara was clearly a distraction. I was also feeling some apprehension about the unusual purpose of my meeting with the national hero. But if I had any notion of dropping the matter, Mr. Grant had other ideas.

That morning, Cheryl Gordon, Mr. Grant's appointment secretary, intercepted me. She handed me a piece a paper, "Here. I made a reservation for you and Chip Johnson at this restaurant for one o'clock today."

"But, why? I didn't ask…"

Initially surprised at my response, Cheryl's features softened and a smile came to her lips, "I see… So, you didn't know Mr. Grant had asked me to make this reservation," she wryly surmised. "You'll have to get used to this sort of thing. If he wants you to do something and doesn't think you're getting to it fast enough, he'll just make the arrangements and let you know where to be. He's done it to everyone. So, don't sweat it. Just don't miss that lunch."

Chip Johnson still exuded the roguish enthusiasm of the swaggering test pilot he had been in his early career. At sixty-seven, he was as fit and nimble as many active astronauts. Though he was mostly retired, Boeing kept him on payroll for times when contract negotiations needed a little star power to win a bid.

As I greeted him at the entrance to the DuPont Circle restaurant, he explained that I was doing him a favor because it helped him keep up his "quota of power lunches that the Boeing brass keeps tabs on."

The hostess greeted Chip by name. He flirted with her while she escorted us to our table toward the back of the restaurant. Chip sat with his back to the wall. He must have preferred that position, as his gaze frequently swept the dining room. Our lunch was interrupted several times by people he knew who came over to say hello. He clearly enjoyed being in public.

"Boeing has the right solution for managing the space station program and getting it back on track, Johnny." I generally disliked being called 'Johnny,' but hearing Chip Johnson use the nickname made me feel I was part of his club. I knew Boeing was in the running to be named the prime contractor for the space station, so it wasn't surprising he would want to talk about the project.

He had placed on the table between my cobb salad and his lamb chops a table-top flip chart and was walking me through the dog-and-pony presentation for Boeing's proposed design and construction of the space station.

"This will be one sweet program. Now, I know there've been a few false starts with the station, but once the White House and Congress settle on a configuration, it should be the start of an exciting new era for spaceflight." I was enthralled by the personal attention. That I had already seen the Boeing presentation at a recent subcommittee hearing didn't matter. My head swelled even more when Chip mentioned how impressed he was by the quality of my questions. "I don't talk to many Hill staffers who can get into the details at that level."

At the same time, I detected a half-heartedness in his presentation. His words at times contradicted his body language in subtle ways. I wondered if I was the problem. After all, why would he want to waste a lunch with a junior staff like me? But, that wasn't it. There was something about the presentation itself that seem to stick in his throat.

Chip was much more animated after he put the flip chart away and began sharing anecdotes about his astronaut and test pilot days. He clearly enjoyed having an eager audience for his stories. I was so captivated I had nearly forgotten to raise the subject that was the purpose of our lunch until it was nearly over. Chip so dominated the conversation that it became very difficult to know how to redirect our discussion.

When Chip signaled for the check, I panicked. Not only did I feel foolish for having waited so long, but the very subject matter made me anxious. There was nothing I could do at that point except blurt it out.

"Chip, I do have something else to ask…" In my hesitation he smiled and said, "You better shoot, son. You already cocked the trigger."

"It's something Mr. Grant asked me to discuss with you regarding the space program… Specifically, why is it exactly that you are so passionate about space?"

"Oh, yes. Seems I recall Harry mentioning that you might want to talk about that kind of stuff." He smiled with a knowing sideways glance at me. He collected himself and seemed to mentally shift gears before continuing. "For starters, I guess you could say I'm just a country boy who always wanted to see what's on the other side of the hill."

"But can you explain why you're so excited about space and what drove you to get into space program?"

His grin was replaced by a thoughtful frown, "Well, let's see. Can't say I get that kind of question often. But, I guess,

if you're asking me serious, I'd have to say the same thing.
I just want to see what's on the other side of the hill. Like
Star Trek, you know: *go where no man has gone before.*

"I always loved flying planes, and pushing the edge of
the envelope nearly every day. But, the space program was
something else altogether. I had always had this thing about
wanting to go places completely different, first where *I* had
never gone, then where no one *I knew* had ever gone, then
where *hardly anyone* else had ever gone. But somehow it was
never enough. When I got the chance to be part of the space
program, I just knew I had to be part of it. But, it wasn't the
test pilot side of me that wanted to go to space...it was the
wanderer side. The side that just wanted to get to some other
place that people had never been before. Hell, just about
every place on this planet, somebody's already been. The
tallest mountains, the north and south poles, deep oceans.
Somehow none of these places had the same attraction to me
as space, and the moon especially."

"So, I think I get what you're saying," I interjected.
"Your passion for space stems from a desire to *see* what no
one has seen before." By this point, Chip had paid the check
and we were getting up to leave. I kicked myself for putting
this part of the discussion off for so long. Now, I was about
to lose the chance to get what I needed from him.

"You've got part of it, Johnny," he said as we walked out
to the sidewalk. "I see we are not quite finished with this
interview. Why don't we walk for a bit?" I was relieved that
he sensed my desire to keep the discussion going. We walked
generally in the direction of the Smithsonian and the Mall.

"Yes," he continued as we strolled, "I wanted to see
what hadn't been seen before, but I was much more excited
about *going* myself where no one has been. You see the
difference. I don't know why that is, it's just the way I feel."
It was during the walk that his good-old-boy banter faded,
revealing a more thoughtful intellect better reflecting his
Princeton education.

"Funny you bring this up. It's the type of question I don't get much, but in my old age, I think about quite often." Chip needed no further prompting. A contemplative monologue took hold and easily flowed from him.

"The way I see it, it's part of human makeup to want to roam, to wander to other places. It's part of our curious nature, but much more. Just think where we'd be if we didn't have this *need* to wander? We would have become extinct before we ever left the plains of Africa, or wherever the hell we started out. Now, not everyone feels strongly about wandering, of course. Some folk will never have any desire to leave their own backyard. We know that. But, there are always some guys, and gals I suppose, that have this urge. They were the ones who chose to go on voyages of discovery throughout history. In prehistoric times they were the scouts who searched for more fertile hunting grounds. In the Middle Ages it was the men who sailed the tall ships of Europe that braved the vast oceans to discover new lands for their kings. You can also look to the Lewis and Clark expedition across this continent. These are some obvious examples, but every age has their wandering sailors and explorers.

"You see, Johnny, we needed to have this drive to see what was beyond our vision, over the hill, on the other side of the ocean—whatever—so that we would eventually wander to every part of this planet, for better or worse. And that's exactly what we did. The funny thing is, now that we reached the end of where we can wander on this planet, the desire doesn't just go away. That desire is still a part of us, and without any land left to explore, we are naturally turning our attention that way," he said, pointing his thumb upward.

"As I said, that desire to wander is a human trait that has enabled us to diversify our population geographically, which had a powerful impact on mankind's long-term survival and growth. Sometimes we wandered to unknown regions because of necessity—scarcity of food, natural disasters, threat of neighboring tribes. Later in our evolution, the prospect of a better and new way of life was as strong a motivator. If we did not develop this uniquely human interest in wandering to other locations, we might well have irrationally stayed in one place regardless of the threats, with the ultimate result of our early extinction."

We turned a corner and just ahead of us was the Smithsonian Air and Space Museum.

He continued, "I guess what I feel is the same as what people have felt down through the ages. Whether it was the tribal villager who wondered what might be beyond the hunting grounds, or the person who lived near the water who wondered what was across the sea. Now that I think about it, it's not so much the wanting to get to a new place as much as it is the excitement of not knowing what to expect on the other side.

"It's like they say, I suppose: It's not the destination, but the journey that counts. But there has to be a place, a specific place that we are journeying to. It's not enough just to be on the road, if you see what I mean. My journey took me to the moon, and I was glad that I had that chance. But, I still feel I would have liked to have gone further."

We arrived at the museum, and without discussion, entered the building.

"But my wandering spirit," he went on, "is not just about me. I actually believe a lot of the NASA press releases. I know I went to the moon as a representative of the human race. Hell, I represented the whole damned planet."

We casually mingled among the relics of the Space Age that once was. A few tourists spotted Chip and asked for autographs, but for the most part no one recognized the aging hero of America's first steps into space.

Chip became silent. Clearly his reflections were not the usual topic for him. Whether he simply loved to talk on any subject, or he was experiencing some kind of release through this discussion, I couldn't really tell.

We had strolled up to an exhibit that included a picture

of Chip in his prime and the two other astronauts on his Apollo flight crew. He stared at the photograph for nearly a minute saying nothing.

Still gazing at the picture, he said, "When I was up there looking out the window at the Earth, really seeing the whole planet in one view, I was mesmerized. I looked and looked. And then I had the strangest experience. My whole body seemed to go numb. My head opened and expanded. I felt this unbelievable sense of connection to the planet. I felt *I was the human race* looking back on the world, rather than just one guy. That feeling stayed with me for a long while as I went about my duties. Eventually, I heard about other astronauts who had similar experiences. A guy even gave it a name. Frank White, I think his name is. He calls it the Overview Effect."

He lingered in some memory for a moment before continuing. "I never felt more fulfilled—before or since— than during that time. And it wasn't the fame or the money or the history books or any of that bullshit. In a heartbeat I would give up everything I've gotten if I could only be a part of that again." He paused, and then apparently snapped out of his reverie, turning to me saying, "To be honest, Johnny, I could give a rat's ass about the space station. Not that it's not important. It certainly is for the all the reasons we talked about. But, we've been to the moon. That's where we should be building a base, and planning trips for Mars and other interesting rocks around this old solar system. Spending billions on a tin can in low Earth orbit so we have a place to send the Shuttle just doesn't make a bit of sense." Then he leaned into my face and said, "And if you ever tell anyone I said that, I'll skin you alive, son." He laughed at my startled reaction. "Don't worry, Johnny. It's no fun if I'm not doing something to piss off the brass every once in a while." We shared a laugh at that.

I wanted to get back to my initial question. "So it's the thrill of exploration that motivates you?"

He turned to me and said, "Yeah, though I prefer the term *wanderer*. And it's not a thrill so much as it is the feeling of fulfillment, and the satisfaction of knowing that I was fulfilling something not just for my own gratification. That I am fulfilling some purpose for the whole human race. I'm not sure how to really communicate that."

He paused looking searchingly into my face. Then suddenly, his signature broad smile appeared on his face. He let out a hoarse laugh and patted me on the shoulder.

"Johnny, you really got this old test pilot going there, didn't you? I hope it all didn't come out like a bunch o' sappy gibberish to you. Just remember, it's the wanderer in us that drives us to reach for the stars. See if Harry Grant is okay with that answer. And another thing: make sure he votes against that stupid Weinstein amendment."

We made our way to curb, and with an exaggerated wave of his hand, Chip declared, "We'll see you on the Hill, Johnny," and he walked back in the direction of his office.

"I met with Chip Johnson, by the way," I casually mentioned as I walked with Mr. Grant to the subcommittee hearing room. The hearing was on the post-Shuttle launch alternatives NASA was studying.

"Oh, good. So what did he say?" A heightened eagerness came to his voice. As I began to share the details of my visit with the astronaut, I was aware that Mr. Grant had changed our course that took us out of the Rayburn Building. It was a sunny day, and we walked over to the grounds of the Capitol Building.

"We have some time, I think. Let's chat out here for a bit. So continue." We sat down on a bench and I did my best to relate the main points of my conversation with Chip Johnson. It was difficult to keep eye contact with Mr. Grant, who had never been so interested in what I had to say.

"The Wanderer," he said forcefully after a pause at the end of my report. "That's as good an explanation as any of the Wanderer Endowment."

"The Wanderer Endowment?..."

"Yes, this Wanderer trait that Chip talked about is an Endowment that emerged in human consciousness early in our development." He paused to allow that to sink in. Ignoring my puzzled look, he explained further, "All species in biology are good at spreading their life in all directions that will sustain them. So the Wanderer Endowment is linked to this primal function. The difference is that in humans, this primal tendency is evolved to incorporate the cognitive faculties of our developed intellect. Once we developed the ability to think abstractly, we could conceptualize, and even fantasize, what life would be like at some far distant location, over land or across the sea...or in outer space."

It was difficult for me to get used to this new side of Mr. Grant's personality that he was sharing with me. His paleontological lecture on the development of human consciousness starkly contrasted with his congressional persona. Nonetheless, I was deeply drawn into the distinctions he was making.

"I can see the logic in what Chip and you are saying: the passion for space is based on the instinctual desire to wander. I kind of get that. But what does all this have to do with the saying on the plaque?"

"Before we can discuss the Obligation, you must first understand the nature of all of the Endowments."

"*All* of the Endowments. How many are there?"

"Six" He smiled. My feeling of overwhelm was mixed with an intense interest to know more.

"Six? ...Well, can you tell me what they are? Maybe I can look them up."

"The best way to learn about the Endowments is to spend time with those who embody the essence of each Endowment. Chip represented the Wanderer Endowment.

Spending time in his presence communicated as strong a message about the Endowment as anything he said. So if you are interested in these matters, you'll have to meet with a representative of each Endowment."

He paused and looked at me for a response. I can only imagine the stupefied look I must have had on my face, because after a few seconds of silence, Mr. Grant burst into a huge belly laugh.

I really wanted to share with Tara the plaque, the Endowments and all of it. I'm sure I would have if our relationship hadn't taken a turn for the worse. I didn't want the Weinstein amendment to come between us, and I know she didn't either. In hindsight, it probably was inevitable. Our conflicting allegiances came to a head on a Saturday night.

I met Tara for Ethiopian food before heading to party with her environmentalist friends. At first we clicked, just as we had a few days earlier. Eating Ethiopian with my fingers was a new experience. Playfully, she demonstrated how to pick up the stewed meats and vegetables with a piece of *injera,* a spongy flatbread. I followed her instructions, but still managed to drop food on my shirt and trousers, to her amusement.

Our conversation easily shifted from celebrity gossip to the serious issues of the day. But, eventually the conversation turned to the Weinstein amendment, and that's where things always got sticky.

"You're just not stating clearly why we need to spend a hundred billion over the next twenty years on the space station. I mean, I have no doubt it will produce valuable research data, but how can a single research facility possibly justify that kind of expense, no matter how valuable the research?"

Our discussions on this topic always went right up to the

line of argument, and we were about to go over it.

I found myself vigorously defending my position. "There are the scientific arguments, and there are the political arguments. As unsavory as it might be, the space station is an important economic driver for many states around the country. The political will is squarely on the side of continuing the program. Your coalition is strong, but ultimately, dismantling the space station budget and spreading the savings around to these other programs will not have enough of an impact to influence enough Members to go to the mat in support of the amendment." I wished I hadn't given a rebuttal. I could see the humor drain from her face as I drove home my stupid point.

We agreed to change the subject for our own good, but a cloud had already formed over the meal. I did my best to lighten things up again, but she seemed less inclined to join me. I had hoped the party would make things right again.

On our walk from the restaurant she reminded me, "As I told you, there will be mostly environmentalists there, so just let me know if anybody comes on too strong. Okay?"

"If I need protecting, you'll be the first person I run to."

The party was in a brownstone not far from my own place on Capitol Hill. It was a nicely sized group, but not too crowded. Tara introduced me to a few people when we first arrived. I was conscious of trying not to be the leechy new boyfriend following her wherever she went. So I feigned disinterest when she slipped away, while I engaged in a conversation on energy policy with a petite woman from the Natural Resources Defense Council.

A half keg was flowing on the back porch. A self-serve bar was laid out on the kitchen table. It had been a while since I had had more than two drinks in one night. The appeal of heavy drinking had worn off for me sometime in my sophomore year. But I made a serious error in judgment by going for innocuous-looking cherry-mango punch. I knew it was spiked, but I was three-quarters through my sixteen-ounce cup before I felt the effect of the extremely high alcohol content of the sweet drink. I could feel the flush in my cheeks and mild disorientation coming over me.

Kyle McAllister, the Executive Director of the CRFS, must have been feeling his punch as well. At first, I was glad to see a familiar face in the room, but within a few minutes I would deeply regret speaking to Kyle or even coming to the party at all.

"Tara tells me you've been in Congressman Grant's office for all of four months. He's been in Congress forever, hasn't he? Like thirty years or something? Talk about job security," he chuckled. I didn't like that he was making fun of Mr. Grant, and when he saw I wasn't amused, he added, "Hey, just kidding, man. He's a great guy." He seemed insincere, which annoyed me.

I said nothing and started to turn away, but he continued to engage me. "So John, I hear you're working on Grant's floor speech for the vote on the space station project," he grinned. Seeing my surprise at this knowledge, he added, "Tara tells me everything." He wiggled an eyebrow that suggested innuendo and I felt an irrational urge to smash him right then. "Funny that Grant would put his ass on the line to save the space station. Does he even have any NASA contracts in his district? What's with that?"

"I'm not sure what you're talking about. We've got plenty of NASA contracts." Yeah, a whopping three million in research grants at the local university, but it was enough to counter Kyle's glib remark. "He happens to believe that the space station project is important for the country and the world. I have to respect that."

"I hope you feel the same way when the Congress votes to cancel the program. You really should try to talk some sense into him. He's on the wrong side of this issue."

"I disagree."

Kyle laughed, "Oh, don't tell me you buy this space and patriotism stuff?" I probably didn't, but I wasn't about to give him the satisfaction of knowing it.

"Let's just say I respect Mr. Grant's opinion. I hope you do as well," I said, in as even a tone as I could. Without waiting for a response, I started to walk past him.

He grabbed my shirt. "Hey, John. Don't be like that." For the first time his voice did not have smarmy edge to it, but it was too late. I had had enough. Reflexively, I pushed him away hard. The cherry-mango punch caused me to exert more effort than I intended. He stumbled backward into a group of partiers and spilled his drink, splashing several people and himself. He slipped on a wet spot, lost his balance and fell hard to the floor. I was as shocked as everyone else at the result of my shove. Suddenly, all eyes were on Kyle and me.

"What's going on?" Tara had appeared as Kyle was helped to his feet.

"It's nothing. No big deal," Kyle insisted to everyone watching the scene. "But Tara, you should see if you can get your friend a thicker skin." He turned to me and stuck out his hand. "Listen, no hard feelings." But I just couldn't immediately accept it. I still felt too much anger and embarrassment.

I looked at Tara, whose gaze was a mixture of puzzlement and disappointment. Just as I noticed her eyes becoming glassy with tears, she turned and walked quickly out of the house. As I made my way after her, I heard someone shout, "Preppy asshole."

Tara was a half block down the street leaning on a low wrought iron fence. A tree shaded the light of the streetlamp, but Tara's silhouette was unmistakable.

As I approached, she got up and walked swiftly in the opposite direction.

"Tara," I called and she stopped, perhaps realizing she couldn't anonymously slip away from me.

I caught up to her. "Tara, that whole thing back there. It was stupid. It got way out of hand. I never would..."

She held up a hand to stop me talking. She was quiet for a moment. "John, I'm confused. I want to be with you. Really I do." She let me hold her. "But right now, with the Weinstein amendment coming up, it seems too hard. We're clearly not seeing eye-to-eye, and that's getting in the way. And now this…"

I felt awful. "Tara, come on. We can get through this. In a few weeks this issue will be over one way or the other."

"Do you really think that will be the end of it? We are on opposite sides of the space issue. As much as you support the space program, I believe it's a waste of money. Will that change?"

"Maybe not, but we can choose not to let that come between us."

"It already has."

"Tara?"

"Look. I need some time to think. Maybe we should cool things down for a while."

"Tara? You're breaking our agreement. You're letting our jobs get in the way of us."

"You did also, back there, when you couldn't control yourself." She started to cry and looked like she had more to say, but gave up. "I can't do this now. I've got to go." She abruptly turned away and headed back down the sidewalk.

I called after her. "Tara?" She ignored me as I watched her disappear into the party house.

THE SETTLER

The intrigue I felt to understand the Endowments was the one thing that elevated my mood after Tara's rejection. It had occurred to me more than once that Mr. Grant might be having a big laugh at my expense. If he hadn't been so intensely interested in this subject I might have concluded as much. But his sincerity and the riddle that he held in front of me were irresistible to me. I gave myself over to his instructions, which meant I would meet with five more individuals. If they proved to be half as interesting as Chip Johnson, there was no downside to the effort. At least I had that to counterbalance to the pain of lost love.

I waited nearly twenty minutes in Professor Jacob Donnelly's cramped office, packed with books and stacks of papers. He had seemed eager to meet with me when I spoke to him on the phone the day before, so I had to assume his tardiness was not from indifference.

I heard the clomp-clomp of footsteps growing louder in the corridor until a tall thin man appeared in the door frame. Thick hair, thick beard, and thick glasses. Professor

Donnelly's physique was not what I expected, though he was just as disheveled as any academic might be. His mild manner immediately put me at ease.

"Ah, John. I have to apologize," he said as he shook my hand and bustled his way over to his cluttered desk. "This is a difficult part of the semester. The students are very *needy*," he said, smiling and tilting his head slightly, as if to say, "you know what I mean."

He landed heavily in his chair. "I have to admit I was surprised to get your call. It's been such a long time since I was involved in space policy matters. But then, given the scope of the space station program, I guess it does make sense to discuss space colonization again."

"Well, Mr. Grant didn't mention space colonization specifically," I lied because I wanted to honor Mr. Grant's insistence that I not discuss the plaque, "but he thought you could help me with a speech I'm writing by explaining to me, in a general way, why you're so passionate about space." I had decided to couch my questioning in the guise of preparing for a speech, which allowed me to avoid mentioning my real purpose.

"Oh …well." He seemed flustered. "To be honest, since the summer study at MIT in 1975, and my subsequent reports and co-authorship of a book on the matter—and that was almost fifteen years ago—I haven't focused much academic energy on space development. There is very little space-related grant money for urban planning research."

"The summer study?"

"Yes. On space colonization." Noting my blank expression he said, "I see you're not familiar with this study. In the summer of 1975, NASA sponsored a three-month study at MIT. They brought together a group of about fifty experts from a wide range of disciplines. I was brought in to give input on the needs for large-scale community development that would fit into the parameters of the baseline technology. It was quite an exciting time. Apollo had just concluded as a huge success that year. NASA was building the Space Shuttle—of course, we didn't know at the time all the problems we would have getting it up and flying. But, for those few weeks in 1975 it seemed like anything was possible—even the colonization of space. So, as I said, I'm not sure what I could offer you of value, if not for my work relating to space settlements."

Feeling that I had no alternative but to stay in the realm of Professor Donnelly's interest and experience, I said, "Okay then, let's talk about that study and see where it takes us."

Heartened, he went on, "All right. Here, let me show you."

From a corner of his book shelf he pulled out a couple of publications that seemed not to have been disturbed in years. The first book was a large format soft cover report of the 1975 study printed by NASA titled *Space Settlements: A Design Study*. This was the sort of publication NASA put out for public consumption. Like other NASA reports, it contained dramatic pictures and artists' conceptions, was written for a lay audience, and offered policy recommendations. I flipped through the book while Professor Donnelly spoke. The pages were yellowing with faded notations in the margins.

The other book was hardbound. Though it was in better shape, the dated dust jacket design gave away its age. The title was *Space Colonization: The Technical & Sociological Implications*. I noted Professor Donnelly's name as one of three co-authors. Glancing at the table of contents, I could see the book was divided into sections, with Donnelly covering urban architecture and sociological topics.

"Take it, John. I can't say this was a best seller. I still have a dozen copies in a box around here somewhere." I thanked him and I felt obliged to ask him to sign the book. He was more than pleased to scratch his name broadly on the cover page and inscribed the message, *"To John, look closely and you will find the purpose in humankind's desire for space."* After reading his inscription, I nodded politely at him in gratitude to indicate *I get your meaning*, though I wasn't at all sure I had.

"I remember your boss, Harrison Grant, during the briefings. He was very interested in the social aspects of what space colonization would mean not only to the people living in space habitats, but also to the people who didn't go. 'How would space colonists interact with the home planet?,' he kept asking. I was very impressed by his level of knowledge of all technical matters. You should consider yourself lucky, John, to be working for him."

"I do." We shared a smile and I continued, "What do you see as the relevance between the 1975 Space Settlement study and the current return from the space station program?" I thought this would help to steer the discussion in the direction of professor's passion for space, and more specifically the Endowment he was to share with me.

"Well, don't you see? It's quite obvious. An orbiting space station is a precursor step that will lead to a future colony. The space station can be a test bed for many of the technologies we'll need for large-scale communities."

I responded, "But no one inside or outside of NASA is arguing that the space station is a precursor to space colonies. As a testing ground for further human exploration of the solar system, yes. Eventually on to Mars, perhaps."

"Yes, I suppose you're right. As I said, I haven't been keeping up with these matters. But, let's forget for a minute about what anyone in Washington is saying about the purpose of the space station. Let's imagine for a moment that the station is operational. It's manned with rotating crews of astronauts and scientists. They help to gain knowledge about living and working in the space environment. Eventually, we return to the moon, and set up a base there. Then go on to Mars even. We continue to build our knowledge base about surviving in the hostile environment of space. Where does that then lead? To more exploration missions? Yes, but then what? Do you see where I'm going with this?"

"Not really," I said honestly.

"You see, it's not just about the exploration. In the long run, it can't be just about the exploration. Eventually, people will want to create a settlement on the new frontier. There are people who are ready right now, no doubt. What is the point of sending humans to explore space, if not as trailblazers who lead the way for the settlers?"

I wanted to agree with him. But when I thought in terms of the political realities inside the Washington beltway, his logic evaporated. Yet, sitting in that cramped office, Donnelly's logic made all the sense in the world.

"But why are you so excited about the space program?" I asked directly.

"What excites me most about the space program is not *how* we get there, but what are we going *to do* once we do get there. Space is not like Antarctica as some people insist. We can't view outer space as a hostile territory meant only for intrepid research scientists. Antarctic research is unique in that the terrain is finite, a precious limited piece of real estate worth preserving as it is for all future generations. The space above the Earth's atmosphere, however, is a whole other story. To compare Antarctica to outer space is like comparing a…a house plant to the Amazon jungle." He chuckled at his own comparison, as if he had never quite put it that way before.

More seriously he said, "Space is where we will eventually build new places for our civilization to grow and develop."

"Chip Johnson says that it's the spirit of exploration that drives us to want to travel to space. He calls it the wanderer in us," I added in the hope of deriving some concurrence between the two men.

Slightly shaking his head in disagreement, he continued, "We're settlers much more than we are explorers or *wanderers*. The settlers of our species far outnumber the explorers, don't they?" He paused, eyebrow raised, waiting for my nonverbal agreement, and went on.

"Once we can adequately provide the means for people to travel to space and live there permanently, there will never be a shortage of pioneers willing to take the chance on a new way of life.

"From my area of expertise in the history of urban planning, I can tell you that some colonies will thrive and many will die. Some settlers will find their new homes in space exciting and exhilarating while others will hate the experience and look for the soonest opportunity to come back home to Earth. That's just the nature of how humans spread. This is the way it has always been.

"So much has been said comparing space colonization to westward expansion in nineteenth century America, but this wasn't a practice unique to Americans, or even with European colonialism of the fifteenth and sixteenth centuries. Every culture in the world is made of settlers and has been since our species first emerged on this planet millions of year ago. Whether it was the promise of more abundant hunting or promise of gold, it has never taken much to inspire the human beings to seek to make a new life for themselves in some new distant land.

"To be space settlers is, in a way, about the most human thing we could do."

He pondered his next statement for a moment and suddenly let out a sharp "Hah!" and startled me out of my lulled attention. Smiling to himself, he explained, "I would argue that *not* to create settlements in space would be about the most *in*human thing our advanced civilization could do," and he looked at me for a reaction. I smiled mirroring his amusement at the insight.

"Just knowing that my species is on the verge of permanently moving off this planet and will create new towns, cities and new civilizations up there, fills me with such a tremendous sense of awe." And he was in that moment. And his awe was infectious as I couldn't help feeling some of the intensity of the possibility myself.

With professorial skill, he then changed vocal tone and launched into another point, "Think about how we define a settlement. What exactly is a settlement? When people settle on a particular piece of geography they are creating a place that protects the population from the surrounding environment. Humans realized very early on that in order to survive they need to employ their ingenuity to build themselves *apart from* the hostile environment that contained so many threats. This primitive need to protect ourselves from the dangers of the wild is at the very heart of the millennia-long growth and development of human civilization." He lifted his eyebrows to make sure I was getting all this so far.

"Along the way, we got really good at thriving even in extreme hostile environments. I like the example of the Inuits. Why in the world would any humans choose to migrate and live at such an inhospitable latitude at the edge of the Arctic Circle? Yet there they have thrived for thousands of years. They developed the technologies they needed to survive in that unforgiving land. They have learned to keep the hostile weather and wildlife at bay. They didn't have to go north. The continent wasn't so populated that they couldn't have found a location farther south. But at some point, the settlements were founded by people who saw the beauty and possibility in the barren frozen wasteland, and who *chose* to make it their home. Such is the case now with the prospect of human settlement of space." He paused again to make sure I was paying attention.

"Now here's my point. It is our uncanny ability to build settlements that protect us from hostile environments that will enable us to develop the necessary technologies for space settlements. In fact, you couldn't find an engineer or scientist who would doubt our ability to do so, as long as there were sufficient commitment of will and resources. In fact, you can already see the prototypes of these space habitats in the world around us. Look at something as commonplace as the shopping mall or the cruise ship. These self-contained habitats support thousands of inhabitants in a controlled atmosphere. It almost seems that without even being consciously aware of it, we have been for many decades developing just the technological know how we will need to build large scale space colonies."

He paused and altered the tone of his voice. "Some people will look at the moon and see nothing but an airless desert. While others will see the raw materials with which a whole new civilization can be built." He stopped and gave me a searching look and asked softly, "Which moon do you see, John?"

"Uh..?" He had again caught me off guard.

"When you look at the moon, what do you see?" he asked again. "Do you see a wasteland or a realm of unlimited potential for human development?"

A response came sluggishly. I had been satisfied a moment earlier with dreamily soaking up the professor's impassioned lecture. I wasn't prepared to be called on to participate. In truth, I did see the moon as a wasteland. I could also see that in some distant future perhaps people might build colonies up there, but such a thought seemed so remote as to be irrelevant. But I knew that wasn't the answer the professor wanted to hear.

"Professor Donnelly, I...I think the moon is a fascinating celestial object and studying it up close with robots and someday with humans may very well help scientists unlock the secrets of the solar system."

He stared at me blankly for a moment or two, than let out a huge laugh, followed by a coughing fit, as if he finally got the punch line to a joke I just told. Still laughing, "That's the biggest bunch of horseshit I ever heard. Forgive my French. I'm not sure what you just said has to do with my question, but it sure sounds like a good way to avoid giving me a straight answer. You should do well in politics, I suspect." He gave me a warm smile to let me know he was only kidding with me and not to take him seriously.

I was still flustered, and before I could formulate a response he said, "Never mind, John. Just take that question as something to ponder."

Taking the opportunity to bring clarity to the subject, I offered, "So, from your point of view, it is the prospect for human settlement of space that excites you most about the space program?"

"Yes…but, I want to be clear that I am not fixated on the particular structure of a colony that we might build on the moon or Mars or in free orbiting space. What I am most interested in is the quality of life for the settlers, wherever they make their homes. I've always seen space colonization as an opportunity to restart civilization with a clean slate. That includes the full range of social interaction, but perhaps the most interesting is in the area of governance. Colonists will have an opportunity to adopt only those parts of our democratic systems that work, and do away with the less functional parts. Each new colony will be like the birth of a new continent—a new America—with renewed opportunity to start over, to refine and improve governance. Eventually, we can hope, the governing structure will evolve to the point that it is so interwoven with the tapestry of the space settlement society that it ceases to even be noticeable.

"What this means for us down here is that we will benefit from lessons learned by our space settler brothers and sisters. We will adopt their ways, just as much of the world adopted the ways of democracy established by our Founding Fathers. Jefferson and Adams are good models for our future space colonists. They seized the chance to take a fresh look at governance, and out of a sincere desire for freedom and ensuring individual rights, they created a remarkable form of government.

"Our government has served us well over the years, hasn't it? And we will likely go many more decades and even centuries with the Constitution remaining largely intact. But let's be honest. Our democracy is showing signs of wear and tear after over two hundred years. If we could start from scratch again today, would we come up with the same system? Probably not. The Constitution, as brilliant as it is, was written by men in the eighteenth century. We are approaching the twenty-first century. We can't pretend to say that what was important and essential to the people in 1776 is just as important for people today, and especially not for tomorrow's generations. So that's where our new colonists come in. They will reconsider anew what it means to govern a free and open society that encourages and brings out the best contributions from each of its members. If we're lucky, the new ideas of social engagement will make their way back to Earth for the benefit of the entire human family.

He paused and smiled at me as if to give me an opportunity to ask questions. As intrigued as I was, I had nothing to say.

"Let's just say I think it's much more exciting to conceive a future for humanity that is expanding out into the limitless regions of the universe, than a future where life remains here on Earth. Doing so is *who we are*. It is an extension of the settler nature that has always been part of our collective psychology. You see?" He looked at me again with raised eyebrows. I nodded.

At that moment I noticed a pair of undergraduates loitering outside of the professor's office. When I turned back to him he gave me that you-know-how-it-is look again.

As he signaled the students to wait a moment longer, I said, "Well, I think I've gotten quite a bit of useful information from our talk. You've been a great help."

"Thank you for giving me the chance to indulge in a favorite topic of conversation. I truly do hope I have given you something you can use. If Congress is planning to look at space settlements again, I would be more than ready to assist."

I detected a visible slumping in demeanor as he brusquely ushered the undergrads into his office.

As I was leaving, something familiar caught my eye. Partially covered by papers, I spotted a simple wooden plaque lying flat on the window sill. Could it have been a copy of the one in Mr. Grant's office? I turned to ask Professor Donnelly if I might have a look. But he was already in conversation with his students, and I decided against it.

As I stepped out the door, he called to me. "And, John, don't forget. Tell Congressman Grant that we discussed the Settler Endowment."

The following Monday, I got word from Cheryl Gordon that Mr. Grant had agreed to speak at the climate change conference in Arizona. This bit of news created a perfect opportunity to reach out to Tara and attempt to make things right after the Saturday night fiasco. I had left her two voice messages and gotten no reply. I assumed the worst. It was over between us. But I wanted to hear from her, and not draw that conclusion from her silence. Rather than call her about Mr. Grant's decision, I decided to catch up with her that afternoon at the HUD-IA committee hearing that I knew she'd be going to.

I spotted her in the third row of the hearing room. The Administrator of the Environmental Protection Agency was giving testimony before the sparsely represented committee. Just five committee members had bothered to show up. Not unusual, but certainly a little embarrassing for both the Members in attendance and the Administrator.

I took a seat three chairs away from her. When she saw me she gave a quick shake of her head and with pursed lips looked straight ahead. I passed her a note, which she reluctantly took. "I have news about the climate conference invite," the note said. She let out a sigh and looked at me.

I followed her into the hallway during a break. She allowed me to approach.

"Good news," I said. "Mr. Grant can make the conference."

She looked to the side with arms crossed. "Great. The conference committee will be glad to hear that."

"And about Saturday. I really feel awful. Can't we rewind? I thought things were going pretty well." I put my hand on her arm and she looked at me, and relaxed her posture a little.

Before responding, she pulled me away from potential eavesdroppers. Very close she said, "It's not just about the party and pushing Kyle. Different things are important to us. I thought we could make it work, but it just didn't. Not for me at least. And there's nothing wrong in that. There's nothing that says we have to date."

"There's nothing that says we can't, either. We can make it work if we want to." I knew there was too much desperation in my voice.

"But, this whole space station thing you're into. It's just too far away from what I'm all about..."

"So what? We can disagree on issues and still be together." I stepped closer, unconcerned about stares we were started to attract. "The question is not about the space station? The question is do you want to be with me?"

Our eyes locked for a few moments of silent communication. Her features softened further, a flush came to her cheek, and a tear formed in her eye. "I...I don't know...I can't think about this now." She broke away, wiping her face, and followed the crowd that was moving back into the hearing room.

It was hard to tell if that was tear of longing or the pain of suffering I represented.

I didn't really have much time to think about failed relationships, and I welcomed the deadlines that dampened my feeling of being a fool for wanting Tara so much. At the top of my list were two speeches I had to write: the floor speech for the Weinstein amendment, and a climate change speech for the World Conservancy Alliance.

Also not far from the front of my mind were the words of Chip Johnson and Professor Donnelly and the mystery of the Six Endowments and the Obligation. Thinking on this puzzle was the only distraction from work I allowed myself. Could I see the moon as a place for a space colony—or even Mars, as the professor had asked? What did he mean by the note he wrote in my copy of his book, *"Look closely and you will find the purpose in humankind's desire for space?"* I wondered what it was all about. Why was Mr. Grant even interested in such things? I looked forward to talking with Mr. Grant about Professor Donnelly and find out who else I would interview. Who would represent the next Endowment?

Organizing my workload, I decided to focus on the Weinstein speech first. The House floor vote on the HUD-IA bill was just three weeks away, and I wanted to prepare as complete a draft as soon as possible to have plenty of time to address any revision Mr. Grant might want to make. After several days of research and consulting with NASA, aerospace contractors, advocacy groups and other sources, my desk was a pile of reference materials and a note-filled memo pad. Finally sitting down to write the first draft, I struggled with how to include some of what Chip and Donnelly had told me, which didn't fit easily into the policy arguments. Ultimately, I included just a smattering of their insights and, after a long evening at my computer, I was satisfied that the document strongly represented Mr. Grant's political view on the amendment. At least I thought so. The floor speech began:

"Mr. Chairman, I rise in strong opposition to the

Amendment offered by the gentleman from New York, Mr. Weinstein, that proposes to cancel the space station program. First, let me say emphatically, I respect the views and position of my colleagues who support this measure. I align myself wholeheartedly with the spirit and intent of the goals this amendment aspires to achieve. I too believe that additional funding should be made available for the other worthy programs to which space station budget could be put. However, I must state without hesitation that now is not the time to turn our back on human spaceflight capability. Since the first flight of Alan Shepard, the first American to pierce the atmospheric veil and touch the heavens, human spaceflight has been part of the fabric of our democracy, and this capability that has been, and continues to be, a source of awe and envy to every other nation on the planet. To shrink from the space station program, the next logical step in space, would send a clear and dangerous signal to international partners and competitors alike that the United States is no longer serious about human space exploration.

In my humble opinion, there are three paramount reasons why we cannot afford as a nation to turn away from the space station: technological competitiveness, national defense and international prestige…"

The remainder of the speech gave supporting data for each of the three reasons. I knew the statement was sound from a conservative political standpoint. Yet, the whole time I was writing, I kept asking myself, *"Where does the Obligation fit into this debate?"*

Several days had passed before I would find the opportunity to discuss with Mr. Grant my lunch meeting with Professor

Donnelly. I had completed the draft speech and placed it on his desk earlier in the day, and thankfully Tara Bingham was nearly out of my head. It was after 6:30 PM. Most of the other staffers had left for the day, and I could hear Mr. Grant rustling in his office.

With one hand leaning on his office door frame, I intruded, "Mr. Grant. I don't want to disturb you, but I've been hoping to speak with you about… Professor Donnelly at some point."

His stern face softened as the purpose of my interruption became apparent.

"Yes, John. Yes. I'm glad you've finally got around to mentioning that. Come in, let's talk a little. Tell me, what did he have to say?" There was an eagerness again in his voice.

As before, Mr. Grant did not interrupt and waited a few beats before commenting once I had finished, "Well, what Endowment did he represent to you?"

"He was quite clear on that point. The Settler Endowment."

"That's right, of course, the Settler Endowment." He expanded, "Like the Wanderer, the Settler is not far from the primal instinct of nesting that protects animals against the elements and predators. The Settler Endowment that emerged in human consciousness enabled the long march from huddling cave dwellers to the mega civilization we are today. Simply put, it is the urge to not only create a settlement wherever new and desirable real estate has been discovered by the Wanderer; it is also the desire to employ the most advanced resources and knowledge to create those settlements."

"I didn't expect Professor Donnelly to talk about space colonies, but once he did I was surprised he didn't speak of colonization as being an *obligation*. Is the Settler Endowment the key to understanding why space colonization is humanity's obligation?" I hoped I could jump to the heart of the matter.

"The Settler Endowment is actually no more or less relevant to the Obligation than any other Endowment. Good question, but once again, you're getting ahead of yourself. You still have four Endowments to go. The next contact is Dr. Judith Falk, a research scientist at JPL, the Jet Propulsion Laboratory."

"Isn't that in Pasadena? Is she in Washington?"

"I'm afraid I'm not sure if she is or not, but I don't think so."

"Then how am I going to meet her if she's on the west coast?"

"Hmm, that will be difficult. But, remember, it is essential that you meet face-to-face with these individuals, otherwise you lose more than half the value."

While I puzzled on his response, he added, "Oh, by the way. Good speech on the Weinstein amendment. Nice and safe." I offered a weak smile of appreciation, not certain Mr. Grant had in fact paid me a compliment.

"And, when will you have the World Conservancy Alliance speech for me? Isn't that just a little over a week away?" I winced. I was terribly behind on my draft of that speech. My tenuous situation with Tara hung over the project as a major disincentive. I gave a weak assurance that he would have it within a day or so.

THE INVENTOR

I barely had time to ponder how I might ever interview Dr. Falk when events conspired to resolve the dilemma.

The day after my talk with Mr. Grant, Cheryl Gordon informed me of his decision to send me to the district office in southern California. As it happened, the chief of staff, Tom Rogers, was forced to cancel a planned trip to the district at the last minute. Rather than pay the airline penalties for canceling the flight, Mr. Grant thought it would be a great idea if I went in his place and got to know how things worked at the local level. I quickly made the connection that the Jet Propulsion Laboratory and Dr. Falk were an easy drive from the district office.

As fortuitous as this turn of events was, I couldn't help raising objections that my workload could not bear my being away for any length of time. Tom Rogers was unmoved, and explained that "...There is never a convenient time to visit the district. The piles of work are always going to be there no matter what. You have to take the opportunities when they arise and keep on top of your work as best you can."

Inwardly I was energized by what lay ahead for me on the west coast. Nonetheless, that meant I had less than two days to prepare for a week-long trip. I was glad to have completed a draft of the Weinstein amendment speech, but worried about getting back with enough time before floor action on the amendment, expected in less than two weeks.

Even more pressing was the speech Mr. Grant was to give in just one week at the WCA global climate change conference in Tucson. I had already gathered some information, and worked on an outline, but to do justice to the piece, I knew I would need to speak with Tara Bingham about the details of the meeting and the audience. With a knot in my stomach I called her intending to keep it as brief and professional as possible. But instead of being cool, Tara was surprisingly eager to talk and insisted that we meet later in the day. I resisted the invitation, but was excited about seeing her despite some apprehension.

We met for a beer at Bullfeathers on First Street. The conversation started out well. Almost too well. Tara apologized for perhaps overreacting about the scuffle on the night of the party. She told me Kyle had explained to her that his falling to the floor had more to do with a wet spot and not as much to do with my pushing him. I insisted it was still all my fault. Though we might have succeeded in neatly getting our apologies out of way, the distance that remained between us was obvious. I assumed we just needed a little time to get used to each other again.

We came to a pause in the apologizing session and the air became thick. Finally, I said, "So, tell me more about this climate change conference."

She smiled as she exhaled, "Yes, the conference! We need to talk about that. Will you be traveling with your boss by the way?"

"No, unfortunately. But, it turns out I will be in California putting in some time in the district office. I leave the day after tomorrow, in fact."

"Well, if you can get down to Tucson it would be great to see you there." It was a courteous reply empty of any desire. At this point, I couldn't tell why she wanted to meet. She was not giving off any romantic cues. We could have handled the conference details on the phone.

Clearing her throat she continued. "What can I tell you about the conference? There'll be three to four hundred people attending, mostly from the U.S. with some international participation. Mr. Grant has twenty minutes with another fifteen or twenty for Q&A. Perhaps he can give an overview of potential for legislative action on climate change, and offer suggestions on how advocates can influence the progress of that legislation. That would be a good place to start."

"And what about the Weinstein amendment? Can he expect any questions on that?"

"The amendment will be on everyone's mind, for sure. Mr. Grant may want to speak to it in his remarks, though in general, the amendment is peripheral to the main topic. Either way, he certainly should be prepared to respond if asked." Then she hesitated before adding, "And I should also mention, John," she said, touching my arm, "There are a few scientists who plan to use the opportunity of the conference to seek to change Mr. Grant's position on Weinstein. I told them it was a long shot, but they plan to buttonhole him just the same."

"I imagine Mr. Grant considered all that before deciding to do the speech."

"But… there is still a possibility that he'll change his mind, isn't there?" I gave her a questioning look. She elaborated. "I mean, his position isn't final until the day of the vote. You said yourself that he is feeling pressure from all sides. Isn't it possible he'll change his vote?"

A cold feeling went through me. "Sure, it's possible, but I haven't seen anything yet that would change his mind."

"I don't have to tell you how great it would be if you could help convince Mr. Grant to support the Weinstein amendment." Though the suggestion came out casually enough, I instantly recognized the calculation in it.

"Mr. Grant is an important swing vote," she continued. "With the right encouragement we feel he might reconsider his position." Coming out of my amorous fog, her true intentions were finally starting to register with me. She must have misread my reaction, because she continued to press the subject.

"We realize that you alone couldn't change his mind, but your involvement could help as part of a coordinated effort." She paused and looked at me directly, "John, I know from our time together that you have strong feelings about environmental issues." The sensation of Tara's clumsy attempt at manipulation filled me with anger and embarrassment.

"Kyle says we have a good chance of winning the House vote if Grant and a few others come over to our side. I just need to ask you straight out if there is any way you could work with us on this."

My emotions were spiking. Before I could say anything, Tara reached across the table and put her hand on mine. I let her touch me, but every fiber wanted to recoil.

"Tara, this is really out of left field. You know how I feel." I could see stress lines appear on her face. "I...I may have different ideas than Mr. Grant, and I might try to express those ideas once in a while. But, the bottom line is I work for him. It's my job to help *him* put *his* agenda forward. Not my own, and certainly not yours… or Kyle's." Her eyes widened slightly.

"If all you intended to do tonight was try to convince me to persuade my boss to vote for the amendment, then I'm sorry you've wasted your time. I had this stupid idea that we could get back to where we started. I'm sorry for being such an idiot." As I was speaking I could see in her face the anguish of realizing she had made a terrible mistake.

"No, you're taking this the wrong way." I could hear the pleading regret in her voice, but it didn't matter. All of my longing for her and frustration came to a head and I suddenly wanted nothing more to do with her.

I stood up without responding.

"John. Wait."

I dropped a twenty on the table and left.

I was over her. Just as well. Realizing there was nothing left with Tara was surprisingly liberating. I was free to focus on preparation for the district trip. There was work I needed to complete, not the least the climate change speech, the one thread that still connected me to her. But, I could go about all of this activity without the gnawing preoccupation of my future with or without her.

Fortunately, that climate change speech would be easier than the Weinstein speech. With Tom Rogers' help I found a similar speech Mr. Grant had given just prior to my joining the staff, providing me a template from which I could generously crib. Though easier, I knew I wouldn't finish the draft until after my arrival in California.

Scheduling a meeting with Judith Falk at the Jet Propulsion Laboratory proved more of a problem than I expected. She could only be available on the day after my arrival in California. That was perfectly fine with me until the district manager, Dotty Rodriquez, took issue with the timing. I had called Dotty to go over my itinerary during my time in the west coast office. When I mentioned my plans to visit JPL, she made it clear that this "side trip" was not appreciated. Not expecting such an objection, I struggled for a convincing answer when she wanted to know the purpose of the visit. I improvised a story that Mr. Grant wanted me to get some first-hand knowledge of the JPL research so I would be better able to manage his space policy agenda. This only seemed to spark more displeasure. My visiting JPL, I would discover later, apparently fed the stereotype that Washington staffers were interested only in policy issues and politics and couldn't care less about the needs and concerns of the constituents who put Mr. Grant in office. I was certainly not getting off on the right foot with my west coast coworkers.

It was on the plane trip that another vision or dream came to me. I worked on the climate change speech for most of the cross country ride, but did take time to gaze out the window and admire the scene from thirty thousand feet. I was reminded vividly of my recurring dream of orbiting the globe. Immersed in the view of the cloud dotted panorama, the sun reflected brilliantly off of lakes and rivers. I began to feel a calm sensation sweep through me, one not unlike that I had experienced on that first day of meditation with Tara. It was a deeply relaxing place. I took in the whole of the globe below me. At some point I lost sensation of my body, and even of the plane around me. I was above the clouds, naked and free. The ground receded even further, and I entered the vision of my dream once again. The world below me pulsated with light, and in the intensity of the moment, I *saw* the world as a single living being. This realization flooded me with awe. I recalled Chip Johnson's experience of seeing the whole Earth from space. He had called it the Overview Effect. That's what I must have experienced, or at least a version of it.

Eventually, I came back to regular awareness, the plane and my speech notes. I collected myself and asked for glass of water from the flight attendant and resumed work on the climate change speech.

The flight landed at Ontario International Airport. I picked up a Ford Taurus rental and drove straight to the district office, a simple storefront on a quiet commercial strip. Everyone was friendly, though the conversations became awkward whenever the subject of my JPL trip came up. "That's too bad. You just got here, and there's so much we want to show you."

Concern for inter-office courtesies dwindled to vapor the next morning on my drive to Pasadena as my anticipation in meeting with Dr. Falk grew with each mile. She met me at JPL's main entrance. She was a short woman, barely over five feet. Her hair was snow white, though her features gave her age to be no older than mid-fifties. She talked fast, and she made no attempt to modify her pronounced New York accent.

Her demeanor was friendly but curt with a tinge of sarcasm. "So Harry sent you all the way from Washington. He must think you're something."

She gave me a brief tour of the facility, starting with the mock-ups of deep space probes on display in the entrance hall, including the historic Voyager spacecraft and Lunar Prospector. We walked through some of the labs where space hardware was under construction or being tested. The scientists we met were eager to talk about their research. She took me to an area where large windows allowed viewing of the clean rooms. Scientists and technicians in white hooded sterile suits talked to us about the projects through microphones. Dr. Falk's explanation for everything she showed me was thorough and deadpan. She responded to my frequent amazed reactions and questions with what seemed to be indifference, although I soon detected a strong sense of pride beneath her tough exterior.

We finally settled in the JPL cafeteria. Her office, she explained, was no place for a meeting as it was a clutter of paper reports and hardware, which didn't matter anyway because she spent so little time there these days. This was a slight disappointment as I had hoped I might spy another copy of the plaque.

The cafeteria was plain and functional. Forgetting my manners, I let my hunger get the best of me and loaded my tray with pasta, deli hero, coleslaw and a large chocolate brownie for desert. When I saw Dr. Falk's small salad and roll, I felt a glutton and wished I had at least skipped the brownie.

We took a table near a window in the back of the room. We spoke for a few minutes about the Galileo space probe mission to Jupiter that she was involved with, but soon Dr. Falk steered to the conversation to the purpose of my visit.

"I'm supposed to tell you about the Inventor, aren't I?" she declared.

"Inventor? No... as I said, you are one of the people Mr. Grant asked me to interview about what motivates humanity to venture into space."

"And, so far you've spoken to Chip and Donnelly. The Wanderer and the Settler Endowments. Is that right?"

"Well, yes. Those are terms they used..."

"And now I'm to tell you about the Inventor Endowment."

"The Inventor Endowment?"

Dr. Falk was not someone who suffered fools well. "I don't know how much Harry has told you so far, but it seems he expects me to give you the point of view of the Inventor."

"Well, yes. Mr. Grant is having me find out about the... Endowments. But he wants me to decipher the nature of each Endowment as they are represented by the people I am interviewing." As I spoke her smile and clear amusement grew to the point of outright laughter. "I have to say, I feel a bit foolish sharing this with you. I know it sounds...eccentric, so I'll understand if..."

Through her laughter, "No, no, John. This is fine. It's just like Harry to do it this way."

"What do you mean by 'do it this way'?"

"Okay, I'll give you a little clue, and then I'll say no more about it. Mr. Grant is sharing with you some knowledge of which very few people are presently aware. He has chosen you, and you apparently are willing, to share this knowledge with in a manner that will allow you to most effectively grasp its meaning. I imagine this all started when you asked about the plaque?"

"Yes, but he swore me not to mention the plaque or its message with you or the others I'm speaking with. But, since you bring it up, perhaps you can tell me…"

"I will say nothing about the plaque," she announced with finality. "But I will discuss the Inventor Endowment. And I suppose we can begin with your basic question. I can tell you simply I am passionate about space because of the challenges that it poses for *invention*.

"I am certainly interested and excited about exploration and settlement—the preoccupation of the Wanderer and the Settler. The Inventor excites me because he makes things easier for the Wanderer and the Settler. The Inventor is the one who creates the tools that will assist both the Wanderer and the Settler in their efforts. A wheel for the Wanderer; a hammer for the Settler. With each generation since the advent of the Inventor Endowment, Inventors have improved on prior inventions. Sometimes in an incremental way. Sometimes taking great leaps. But always solving problems in a way that's never been done before. Sometimes technologies are lost to time, but many are still with us today.

"The ability to invent or, more simply, problem solve, is of course what sets us apart from the animal kingdom. The Wanderer is actually just a short leap from the tendency to spread out geographically that we see everywhere in nature. A little overcrowding is all that is needed. In a similar fashion, the Settler trait is not much of an evolutionary change from the nesting habits found in nature.

"But, the Inventor,…" she used a big voice for emphasis, "The Inventor represents a big leap in consciousness for humankind. Once we gained the Inventor Endowment, our species took off and never looked back."

From the pocket of the light jacket she wore, she produced a small wooden box.

"Here, look at this," she placed the box on the table, and opened it. Inside, sitting on a bed of velvet cloth, was an oblong jagged rock.

"This was given to me by an archaeologist friend at St. Mary's. He discovered a load of artifacts like this at the site of one of the oldest known human settlements in Kenya dating back two-and-a-half million years. He would be in serious trouble if anyone knew he gave this to me."

Only seeing a stone, I was forced to asked, "What is it?"

"It's a simple cutting tool."

She carefully handled the object without inviting me to hold it. At first glance there wasn't much to the piece of rock. But on closer inspection, it was clear that a sharp edge had been chipped into the stone on both sides. I could image how this stone might have been attached to a wooden handle.

"Whenever I look at this it reminds me of the earliest inventors. The first problem solvers who asked themselves, 'How can we more efficiently remove the meat from the bones of the animals we kill or find?'" She took another admiring look at the tool before returning it to the box and her coat pocket.

"At some point early in our development there evolved in our consciousness the capacity to be an Inventor. It is the Inventor who enabled everything we know ourselves to be beyond our purely animalistic qualities. Every manufactured object was first conceived by the Inventor. Without the Inventor Endowment there would be no human civilization. We would still be scavengers and crude hunters—if we survived at all.

"And without the Inventor," she paused and bore her eyes deeper into mine, "there would most certainly be no space program."

She held a pause before continuing. My first reaction was to think her statement an obvious one, but her emphasis forced me to wonder what more there was to it.

"What truly excites me is finding ways to answer the big scientific questions. The inventor, in the way I am talking about it, includes all of science and technology. Invention is about gaining a level of understanding about a problem or challenge combined with a deep knowledge of natural laws and applying that information to address a practical purpose. With space exploration, for example, the challenge is getting your instruments, or people, to the part of the solar system you want to study and making sure those instruments, or people, are working properly so they can collect the information you need in a form that you can dump into your computers so you can get some idea what is going on out there." She pointed her eyes upward with that. "Experimental scientists have to be inventors if they are to create the instruments they need to find the answers they're looking for.

"Fundamentally, the Inventor represents the human capacity to understand the nature of his physical world and with that understanding manipulates his environment in creative ways to suit his purposes – whatever those purposes may be.

"You could say that the Inventor is like the Wanderer, but he wanders the 'inner' spaces of his mind rather than the 'outer' spaces of geography. Internally, she wanders, searching for the new linkages in order to advance her understanding of the physical world, and solve the problems she has set for herself or were set for her by someone or something else."

I dared to interject. "But, tying this back to your passion for space…?"

"Well, that's simple. Space is the realm of the biggest unanswered questions. Those questions inspire deep scientific inquiry. Each answer, or partial answer, creates a set of more refined questions. To answer these questions in a scientifically rigorous fashion requires the inventions of appropriate instruments. Rocketry is a prime example. As I mentioned, just getting people and equipment where we want it to be requires extraordinary creativity. From a technological standpoint, the challenge of space is irresistible. Goddard, von Braun and others were driven to solve the puzzle of building a vehicle to carry people into space. Yet, there is so much we don't yet know how to do in space. As amazing as our progress so far may appear, we have barely begun to develop our capability in space, both in terms of the vehicles we use to get there, and how we will manage our activities once we do reach the moon, Mars and other destinations. If we expect to eventually conduct lunar mining operations or Martian habitat construction, we are looking at a scale of invention that dwarfs anything we've done so far. But it's the vision of such possibilities that captures the heart of the pure Inventor. Such intense desire can be found in other terrestrial endeavors, but nowhere is it stronger than it is in the space arena.

"Ultimately, the biggest technological challenges we will face as a global society will be out there, not down here. I don't mean to minimize the importance of terrestrial sciences and technologies in the least. Obviously the leading edges of information and biotechnology research are posing enormous challenges and yielding enormous benefits. But, when comparing the full range of challenges that technologists can take on, the space studies stands alone, in my opinion.

"But, it's important to understand that the true Inventor in any field is driven by uncontrollable curiosity, always asking 'what if?' 'How can this be done better?' 'How does that work and can it be improved upon?' Such people exist in all walks of life, and most people exhibit some of the Inventor trait from time to time. Inventors are in business, the trades, technology, of course, academia, the arts. My mother, for God's sake, was a great Inventor." She laughed unexpectedly at the sudden recognition. "She made a science out of stretching a teacher's salary to care for five kids. She was quite an innovator of her domestic world. We had schedules for everything. Coupon clipping was a family activity. And she never made us feel that we lacked for anything. Whatever any of we kids really wanted, she applied her Inventor traits to figure out how to get it for us. My friends were always amazed by what she could do, and had no idea how meager our household income really was."

Dr. Falk was so animated at that point that I wondered if the entire cafeteria might be listening to her exposition. But, a discreet glance around the room revealed no sign of eavesdropping.

"Now, let's get back to space development in particular. On the surface, it's easy to conclude that inventiveness with regard to rocketry and space travel is merely an extension of humankind's age old capacity to invent. In a way, all of our inventions down through the millennia have all been *in preparation* for our taking on the challenges of making our way into space. Does that make sense to you?" I wasn't really sure, but nodded anyway.

She continued, "So the Inventor is endlessly intrigued by, and drawn to, the challenge of *conquering the high frontier*," as she exaggerated latter words with mock bravado.

"Many, many other fields draw on the Inventor in all disciplines, but space remains the Holy Grail for the Inventor. It beckons us like no other. Like the wings of Icarus, we desire to build that which enables us to ascend to the sun. We don't care if we get burned. Therefore, where the Wanderer and Settler Endowments create the initial yearning for space travel and migration, ultimately, it is the Inventor Endowment that provides the means by which the physical world can be manipulated in such a way that makes space travel possible. The Inventor is, in effect, an evolved version of the Wanderer. Very different, but similar on a basic level." At this she stopped and studied my face.

"Each of us has some amount of the Inventor in them. They also have some amount of each of the other Endowments. So, let me ask you," she said, pointing a finger at me, "In what way have you exhibited the Inventor Endowment? It's not a trick question. Think about it."

"Let me see. I'm not sure. It's an interesting question." I stalled, hoping an idea would come to mind. "I can't really think of anything. I've never been mechanically inclined…"

"Remember, the Inventor is the creative problem solver. Mechanical technology is just one place where it can be exhibited. Your experience might be creating a piece of art, or solving an interpersonal problem, or addressing a home repair project."

Suddenly something came to me. "Well, I guess one thing comes to mind. It will sound dumb…"

"Ah, ah, ah. In science there are no dumb ideas," she admonished.

I continued, "In grammar school…I went to Catholic school…I had to make a diorama depicting a scene from the story of the Exodus—the Moses story. I got it in my head that I wanted to dress my *G.I. Joe* doll as Moses, but realized it would never fit in a shoe box that was always used for dioramas. So I created a diorama from a much larger box to fit my nine-inch Moses. Instead of paper cutouts and glue, I used papier-mâché over a wire frame to make the mountain Moses walked down carrying the Ten Commandments. I created trees and shrubbery using sticks and leaves from my backyard…Is that what you mean?"

"That's a great example! Had you ever seen anything like it before? No. Did you solve a problem? Yes. Did you combine seemingly unrelated knowledge to create something new and functional? Yes…You would do well to continue to emulate the person you were in Catholic grade school."

She smiled at me for a moment before continuing, "So now you know essentially everything I have to say about the Inventor Endowment." She looked at the thick watch on her wrist. "Well, it has been wonderful speaking with you, John. I hope you got what you needed. If it is all right with you, I have a two o'clock briefing I need to get to. Can I leave you here? You should have no problem getting back to your car."

We shook hands, lingering with eyes locked. "Consider yourself fortunate, John," she said. As I watched her quick stride carry her from sight, I thought about that grammar school project. I recalled the excitement I felt working on it, as well as the praise I received from my teachers and classmates for going so far beyond the scope of what the assignment required.

Several hours later, I was pondering what I had learned from Dr. Falk while manning the front desk of Mr. Grant's district office. Dotty Rodriquez said answering the office phone was a good experience that would give me a solid overview of the rhythm of how things worked. She explained the proper way to answer and forward incoming calls, and then left me on my own. I was happy to get into the swing of the office, and demonstrate my eagerness to be part of the greater Congressman Harrison B. Grant team.

Between phone calls, I skimmed through a stack of pending case files and thought about the Endowments. There were three Endowments that I had so far learned about: the Wanderer, the Settler, and the Inventor. On face value, I didn't see anything particularly special about these human traits. Yes, these were important dimensions of human consciousness, and certainly discussing them with such extraordinary people was thought provoking—inspiring even. But, where would understanding all the Endowments ultimately lead?

I also wondered when I would have the opportunity to discuss the meeting with Mr. Grant as I had with the others. I knew he was scheduled to fly into to California from

Washington the next day, but I had no expectation that I would be able to spend time with him to discuss the Endowments.

This thought reminded me that I needed to complete the draft speech for the global climate change conference. I was nearly done. I had taken a copy on a floppy disk so I could finish it on the district office computer.

The phone rang.

"Good afternoon, Congressman Harrison Grant's office. How may I help you today?" I answered with a bit more cheery eagerness than was necessary. I had joked with Dotty that the way she instructed me to answer the phone made me sound like an order taker at a fast food restaurant.

To my surprise, the caller asked for me.

"This is John," I allowed my voice to drop a few octaves in the hope of projecting more authority. It vexed me that that the caller might think I was the receptionist.

"I see…I'm calling from Evan Phillips' office at Starblazer Launch Systems. Mr. Phillips asked me to call to see if you may be able to meet him at our engine-test facility out in the Mojave Desert tomorrow morning."

I was baffled. "Are you sure you were calling for me? I haven't been in communication with Mr. Phillips."

"Mr. Phillips said he had gotten word from Congressman Grant that you should be called in for a meeting. Mr. Phillips thought you would find it interesting to see the facility. Do you think you can make it tomorrow?"

It all became clear. Evan Phillips was my contact for the fourth Endowment, though I wished Mr. Grant had given me some warning. Phillips was a wealthy entrepreneur who intended to make his next fortune selling rockets that could put satellites into orbit. Starblazer would serve the small satellite market, under five hundred pounds, which Phillips saw as a very lucrative niche. I had read that Starblazer Launch Systems was conducting rocket engine tests. Though he had not actually launched anything yet, Phillips had managed to raise significant venture capital and collected enough letters of agreement from prospective customers to create a stir in the space industry.

"What time?"

"Six AM," she said. "And, for Mr. Phillips' information, John, what *is* your exact title?" I cringed that she would ask the question, but was happy to set the record straight.

News that I was off again on another *outing* didn't sit well with Dotty and the other staff. A rushed call to Mr. Grant, however, confirmed that it was his wish that I keep the appointment. I assured Dotty that, because of the early hour of the meeting, I would be back in the office before noon.

It also meant I would have to complete the climate change speech before leaving the office that evening.

There was a packet for me in the afternoon mail. From Tara. The envelope contained information she thought would be helpful for the speech. Along with the background material and neatly typed cover memo, there was a handwritten note.

John,

> *I need to tell you how awful I feel about last night. I didn't mean to use our friendship to gain your help on Weinstein. I didn't realize what I was saying, or how it came out. I actually thought (or convinced myself anyway) that you might want to help. I was wrong for thinking that way.*

> *I just want you to know I'm sorry, and I wish I could take it back.*

I miss you,

Tara

I read the note two more times. "*I miss you,*" were the only words in the apology that meant anything to me. As angry as I was that night at Bullfeather's, those three words reignited feelings I thought were gone.

THE BUILDER

I made the two-hour ride out to the test facility on four hours of sleep. I had stayed in the office late completing the climate change speech, which I promised would be done by that day. Though it was largely a cut-and-paste exercise, I didn't want it to look that way. So, I put in a few extra hours to make it something I felt good about.

The faint glow of dawn was just beginning to illuminate the landscape. The road twisted and turned up and down the sloping terrain of the desert. A building finally appeared on the horizon directly ahead. As I drew closer, I saw that it was surrounded by a fence topped with barbed coil. It was an old Air Force facility that had been mothballed for years before being sold to Starblazer eighteen months earlier.

The gate was open and I eased my Taurus through the opening onto the gravel driveway. There was an area where about two dozen vehicles were parked. The building was a low one-story bunker with windows on one side facing away from the gate entrance.

My attention was drawn to a spot at least a thousand feet out into the desert. From what I could make out from that distance, smoke or steam was puffing from an oblong piece of machinery, which I recognized as a rocket engine. Hoses ran from the stand with the engine to two trucks that I assumed would feed the necessary fuel and oxidizer to the engine during the test. There were at least a half-dozen men at work around it.

No one paid much attention to my approach as I parked the car, and made my way toward the building. When I was nearly at the bunker a man of medium build emerged, whom I recognized at once as Evan Phillips. He had a full mustache, graying brown hair and a broad toothy smile.

"John from Grant's office?" he asked expectantly. When I nodded, he added, "Glad you could make it." As we met, he barely slowed his stride to shake hands and gestured me to walk with him.

"It's almost time, so our chat will have to wait. You just stick by my side. I think you'll find this interesting," he said with a grin.

We walked over to a Jeep, got in and drove directly for the test stand. We didn't speak for most of the ride as Phillips was continuously on the walkie-talkie or in focused thought on what was about to take place.

At one point Phillips turned his attention to me. "Know what you're looking at, John?"

"I assume it's a rocket engine," I responded. Then added, "I presume you're conducting a test."

"Exactly," he said approvingly. "That's the first stage engine that will take my launch vehicle, the OmegaStar, into orbit. Today is my final test of the rocket engine before our maiden launch six months from now, if all goes well."

Three engineers met our Jeep as we pulled up to the test stand. The rocket was much larger than I could tell from the bunker. With a close-up look I made out details such as the exhaust nozzle and the gnarl of piping, tanks and wiring attached to it. The engine was securely bolted to the stand. Two video cameras twenty feet away were aimed at it.

"Well?" Phillips asked an engineer.

"I think we're ready to go," he replied confidently. The other engineers nodded in agreement.

Holding out a clip board for Phillips to review, the engineer said, "Everything is right where we need it to be."

Phillips studied the checklist. He looked into the eyes of each engineer. He approached the rocket, and made a slow walk around the entire structure, looking for the slightest flaw, frequently referring to the checklist. He walked back over to the engineers, head down massaging his chin, still searching the clipboard and his thoughts for anything he might have missed. After a long pause he finally looked up and said, "All right boys, let's light this sucker!" And with that his face broke into a broad smile once again. The engineers responded enthusiastically and dashed in different directions to make final preparations.

I rode back to the bunker with Phillips and his principal engineer, taking the back seat. What struck me most about Phillips was how absolutely calm he was when everyone else was understandably tense with anticipation. The tension he had exhibited on the way out to the stand was gone. If not for the buzz of activity swarming around him, you would not be able to tell he was moments away from a critical multi-million dollar test on which the future of his company depended.

I followed him into the bunker, a cramped space knotted with wires and equipment. TV monitors showed live video of the engine. The windows in the cinderblock structure were long and narrow and made of thick glass. A portable air conditioner helped to manage the heat that would have otherwise built up in the enclosed space. A team of about eight engineers manned the monitoring equipment. Other employees and friends expectantly stood by waiting for the show to begin.

"Here, you may want to use these," Phillips thrust a pair of binoculars and ear plugs at me.

"We're coming up on five minutes," announced an

engineer, his eyes fixed on his instrument. The room became very quiet, punctuated by occasional status checks about fuel pressure or internal temperature.

Eying Phillips' calm demeanor again, I couldn't resist asking, "Mr. Phillips, you seem...awfully relaxed with all this going on. Aren't you at all...nervous?"

Without taking his eyes off his binoculars he said, "Well, it's at times like this I remember what Chuck Yeager once told me. With any big event, the person in charge is like a general going to battle. You do all you can do to plan for victory in advance, but once the battle has begun, there is nothing more you can do, so you may as well sit back and enjoy the ride."

"Sixty seconds."

Phillips stood casually peering through his binoculars. Then there was the final countdown from ten, and I hastily stuffed the plugs in my ears and pulled up my binoculars, "...three, two, one, ignition."

At first there was nothing from the engine stand. Then a spark, and a bit of smoke. Then suddenly, a column of flame rushed out of the nozzle. A fraction of a second later, I felt, more than heard, the engine roar. The vibration was alarming.

In a few moments my ears, aided by the plugs, adjusted to the crackling rumble of the lit engine. Even from that distance, the exhaust etched momentary bright spots in my cornea.

"Engine's at ninety-five percent," came the barely audible voice of an engineer. The engine was at near maximum thrust. This part of the burn lasted for sixty seconds. I looked at the video monitor that captured close-ups of the engine. A strip recorder swung its arms back and forth, etching the vibration onto paper. The guests were all captivated, some wincing and covering their ears from the noise. Engineers were immovable from their stations.

Then the engine flame diminished a little. "Down to eighty-five percent." The engine was gradually reducing thrust to simulate reduced demand for power as the rocket burned off its massive propellant load, rising into the atmosphere. The engineer announced each percentage threshold in increments of five.

After two-and-a-half-minutes, when the thrust was down to sixty-five percent, Phillips finally said, "Alright, let's open'er up all the way." With that command, the engine exhaust flame expanded, burning more intensely than it had at any previous time during the test. "A hundred and ten percent." After twenty seconds at that power level Phillips gave the signal to cut the engine.

Following a beat of ringing silence, the room erupted in applause, hand shaking, and back slapping. Phillips limited his outburst to a broad grin. The moment was gripping and I found myself caught up in the excitement.

The celebration was quickly replaced by a giddy buzz of activity to analyze the results of the test firing. Overall, they were all pleased with the engine's performance, despite a few areas of minor concern. Occasionally, Phillips would shoot a glance in my direction.

Finally, Phillips announced, "Okay, let's go have a look at 'er." He motioned me to come with him.

We walked to the Jeep again, just the two of us.

"I think you can tell, this is a good day for Starblazer," he chuckled, his satisfaction still in full bloom. "I've seen everything I need to see to convince me we're on target, and ready for a full-up suborbital launch.

"So now, John, did our little engine test help answer your questions?"

His shift in attention to the reason for my visit caught me off guard.

"Well,…it certainly does on an emotional level. Now if I can only describe that feeling in words…"

He chuckled at that.

I wanted to know more about his rocket, and asked, "How long did it take you to develop that engine?"

He looked at me quizzically, "Develop it?" as though I had asked a dumb question. "I would say it took us exactly... zero days." He laughed again, and then explained, "I didn't develop anything. This was strictly off the shelf hardware, my friend. That's an Aerojet LR-87 engine. It's been pushing military and civilian rockets into space, and who knows where else, for years. The Defense Department spent $1.8 billion to develop it. And I'm glad they did... so I didn't have to.

"But, the test, and..."

"...Standard integration testing is all. God, what do you think I am, some kind of *inventor*? The last thing I want to do is invent from scratch – I'm a Builder, John."

We arrived at the rocket stand, putting our conversation on hold. Phillips spent forty-five minutes with his team examining how well the hardware had endured the test. I was becoming anxious. The morning was getting on, and I began calculating and recalculating approximately when I would make it back to Mr. Grant's district office.

Perhaps sensing my impatience, Phillips finally came over and motioned me to walk with him again. This time we walked away from the stand out into the open desert, the cracked lakebed surface crunching under our shoes.

I brought the conversation back to where we had left off. "You said you weren't an inventor. That you are a *builder*. What did you mean by that?"

He mulled this for a minute, "In my opinion, the Inventor is overrated. The Builder is the one who takes the inventions and puts them into common use. What good is an invention if it is not widely adopted? It takes visionaries like me, in all modesty, to replicate invention for the benefit of the masses. The Builder finds out what works, and keeps doing it."

"Are you saying the Builder is one of the Endowments – the fourth Endowment?"

He gave me a look that said he knew what I was talking about. "I suppose you can say the ability to replicate good ideas is a critical human *Endowment*."

We had walked about fifty yards into the desert with the engine stand between us and the bunker. The landscape was barren and majestic. The air was warming up as the sun rose at the horizon but still comfortable. The only sound was the occasional shout from an engineer at the test stand, or the clank of metal on metal.

"Replication and application of invention is the very engine of civilization. By themselves, inventions are nothing more than one time novelties that maybe provide some utility to the Inventor and his neighbors, but in the end a one-off device or process leads nowhere. Without the Builder we'd literally still be living in caves, except for the occasional guy or gal that would *invent* a hut." He laughed at this.

"Of course, we can't even imagine such a thing. We are such good imitators that the thought of *not* being able to use what has come before, and copy it, is a ridiculous notion. The Builder and Inventor work together to advance civilization. The Builder copying what the Inventor creates. The Inventor improving on all that the Builder disseminates throughout society. This partnership has created a dynamic spiral of upward technological and social progress throughout human history, from the first caveman tools to supercomputers and Saturn V rockets. Inventors and Builders depend on each other." He paused looking for my reaction. "Pretty interesting stuff, huh?"

Noting my attentiveness, he went on, "But let me clarify the definition of the Builder a little more, as an *Endowment*. The Builder Endowment, more broadly speaking, is our capacity to learn or be educated and express what we have learned in some fashion. Some of us take what we learn and invent new things, but most of us are perfectly happy with living in the realm of what is already known. The best of those individuals we call experts, artisans, scholars, craftsmen and business managers—the people who take great pride in doing a good job. For example, we want the electrician we hire to really know the right way to wire a house. We don't want him to be an inventor. We don't want him to tinker with what already works—especially not in our fuse box. A little inventiveness is great, but we want *and need* people who can get very specific predetermined jobs done well. Professions in this category include librarians, truck drivers, nurses, firefighters, as well as bricklayers, steel workers, and carpenters—all these people perform the critical functions that keep society humming. They are all the Builders in our culture.

"The business world, of course, is dominated by Builders who can take products and services that are known and proven and market them to the population. As I said before, I have no interest in inventing a new kind of rocket engine. I'm excited about taking what has already been developed by people much smarter than me and making copies – lots of copies – and selling them for as much as the market will bear. And yes, I would like to get rich on selling rockets, but ultimately money is not what the Builder is really after. The true satisfaction will always come in the building itself."

We had strolled making a wide circle looping out from the test stand. The sun was getting higher in the cloudless sky. Its heat prickled my exposed skin.

After a pause in our discussion, I said, "But I don't see how you could have come as far as you have without being something of an inventor. I mean, you invented your company and a model for how to make money with these off-the-shelf rockets."

"Good point, John." Phillips thought this over for a few moments. "Though I consider myself a Builder at the core, I am also an Inventor to a degree…There is some Inventor in me, maybe a lot, and I suppose that's what gives me an edge against the competition. I suspect every successful Builder has some Inventor in him. Henry Ford, my inspiration, would fall into that category.

"And every successful Inventor has some Builder Endowment in him. Thomas Edison is an example of someone who was both a towering Inventor and a shrewd Builder. The Inventor will likely dream about his inventions being adopted by the masses, but it is the Builder who will ultimately make that dream come true. If the Inventor is also a Builder, he or she will reap the financial rewards of his or her inventions. If the Builder endowment is not strong in the Inventor, others will take his worthy creations and make their fortunes from it, leaving the Inventor with little financial reward to show for their genius."

He paused, took a deep breath. Smiling, he said, "Now, are you getting what you need?"

Although the conversation was fascinating, I realized I needed more clarification relating to my central question.

"Well,...I think I understand the logic of what you're saying about the Inventor and the Builders. But, this logic seems to be true for all of civilization. How does this relate specifically to your interest, or passion, for space development?"

He thought for minute, looking up. "Space and space travel have a pull like nothing else. For me, the development of space requires the fullest and best application of our collective technological ability. To be part of making it easier and more affordable to get into space, to my mind, is to be part of an unbelievably important period of human history. But without the Builders like me, we'll have nothing to show for our efforts in space except flags and footprints on the moon. The Inventors have been tinkering around up there for too damn long, and the Builders are chomping at the bit to get a piece of the action. Space can't be the exclusive realm of scientists. Of course, there are some bright spots on the horizon. With communication satellites and remote sensing satellites, we're starting to see the emergence of a commercially viable space business model independent of federal government contracts. And I intend to be right in the mix offering superior cheap launch services."

He paused again, gazing in the direction of a distant mountain range. "But satellites, and even my launch business, are just the very beginning, John. The Builders who feel a sense of urgency about space have their sights set on building new civilizations beyond Earth. We're itching to build the space colonies that will allow humanity to begin a whole new chapter of existence." With that he turned to me, smiling. He sensed my surprise at his mention of space colonies, and broke off in a fit of laughter. The engineers at the test stand looked in our direction to see what had set Phillips off.

"I like shooting off rockets as much as anyone likes a good fireworks show. But putting a few dozen satellites into orbit—even a few hundred or few thousand—only goes so far. The real action begins when people—regular people like you and me—start making the trip into space, up to a space station and eventually to space colonies."

Maybe I should have expected it, but Philips' proclamation about space colonies still caught me by surprise. For him to be passionate about space colonization seemed out of character.

I finally responded, "It's interesting to hear you speak about space colonies. I would have guessed such ideas would have seemed to you to be...impractical."

"Space colonies are completely impractical...*today*. I'd love to open a hotel on the moon tomorrow—but I know that can't happen. Therefore, I'm looking at what I can reasonably do right now to help move us in that direction—and right now the name of the game is *cheap access*: driving down the cost of getting to orbit as much as possible.

"But the barriers to human settlement of space go beyond the price of a launch. We currently have a global culture that has yet to even consider the possibility. Despite the best efforts of Gene Roddenberry and George Lucas, most people can't comprehend a human settlement on the moon or Mars any time in the next two hundred years. And

NASA and the government are staying as far away as they can from any mention of space colonies.

"What this has created is an imbalance in the Inventor/Builder relationship when it comes to human space activity. The *invention* of the means to enable people to live and work in space has not been followed by the *building* or replicating of those means so that all who wish can do the same. Once we can bridge the gap between the Inventor and Builder, we will see an explosion of human expansion throughout the solar system.

I asked tentatively, "Do you see this happening in your lifetime?"

"It doesn't matter to me if it happens in my lifetime or not. All I can do is conduct myself in a manner that assumes *it will.*"

Just then Phillips was hailed by one of his engineers, and I knew our talk was over. I caught a ride back to my car with one of his team who spoke of Phillips as a devotee would of his guru. I could see the appeal. If anyone was going to build a new civilization in space, it could very well be Evan Phillips.

I arrived back at the district office a little before noon. I could sense a heightened energy level, and when I spotted Mr. Grant among a cluster of staff, I realized he was the source.

As I approached the group, Mr. Grant broke from his conversation, saying as he pointed at me, "Him. John. John will drive me." The other staff, Dotty among them, seemed just as taken aback as I was by this outburst. Mr. Grant was in town for a planned trip, which included appearances at a series of local events. On the agenda that day was a luncheon presentation to a Kiwanis Club, and apparently I was to be the chauffeur.

It was not clear whether Mr. Grant preferred my company, or if it was the company of other more demanding staff he wished to avoid. He marched to the door and said, "Let's go." A flustered and clearly annoyed Dotty Rodriguez thrust a folder in my hand and told me that I'd better get going. The folder contained his speech and a sheet of meeting logistics.

"You drive." He tossed me the keys as I approached his Buick Skylark. Despite the suddenness of the situation, I knew this assignment created an opportunity for me to discuss my experiences with Judith Falk and Evan Phillips. After the incredible morning at the rocket test facility, I was bursting to share the details with Mr. Grant. I attempted to open the discussion as soon as we pulled onto the road. He just smiled and patted my arm saying, "There'll be plenty of time. At the moment, however, we are late, and we need to concentrate on getting where we need to be." Mr. Grant did not say anything more except to occasionally bark directions to the Kiwanis hall.

Once inside, Mr. Grant became his jovial self, glad handing and joking with his old buddies while sipping a scotch on the rocks. It was his element. I sat at the head table, mostly listening to the conversation dominated by humorous anecdotes by Mr. Grant to everyone's enjoyment. Just before he stood up to make his way to the podium I tried to hand him the folder with the speech, but he waved me off.

In the next thirty minutes, I witnessed a masterful off-the-cuff speech that entertained, informed, and inspired the crowd. Most people even stood up during the applause. Mr. Grant knew his audience, and they loved their congressman.

It was after 2:30 when we left the hall. Mr. Grant settled into the passenger seat satisfied by how the event had gone. "Do you feel like taking a little ride?" he asked. "I'd like to hear about your time with Dr. Falk and Evan Phillips." I was thankful that he wished to engage in that subject. The luncheon had not dampened my desire to speak with him about the Endowments.

"Of course…where to?"

"I'll show you. Go straight to the second light and make a left." Within a mile or so, the road narrowed and we passed fewer houses. "Turn here," Mr. Grant commanded just as I made out a sign that read "Box Springs Mountain Park." It was a large park with recreational areas and hiking trails. As I followed the twists and turns according to Mr. Grant's instruction I felt the increasing elevation. Finally he had me pull into one of the available spots in a gravel parking area.

We hiked along a short inclined path that opened to a grassy plateau. There were benches and picnic tables scattered around the clearing. The opposite end of the field was a cliff's edge that provided a magnificent overlook of the valley below and views of the mountains in the distance. There was no one else there. We sat on a bench overlooking the cliff. The silence was disturbed only by a light breeze blowing through the trees and the occasional bird call.

After a minute or two of taking in the surroundings, Mr. Grant began, "So, what do you think of the Endowments so far? Is the picture starting to come together?"

"What's becoming clear is that there are distinct reasons why people are passionate about space travel. Each reason is linked to an endowment, and the desire for space travel manifests differently depending on which endowment it is springing from."

"And what can you conclude from that?"

"Uh…that human interest, or passion, for space travel is an expression of certain basic human traits,… the Endowments."

"Mmm…that's pretty close, considering you don't have the full story yet." His less than enthusiastic reaction took the wind out of my sail. I thought I was doing pretty well. He chuckled. "Don't worry about that for the moment. It will become clear later. What you should begin to understand about the Endowments are two things. First, that the second two endowments are evolved versions of the first two. Second, the Endowments are pairs with masculine and feminine characteristics. With the first two Endowments, the Wanderer is masculine and the Settler is feminine. The Wanderer is the tendency to strike outward in an aggressive archetypically manly way. The Settler is feminine; she wants to make a safe place for herself and her offspring. It's related to the nesting instinct. Please don't confuse these with gender roles of man and woman. You'll only get yourself into trouble if you do."

He paused, turning his head away from the view to look directly at me. "Now we move onto the Inventor and the Builder. The Inventor, a masculine Endowment is an evolved version of the Wanderer. You see?"

I interjected, "Yes, Dr. Falk talked about the relationship between the Wanderer and the Inventor. She said how the Inventor wanders in the confines of his own mind to solve problems and create innovation."

"That's right. And similarly, the Builder, a feminine endowment, is the evolved version of the Settler." Though there was nothing feminine about Evan Phillips, I understood the point Mr. Grant was making.

"The Builder builds cities, as Evan Phillips no doubt told you. In a sense they are seeking to achieve the same safety and comfort for the population that the Settler wants to achieve. Both the masculine and feminine are needed for balance and survival."

I was reminded of what Phillips had said about there being an imbalance in human space development. "Evan Phillips said that there was a great deal of focus on the Invention aspects of space travel, but at the same time, the ability of the Builder to participate was severely restricted."

"That's a very interesting point. There is a verse in the Tao Te Ching, the ancient book of philosophy, that says, 'All things stand with their backs to the feminine, facing the masculine. When male and female combine all things achieve harmony.' Phillips recognizes that our space program is seriously out of balance."

He paused at this. I was beginning to see the larger context and pattern of the Endowments. There seemed to be a principled link between them.

"Now, what does all of this mean for the next pairs of Endowments: The Visionary and the Protector?"

"The Visionary and the Protector?" I absently repeated it to Mr. Grant's gleaming smile.

"Yes. So, based on what I have said, what can we expect about the final pair of Endowments?"

"...That they are evolved versions of earlier Endowments: one will be feminine in quality and one will be masculine? Is that what you're saying?"

"I think you're starting to understand."

As strange as it seemed to me, the pieces were coming together, though I still had the sense that I was only seeing one corner of a much larger picture.

"So, the next Endowments...Who will I learn about those from?"

"The Visionary, I'm afraid, will have to be a surprise." He exaggerated the statement with raised eyebrows, and laughed at my blank expression. The rumble of his amusement echoed out into the valley below.

THE VISIONARY

Two days later I was on my way to see the Visionary.

As far as Dotty Rodriguez and the others on staff were concerned my excursions to JPL and the Mojave Desert related to research I was doing for the space subcommittee. My next outing to visit the Visionary and the Protector were a whole other story.

Outside the closed door of Mr. Grant's private office I could clearly hear Dotty's vehement objections to my taking another three days out of the office. "What about the expense...The time away...He's just a junior staff." Mr. Grant's baritone voice was an unintelligible rumble through the wall, but from the tone of his voice, he was apparently unmoved by Dotty's arguments. She finally emerged stone faced.

Without making eye contact she explained my itinerary for the coming days. Her voice flat and cool. "You're to contact Terry Li at the Kitt Peak National Observatory in southern Arizona and arrange to meet with him there tomorrow evening. The following day, you are to meet Mr. Grant at the climate change conference in Tucson. You should plan to leave early tomorrow. It's a long drive. Sorry, we have no budget to send you by plane, especially on such short notice." I thought I should say I was okay with driving, but the situation was awkward enough.

"Oh! One more thing. On your way to Kitt Peak, you're to make a stop in Scottsdale. Here's the address." She handed me a piece of note paper with a street address in Arizona. "Mr. Grant didn't say who you are to meet there. He said you'll know when you get there," she said with a slight roll of the eyes. "And make sure you're there by three PM tomorrow."

I was embarrassed that my exploration of the Endowments was causing so much disruption. At the same time, I was captivated by the process of discovery Mr. Grant was guiding me on, and nothing else was nearly as important.

I attempted to say something about the awkward situation Mr. Grant had put us both in, but she just sighed and shook her head on the way back to her desk.

For an instant I grasped for some positive acknowledgment. Then, the realization hit me. Tara Bingham would be at the Tucson conference. That meant I would not have to wait until I got back to Washington to see her. "*I miss you.*" Her words I had repeated to myself a hundred times since I read her letter. With the Tucson trip suddenly on my schedule, my mixed feelings about seeing her wonderfully competed with my intense desire to decipher the meaning of the Endowments and the Obligation.

Things were accelerating and I didn't understand why. My co-workers were distant the remainder of the afternoon as I absently sorted casework files for the rest of the afternoon, planning the next day's trip in my head. Mr. Grant gave me a wave as he left with Dotty for a fund raising dinner. He didn't say a word.

The following day I arrived at my first destination at 2:30 PM, a half hour early. The drive was long, over seven hours. I had never driven that part of the country before. The shifting scenery was beautiful and alien, making the drive easier than it might have been. The address was of a ranch house in the affluent town of Rio Verde, just outside of Scottsdale. The house was smaller than most in the neighborhood though clearly well appointed. It was southwestern style with a stucco façade and clay tile roof. I debated whether to ring the bell and introduce myself right away, or wait until three, the designated time. As I pondered this question, a middle-aged woman with long straight gray hair pulled back in a loose pony tail came out of the house, and looked in my direction shielding her eyes. I had parked across the street from the home. She walked down a footpath to the gate of her three foot high stone fence, leaned forward and said something that I couldn't hear with my windows up and air conditioner blasting. I rolled down the window, and she repeated herself.

"John? Are you John from Harry Grant's office?" Seeing her more clearly and hearing her refined British accent, I felt I knew her from somewhere.

"Yes. Yes, I am. It wasn't three yet, and I thought that I shouldn't intrude earlier than expected..."

"Nonsense. Nonsense. Come on in. I've been waiting for you." And she turned and headed back to the door without waiting for me to get out of the car. I scurried after her. She didn't linger for me at the front door either, which I closed after entering, allowing the air conditioned equilibrium to return to the room.

"I'm in the kitchen," her voiced echoed off the terracotta tile floor.

I finally caught up with her in a spacious kitchen where she handed me a tall glass of lemonade. "Here you are." Looking at her close up, I saw how tall and slim she was; easily an inch or two taller than me.

"Thank you." I took a long drink. It was cold and refreshing with just the right amount of sweetness. The spent lemon rinds still littered the counter, evidence that the drink was freshly made.

"This is wonderful. I have to apologize, but Mr. Grant only gave me the address. He didn't say who I'd be meeting, but you seem so familiar."

She laughed at that. "I suppose it was Harry's idea of protecting my privacy...Well then. My name is Barbara Everheart. Pleased to meet you." She stuck out her hand to shake as the recognition hit me. Barbara Everheart, the famous science fiction author who had written many of the best known classics of the genre. You didn't have to be a science fiction fan to recognize the trademark features and personality.

"Yes, of course. A great pleasure to meet you. I should have recognized you right away." I contained another surge of embarrassment, but she seemed only amused by the situation. She wore a beige cotton tunic over light green linen shorts. Modest jewelry of silver, wood and turquoise adorned her wrist and neck.

"Let's sit inside, shall we?" She led the way. "I think we have some things to discuss. Hmm?"

Everheart's upper class British accent was warm and inviting, and put me at ease. We sat in her living room facing the glass sliding doors that looked out onto the cactus desert and distant jagged mountains. She sat in an oversized leather arm chair, and I sat on a soft couch with rolled arms. The décor had a distinct southwestern overtone, accented with African, Indian, European and Chinese elements among the furnishing and art. But, the one object I hoped I might see was not in sight.

"Looking for something, John?" My casual sweep of the room had apparently crossed the line from admiring to searching.

"No, just appreciating your beautiful home."

"Oh. I thought you might be wondering where I hang my *Obligation plaque*." She smiled impishly. "I prefer to keep that in my bedroom," she teased, as I felt my cheeks go flush.

"I understand you've been having some interesting conversations about the Endowments."

"Yes."

"The Wanderer and the Settler, and the Inventor and the Builder." She stirred her lemonade with a straw and took a long sip, eyeing me. There was such a playful quality to her. The aging woman I first saw at her front gate was replaced by a youthful presence who challenged any assignment of age.

"Yes, those are the ones I've heard about..."

"Now we come to the next pair of Endowments: The Visionary and the Protector." She leaned back putting her feet up onto a round leather ottoman. "I want to make sure we are in dialogue about this information, so why don't we start with you telling me what you think the Visionary Endowment might mean in the context of all that you have heard up to this point."

"Well, let me see..." It took me a few moments to consider the question. "When I think of a visionary, I think of someone who has big ideas about the future. Maybe he's someone like Henry Ford or Steven Jobs, or maybe the Founding Fathers...of the United States."

"Yes, those are good examples." She looked out at the scenery for a moment before continuing. "The Visionary, in the way we are discussing it as an Endowment, is the capacity to conceptualize expansively and holistically about things that do not yet exist. Through the visioning process, consciousness is pushed to a level beyond the problem solving of the Inventor. The Visionary is the one who sees the big picture possibilities for himself, his community and the world. A vision may be as expansive as a utopian city or form of government or a pyramid. The great leaps in civilization were not possible before the emergence of the Visionary endowment in human consciousness. The Visionary may also have more modest visions as well, such as that of a beautiful rose garden or a work of art."

I asked, "But what about the Inventor and the Builder?

I thought those Endowments made civilization possible."

"Yes, the Inventor and Builder were essential to the evolution of civilization, but the great leaps forward required the Visionary to define the challenge to which the Inventor and Builder applied themselves. It may have been the Inventor who solved the engineering challenge of building a clay house so that its occupants could be protected from the elements. And it may have been the Builder who copied the technique over and over again so that the whole community could have the same kind of dwelling. But it is the Visionary that sees how the technology could be applied to build a temple for worship and an entire city for the masses. There is a higher conscious intent in the Visionary's design."

Recollecting my last talk with Mr. Grant, I surmised, "So, you're saying the Visionary is an *evolved* version of the Inventor Endowment."

"That's exactly right. The Visionary Endowment is a manifestation of the universal outward expansion, the Yang or masculine force, like our impulse to wander and to invent. To become a Visionary, the Inventor evolves from being a problem solver to someone who can envision how their inventions—whether they exist yet or not—can be used to change the world in which he lives. So it's not just about the object or process, *per se.* It's about the whole future condition that can be brought into being. The Visionary may not necessarily know just how his vision can be brought into reality, though he may have some ideas, or many ideas, how it can be achieved. The important thing is the vision itself, and the action the Visionary takes to make that vision a reality. If the vision is something the Visionary can accomplish on his own, he needs to take decisive steps to bring it about. If he needs help, it becomes necessary to effectively communicate the vision. The Visionary then provides the inspiration and motivation to the Inventors and Builders to create the means by which the vision can be realized.

"The mind of the Visionary knows no limits. She can see with her mind's eye all the possibilities. Though it may seem obvious, but it's important to emphasize that only by first having a vision is it possible to create that vision in the physical world. It is the capacity to be open, to see something where there is nothing. Many Visionaries speak of their visions as being *revealed* spontaneously. I know in my writing this is often the case. When I am in that writing *zone*, it seems all I have to do is copy down the details of the vision that appears before me… I like to believe that somehow the future is communicating with me directly, showing me which alternative future most needs to be expressed in my prose." She laughed at her last statement with a hand over her mouth. "I hope that doesn't sound too strange, John? I wouldn't want you to get the wrong idea."

She took another sip of lemonade and continued, "Now let's be clear on something. Someone might say they have a vision of one day owning a new car or house. This is not a vision but a desire, however vivid it might be. Wanting or desiring something for yourself that already exists does not constitute a vision as defined by the Visionary Endowment. This desire would be more closely aligned with the Builder, whereby you want to reproduce something that is already in the world for your own benefit. There is nothing inappropriate, by the way, in the desire for material things. This desire has been, in a sense, one of the engines of our evolution. Anthropologically speaking, if we didn't covet the finer things of our neighbor, there never would have been triggered the spiral of introduction of something new, followed by widespread adoption, followed by something new, etc… I do hope I'm making sense, John."

I assured her she was.

"I should also be clear that visions are not necessarily selfless conceptualizations. In fact, they rarely have been. The Pharaoh's vision of constructing for himself the largest pyramid ever built is something that certainly advanced human capability. Architects, engineers and artisans toil to make that vision a reality, and in the process invented new building methods and techniques. I imagine that the visions of most large transformative construction projects sprang from the vanity of a self-absorbed ruler or ruling class. And the interesting question here is why these, mostly men, chose to express their vanity with a pyramid, temple or skyscraper? It's interesting, isn't it, that we have been so fixated on the central projects that involved constructing buildings and monuments that reach as high as possible above the ground, attempting to touch the heavens." She paused to pull me into the point. "Something to think about, isn't it?" She was leading me down a logic path, but didn't quite finish making the connection before moving on.

"But, we're focusing here on the Visionary. Vanity, pride, show of strength, and insecurity. These are all base emotions that have stimulated visions that, despite their selfish nature, have spurred Visionaries of great things. In most cases, grand visions were enthusiastically embraced by the community that would build and live in the presence of these structures. To be a laborer on a cathedral in the Middle Ages was a great honor, a religious experience.

"More recently, the Apollo moon program could be described as a central project put forth by politicians who were more interested in showing off their technical prowess to a rival super power than reaching out to the moon for its own sake. Many critics have labeled the moon missions as little more than a Cold War stunt. But the Apollo program can't be dismissed so easily. We know that. Men and women worked on that program with breathless devotion. The nations and people of the world cheered the program on. We came together as a human family in July 1969 like never before to witness something that transformed life on this planet forever. That was a moment of a vision fulfilled. The true Apollo visionaries, like Wernher von Braun, could care less about the race with the Soviets. In the scope of human history, it will be the mission itself that will be remembered long after the Cold War is forgotten.

"The Visionaries could be rather deranged fellows as well. Caesar, Genghis Khan, even Hitler, were all men of vision, you could say. They were also monsters. In their twisted minds, they saw their role as bringing nations together. Visionaries plunged Europe into the Dark Ages with the Inquisitions and holy wars, and have shackled the hearts and minds of populations in nearly every age."

I was becoming uneasy with the direction Everheart's instruction was taking, and it must have shown on my face. "Didn't Harry discuss this with you?"

Just then, a tall man appeared from a side room. He was slender like Everheart, with bony handsome features and several days' gray growth on his chin. His sudden presence disarmed the conversation.

"Oh, Bill. There you are. I thought you might've stayed in hiding the whole time our friend John was here." I shook hands with Bill, who was an American about the same age as Barbara. I didn't ask but assumed he was more than a friend.

"I hope you're not trying to freak this fellow out. We wouldn't want him to go back to Washington with all sorts of crazy ideas." He smiled in my direction, and I wondered if his entrance was specifically intended to relieve my anxiety.

"Don't be silly," Everheart laughed. "What I'm trying to explain, John, is that the Endowments are ethically and morally neutral impulses." Bill smiled and headed to the kitchen. "Fortunately, humanity has been on a moral and ethical evolutionary path as well, and more and more we are seeing Visions conceived and realized in the context of selfless moral and humanitarian ideals."

"So it is that, somehow, despite the questionable morality of many of our forebearers, this huge cauldron of humanity, acting in response to the Endowment, generation after generation, in literally billions of ways, has somehow emerged from history, on balance, looking pretty good. We survived, haven't we? We made it!" I got what she meant. Just sitting in that beautiful home with nothing really to fear, looking out on an exquisite landscape, life was indeed pretty good. It was at that point I realized I had slipped into a state of heightened receptiveness. The sensation had come over me so gradually I barely noticed.

A thought occurred to me. "For us, things may have worked out. I mean here in the U.S. and Europe and some other parts of the world, but there are many places where life is still extremely difficult, struggling with hunger, brutality, environmental devastation."

"Yes, you're right. And this is where the latest generation of Visionaries is at work. They see a world where no one goes hungry, children are educated, and everyone is ensured basic human rights. There is a rise in the number of Visionaries who are indeed selfless, which is an excellent development. These Visionaries are here. You don't have to look very hard." She was right, of course. Being in Washington, I saw firsthand such Visionaries addressing global issues trying with all their heart to make a difference. Tara Bingham was one of them, I assumed, doing her part for the environmental cause. Bill, who had stood listening, winked at me and drifted to the kitchen, apparently satisfied he had served his purpose.

Everheart continued, "As I mentioned earlier, Visionaries can also be the creators or inventors of their own visions. These are the solitary writers, artists and researchers who will move easily from seeing a vision in their mind to giving it form with their own hands. Like an artist creating a painting or sculpture. Take me, for example. I have created visions of alien universes and civilizations, with technologies and cultures that we can't imagine existing in the real world. These are solitary acts of art. At the same time, I believe they also inform and inspire our culture to reach for new possibilities."

This was true. Everheart's stories had inspired generations of scientists, artists and entrepreneurs.

"With art, we speak of its *uplifting* quality. We are moved, motivated. It all adds to the great soup of our collective advancement. On the other hand, for visions that have direct societal impact, or any that involve significant commitment of resources and political will, the vision's fulfillment requires the enlistment of others to agree with your vision and become emotionally invested along with the Visionary. That's where articulation of the vision comes in. Others have to know about the vision, don't they? This is risky, of course. By his nature, the Visionary thinks outside established norms, and therefore his ideas are easily labeled impossible, crazy, ridiculous or worse. The successful Visionary is able to present her vision in a compelling fashion. The sad reality is that the majority of Visionaries never see their visions blossom because they are either unable to effectively communicate them, or they don't even try." Her voice had trailed off to a melancholy place as she stared out the window. "This is a tragedy."

She turned back to me and straightened her posture before continuing more cheerily.

"Fortunately for the planet, of course, there have been many Visionaries who have succeeded despite all odds— either they themselves succeeded, or their devoted followers succeeded in their name. A vision can, of course, be carried from one generation to the next, or span many generations, before it comes to fruition. This is the power of the evolutionary forces we are dealing with here. They are not dependent on a particular individual. Sometimes visions will take centuries to become realized. And the last hundred and fifty years or so has certainly been a time when ancient visions were fulfilled. The horseless carriage, flameless light, the airplane, the end of legalized slavery. It is all the realized visions in history strung together that tell the story of the advancements in human civilizations over the last ten thousand years. We have had visions of making a new village – and we have done it. We've had visions of building better tools – and we have done that. We've had visions of building great towers that touch the sky –we've done that. We've had visions of walking on the moon – and we have done that, too.

"The story, of course is far from over. The twentieth century also gave birth to new and spectacular visions, some of which will take decades or even centuries to fulfill. Speaking in a social sense, Martin Luther King, Jr. had a vision, right? A dream of a post-racial world where everyone had an equal chance at making the best lives for themselves regardless of the color of their skin. Though Dr. King is dead, we are reminded regularly that his dream is still alive. And indeed it is."

She looked at the floor, considering her words. "I think we should speak a little more about what the Visionary is *not*. Visioning is not daydreaming, though a vision can start as an idle daydream that develops over time into a true vision. Visioning also has nothing to do with wishful thinking, wanting something good to happen to you personally, as we discussed earlier, or even wishing that things would be better for larger society.

"It is also possible for the Visionary, if he or she is not careful, to get lost in a vision, even a sincere selfless one. A vision can become a gilded cage of the mind, a dream world where we fantasize about how things will be once our vision becomes reality. This is not authentic visioning, and could devolve into a form of delusion. Therefore, I stress again that a vision only has value if action is being taken to bring it into reality, or in some way it is shared with others. Otherwise, the potential of this Endowment will have been wasted." Her stare lingered in the silence after these words, and again there was the flicker of sadness in the corner of her eyes.

Breaking the quiet, I asked, "Can you speak more about how the Visionary relates to space exploration…and settlement?"

"Yes, of course. We wouldn't be here in dialogue if all of this didn't tie back to outer space." She smiled with closed lips. "The Visionary Endowment is the Endowment most responsible for the advanced civilization we live in today, as I've explained. And, it is only with the Visionary Endowment that we can envision the creation of new civilizations beyond Earth. So, as with the other Endowments, the Visionary was not only integral to enabling us to come this far, but is also the very capacity we need to light our way to the stars.

"The visions of great cities in space are out there. God knows, I created many of them. Serious scientists have put forth visions as well, like my friend Gerry O'Neill at Princeton, who developed detailed designs for free orbiting space colonies that could support populations of ten thousand and larger. NASA even sponsored a study on space colonies in the mid-seventies."

"I believe Prof. Donnelly told me about that study, and even showed me the published report."

She nodded, and continued, "The Visionary understands that extending civilization into space will bear fruits far beyond anything currently imaginable. Many thousands or perhaps millions of people are drawn to these visions. As these visions filter through the global culture, with each generation there is the hope that eventually a group of influential and adventurous souls will find the pathway to building those great cities in space." As she said this she looked straight at me with raised eyebrows, almost asking if I might be one of those souls.

"With my writing, I create fictional worlds, a form of art that can excite and stimulate the mind of my readers. There are Visionaries right now who are contemplating the stepping stones leading toward human settlement of space. There are many visions of how to improve life on Earth, and all of these visions are essential and valid. But, the Visionary who contemplates the migration of humans to space is unique— and critical.

"It is humbling that there are those who dare to even suggest such things. Yet, not only do we suggest it, there are millions around the world who willingly embrace space migration wholeheartedly. If you have a heart, John, you must be humbled by this dimension of the human family.

Her point hit me more physically than cognitively.

We sat in a relaxed silence for about a minute, before she said calmly, "Well, I think that will have to do for now, John. I hope this has been helpful."

"Yes. Yes it has. Very much." Almost on cue, Bill reemerged from the kitchen with a tall glass of lemonade.

"Well then, can I get you a refill?"

THE PROTECTOR

The sun was low in the sky when I finally reached Kitt Peak National Observatory. The sprawling research center was situated high above the Sonoran Desert on the Tohono O'odham Reservation. The facility was home to more than twenty optical and radio telescopes and represented eight astronomical research institutions.

I was light headed all the way from Barbara Everheart's. I wished there had been more time to digest her words before meeting the next, and last, Endowment representative, Terry Li. When I asked Ms. Everheart about the Protector Endowment, she only said that he probably wouldn't be what I might expect.

I followed the signs to the visitors' parking area. Getting out of the car, I felt a stiff wind. Up on the mountain, the temperature was at least twenty degrees colder than it was at Everheart's place.

Standing at the main entrance of the administration building was Terry Li, the principal investigator of Spaceguard, a program to identify and catalog near-earth orbiting objects. Terry was short and very thin with straight black hair that fell over his ears.

"Welcome. Welcome, John. It's so good you could make

101

it all this way." Terry spoke with a slight Asian accent and exuded an enthusiasm that made him seem perpetually on the verge of all-out laughter.

We had dinner in the cafeteria with two other scientists from his team who casually joined us. I thought briefly about my lunch with Dr. Falk in the JPL cafeteria just a few days earlier, which felt like weeks. Over a corned beef platter and hot minestrone soup, Terry mentioned nothing about the Endowments, but gave me an excellent overview of Kitt Peak and its many telescopes and areas of research.

After the meal, Terry asked if I'd like a driving tour of the center. The sun had already disappeared behind the mountains, and the last vestiges of its light provided just enough illumination to make the tour worthwhile. Terry described the focus of research of each observatory as they passed by my window. He stopped the car at an unusual building that looked like the bottom half of a giant letter "K." It was the Solar Observatory, he explained, and thought I would be interested in having a closer look. The angled portion of the structure, at two hundred feet in length, was the above ground section of the telescope. The telescope shaft extended another three hundred feet down into the mountain. Scientists used the telescope to measure the sun's magnetic fields and chemical composition.

Our next and final stop was a domed observatory of modest size. It was the Steward Observatory, the oldest at Kitt Peak. The observatory was a plain white structure with the base footprint not exceeding the circumference of the dome, which was about fifty feet in diameter. We entered the building and went up a flight of stairs, and made our way to a spacious control room where one of Terry's team members, Bill Powell, was working at a computer station. The office area was a modest space whose purpose was to take scientific measurements of the sky and little else.

"Hi Terry. I was just about to do the pour."

"Super." Then to me, "You'll be interested in this." We

left the control room and went up another flight of stairs to the main observatory level. The retractable door of the dome was open wide, letting in the cold mountain air and stars from the cloudless sky. In the dimly lit space, the 36-inch telescope loomed overhead, reaching up to the opening in the dome. Curious about the mechanics of the telescope, I asked Terry where the eyepiece was located. "You expect to see an eyepiece like the telescopes you had as a kid?" He chuckled. "With this kind of instrument we use a charged-coupled device, or CCD, that allows us to record the image digitally. Then we look at it in the control room. With CCDs there's no more need for film." He waited until I was good with his response, and then turned my attention to Bill who was standing on a small platform next to the telescope. With heavy work gloves, Bill held what looked like a large thermos. He pressed a button on the rail of the platform and with a slight jolt it began to rise slowly.

"Bill is going to pour liquid nitrogen into the apparatus. We're dealing with electrons that prefer to be super cold for the best images, and the heat of the CCD itself can really screw up the quality." Bill elevated himself ten feet to the top of the telescope. He removed the cap of the canister and, with a funnel, he poured the super cooled liquid into an opening. Ice cold nitrogen vapor billowed all around him.

"We'll see everything we want to see downstairs." Back in the control room, I finally got a good look at the array of computer screens that guided, monitored and recorded the observations. The room was dark with most of the light coming from the screens. Bill explained that they kept the lights low so their eyes didn't have to adjust when making frequent trips up to the dome.

"Now we wait, and every twenty minutes we take a picture of the same part of the sky. The computer compares each new picture with the previous one, and if it finds anything different it lets us know. Any change is an indication that an asteroid or comet has come into the field of observation." He went over the one of the computer screens and began typing on a keyboard.

"Here, let me show you what I mean." A star field blinked onto the screen. It was interesting enough. Then he pressed the enter key and the field changed slightly. I noticed a new star appeared near the center of the field. He press the key again, and then I realized the second star had disappeared and a new one had appeared in the lower left part of the monitor. He kept tapping the enter key, and I saw a repeated pattern of three images of an object in the upper right, then center, then lower left. The pictures depicted the path of an object moving through the star field.

"We recorded that a few days ago. That's an asteroid heading for Earth. If it hits us at the right place, it could completely destroy a city the size of New York."

He waited for my look of surprise, and then added, "Of course, it will miss the Earth by three-and-a-half million kilometers, or about nine times the distance between the Earth and the moon. In celestial terms, however, that's a hair's breadth. We will be lucky this time. But the truth is asteroids of significant size come close to Earth quite often. So, the question is not *if* a city destroying asteroid will hit the Earth, but *when*."

I knew that Terry Li was the principal investigator of the Spaceguard Project, a program partially funded by NASA. I asked him about it. "It all started very modestly in the early 1980's, with just one observatory looking for NEO's—Near-Earth Objects. Interest has grown. Other observatories have joined the search, but we are a long way from what is needed to identify potential blockbuster asteroids, never mind coming up with ways to mitigate the catastrophic effect if and when we do identify a really nasty one heading straight for us."

Noticing that Bill had moved to the other side of the room, out of ear shot, I took the opportunity to ask. "Is this work related to the Protector Endowment?"

He gave me a searching look that quickly morphed into a broad smile. "Yes, of course it does. But, first…coffee." He led the way to a kitchen area, with a refrigerator, microwave, and coffee pot. He poured two large mugs and handed me one. Nothing could have been more welcome in that moment, as I was feeling the effect of a long day that had begun very early in Riverside, California. The coffee was a strong gourmet blend.

I expressed appreciation. "We take our coffee very seriously around here," Terry proclaimed. "Let's go back upstairs. Here, put this on." He handed me a parka, which I appreciated almost as much as the coffee.

On the dark observation level, Terry went over to a panel on the wall and pressed a button. With a shudder, the dome began to rotate. Over the sound of the motor that turned the dome, Terry said, "I need to adjust the opening to face the part of the sky we'll be viewing tonight." Watching the rectangle of stars slide past the dome opening against the black interior was disorienting.

We sat at a console next to the telescope and Terry spoke briefly to Bill via intercom to ensure the rotation was correct.

Without my prompting he began speaking about the Protector Endowment. "We are finally coming to some appreciation that the planet we live on exists in a galaxy that in many ways is perpetually threatening humankind's very existence. NEOs are just one threat that could spell doom for Earth. We know the sun eventually will become a red giant and turn our planet into a cinder. But the sun is somewhat unpredictable and could at any time erupt in powerful flares that could do serious damage. It's happened before in fact. A solar event in 1859 caused telegraph lines to heat up and catch fire. A similar event today could destroy much of our electronic infrastructure and send us back into the nineteenth century."

He seemed to change his tone and cadence in a way similar to that of the others, once it was time to talk about the

Endowments. There was information that needed to be conveyed in a certain way with a certain amount of detail. It was not that the Endowment representatives became different people, but that there was a deliberateness with regard to how they spoke about the topic.

"The point is there are risks on many levels that could bring an end of our species or to all life on Earth. This is what the Sixth Endowment is about. The Protector Endowment is the capacity in some people to assess broad environmental risks, and search for ways to avoid those risks. Like the Visionary, The Protector has enormous capacity to envision all possible futures, but in the case of the Protector the visioning is oriented toward protection and preservation of a particular population or even the species as a whole.

"The Protector realizes that we must take decisive action to be ready to deal with catastrophic events that are likely to occur. As we become ever more aware of the dangers that threaten human existence, as we've started to discuss, we sense the survival imperative to do something before it's too late.

"The Protector is a feminine or complexity trait, right. I think you know by now what I mean by that." I nodded. "So, it has similarities to the Settler and Builder Endowments. The Settler and Builder Endowments are also about protection, aren't they? They are intent on removing from our environment the dangers of the wild, or from each other, so that we are safe and protected. The Protector is the one looking ahead now, looking for what dangers might threaten us in the grandest and perhaps most improbable of ways. These are folks who look up at the mountain and think rock slide, who look out into the ocean and see tidal waves, and look up into space and see falling asteroids. He may be the *chicken little* of our society, but the Protector is essential to our survival and development. In one sense this is no different from the smallest animal in the jungle that is ever vigilant of some imminent danger.

"The Protector creates all forms of emergency preparedness programs: earthquake monitoring, weather watch, construction of levees. He wants to guard against natural disasters. In medicine, it is the quest to protect the population against infectious diseases. Then there is protection against the threat of our neighbors. In ancient times it took the Protector to envision great walls to protect castles from invading armies, design moats and boiling oil to pour on the enemy. There are many gruesome examples of military protectors, not the least being the maintenance of standing armies. The Great Wall of China, in my home country, was built to protect the ancient Chinese empire from the northern hordes. A Protector envisioned a fortification that stretched thousands of miles, that took hundreds of years and millions of workers to complete.

"We now live in a world of 'safety first,' don't we? Cars are safer, because of seatbelts, airbags and drunk driving laws. There are safety regulations governing air and sea travel. The world in many ways is much safer than it was even fifty years ago. The Protector is ever at work to systemically reduce the risk of bodily injury or death. Sometimes, or quite often, the Protector has been ignored leading to horrendous consequences.

"The Protector has thrived with the rise of democracy. Once *the people* had a voice in politics and could sway public policy with their vote, the Protector was hugely empowered. Child labor laws, occupational-safety and health laws, environmental protection, food safety laws. Right?

"Diplomacy, to negotiate peace terms and avoid war, is the Protector at work as well. He always wants to keep things nice and predictable and everybody happy and safe.

"In the last part of the twentieth century, however, the Protector found himself face to face with his biggest challenge ever. Our knowledge of the Earth and the solar system has progressed to the point where we can now conclude without a doubt that the ancient prophets were right all along: life on Earth will most certainly come to an end."

He paused for emphasis.

"We live in a hostile and unforgiving universe. The only thing more amazing than the fact that our existence hangs by a celestial thread, is that life on this speck of a planet was not extinguished long ago, or that it even came into being in the first place. That we are still here is as much a testament to the resilience of life to endure as it is to sheer luck.

He laughed. He had taken on a more somber tone, but the humor was still intact.

"This is a tough situation for the Protector. How is he going to save the world from certain death? It seems that the list of existential threats to human life keeps getting longer and more imminent every year. The risk to civilization by asteroids is real. We've done a good job of identifying the big rocks out there, but there are many thousands yet that we have not found. You know about the asteroid that sent the dinosaurs to oblivion sixty-five million years ago—at least that's what most paleontologists believe. There's a ride at Disney World that does a good job of reenacting that last moment before the asteroid impact." I had actually been on that ride. Park goers pile into time traveling jeeps to visit the dinosaur age. A slip of the time dial places riders at the very moments of the asteroid impact. The jeep narrowly dodges dinosaurs and asteroid fragments exploding at every turn. Just as the big one hits, the jeep jumps back through the time portal, delivering passengers safely to the Disney World Park ride attendants. The ride was more fun than most, but any thought that such a fate might actually be repeated in my lifetime had never occurred to me.

"That asteroid that took out the dinosaurs was seven-and-a-half miles wide. But if you want a more recent example of the damage a near-earth object can do, you just have to look back to 1908 when a comet a mere forty feet in diameter destroyed over eight hundred square miles of forest with a force a thousand times more powerful than the bomb dropped on Hiroshima." He paused, looking for my reaction to that frightening statistic. "That's an impressive amount of destruction for a rock about the size of a house. And if that asteroid had been delayed by just three hours, Moscow would have been the impact site, wiping out the city and its population, instead of just a few million trees."

Terry wanted this to sink in. The LCD lights of the instruments reflecting off his eyes gave them an otherworldly glow.

"We know these NEOs are whizzing by us all the time, and sooner or later another major impact is going to happen, and next time we may not be so lucky. We're starting to look for and catalog NEOs, but we have only begun this process and we have a very long way to go. Many of the biggest objects are missed by our monitoring until they've already gone past the planet. This blind spot is caused by the light of the sun, which overwhelms the dimmer light of anything coming from its direction. Not to cause you alarm, but the next big one, a city buster or bigger, could be on its way here tomorrow, and we'd have no idea it's coming."

Again his penetrating stare focused on my eyes for emphasis. "The point I'm making is that there is no way we can guard against asteroid danger completely. Not now, anyway. And asteroids are just one of the many dangers that threaten our civilization's survival. I probably don't need to tell you that. We can tick some of these off: the risk of new plague or biological weapons, creating a runaway virus that is both highly contagious and beyond limits of medical science to respond; nuclear weapons in the hands of terrorists, or rogue governments could trigger an exchange of warheads that could bring about Armageddon.

"I guess you can include some of the extreme predictions made about global warming," I offered this, as I had heard sensational claims about how global warming might cause extreme climate shifts that could bring down civilization.

"That's right. We have to appreciate the fact that to a large extent, we really don't know what affect Global Warming will have on the world and our ability to survive the changes that are coming with rising ocean levels and more severe weather patterns.

"Volcanic outgassing is another unknown. There is much we don't know about the volatility of the magma deep below us. Have you ever heard of a supervolcano?" It sounded familiar. "A supervolcano eruption is thousands of times greater than any volcano we've experienced in known human history. By comparison, Mount Saint Helen's was just a hiccup. There are six known supervolcano sites, including one at Yellowstone National Park."

That jogged my memory. "I remember seeing a Discovery Channel program about that."

"That was a terrible documentary. But the damage a Supervolcano can do is global, interrupting food production, affecting air quality, perhaps pushing the human race toward extinction. A supervolcano eruption in Indonesia almost took out the human race seventy-five-thousand years ago.

He took a deep breath and leaned back. "But hey, we don't want everyone to sit around worrying about this stuff. At the same time, some of us should be taking it all very seriously. We live in a world that is perpetually at risk from extinction-level events."

Terry paused, and I felt I needed to summarize the characteristics of the Protector. "What I'm getting from you is that the Protector has the ability to recognize large population threatening risks and do his best to communicate those risks in order to stimulate the responses necessary to remove or reduce them. So, with the NEOs, for example, if we know that a big asteroid is heading to Earth, perhaps we can take some action to divert the rock's course. Right? And, I guess the same goes for other global risks. Bring enough attention to the potential global hazard so that the people in charge will do something about it. So, I guess you're saying that we need a strong space program now in order to develop the capability to divert asteroids out of Earth's path when the time comes."

"Well, yes. We do need to create such a capability. Diverting asteroids is one strategy we'll have to pursue. But, there is one other response to possible global extinction that is much more relevant to you and your travels to understand the Endowments. The Protector recognizes the need to diversify our population beyond this planet as an insurance policy against the worst case scenario that might befall us. Ultimately, to safeguard human life against existential risk is a powerful reason to build colonies on the moon and Mars and to eventually send space arks to other star systems where perhaps we can find planets like our own to call home.

"This house—our planet—may be perfectly safe for us for millions of years to come, but because we now know that it might not be, *and* we have the capability and the means to spread civilization outward, the Protector impulse demands that we act on that capability and colonize space as soon as possible. I like to think that our knowledge of the many threats to our existence is God's way of telling us that it's time to build a new ark."

"An ark," I repeated.

This thought had already been forming in my mind. A space settlement was like the biblical ark in that it potentially held all that made up our civilization and, in theory anyway, might be able to repopulate the world if necessary in the aftermath of some cataclysm. A space ark could even house many animal species as a guard against their extinction as well.

"As we come to think of the entire globe as a single-point failure, it makes sense to think in terms of moving some small portion of our population to other parts of the solar system as a safeguard against annihilation. What ship would set sail without adequate defenses, insurance and lifeboats? None. But here we are, fully conscious of the risks both man-made and natural, from on this planet and from space, and yet we are doing nothing to protect ourselves against a total system failure. One of the best strategies to mitigate a potential risk is to simply be out of harm's way if something should go wrong. We can't move everyone to a space colony, nor would we want to, but we can ensure that at least some of us can stay safely out of the way, just in case."

My coffee was cold as I tipped the mug for the last swallow. It still tasted good. Barbara was right. The Protector was not quite what I expected. It was too practical, especially compared to the Visionary.

Terry assured me that he had told me as much as there was to say about the Protector Endowment for the time being. I thanked him and said my goodbyes to him and Bill, who still had long hours of work ahead of them on such a pristine cloudless night. On my way to my car I stopped to take in the night sky which was thick with the stars of our galaxy.

THE PRIMARY
OBLIGATION

It was a restless night in the motel where Dotty had made reservations for me. I woke several times, my head trying to hold and integrate the significance of the Endowments. Three pairs of Endowments. Masculine and feminine. Each pair evolving from the previous. My mind swung between trying to grasp some grand meaning to it all and concluding that there really wasn't any.

And then there was the dream again—of orbital flight. I floated a little further out than usual with the Earth just barely in full view of my vision. About a fifth of the orb was in shadow. The planet glowed and pulsated. It was alive. It whispered in my ear, but I couldn't recall what it said once I awoke. Was it the words from the plaque? I couldn't tell.

In the pre-dawn hour, moonlight filtered through the window, cutting a diagonal path across my bed cover. It beckoned me from the room. I stepped out into the cool desert night with the nearly full moon showing with unusual intensity and dimming the blazing star field I saw at Kitt Peak. Barefoot and in my jeans, I walked beyond the glow of the motel lights to get a better look into the immensity of the

Arizona sky. Craning my head, I felt immersed in the cosmos, and in no way separate from it.

I might have stood there an hour if the sound of movement hadn't broken my reverie. Looking back to the motel, a silhouette of a large man walked over to a picnic table and sat down. The posture and stride were unmistakable. I moved closer to inspect.

"Hello, John. You're up early," Mr. Grant's deep soft voice came from the dark figure as I approached.

"Mr. Grant? Is that you?" He was backlit, his features obscured, which prolonged my sense of disbelief.

"Don't just stand there, son. Have a seat." He motioned me to sit opposite him.

There were two Styrofoam containers of coffee and a white paper bag set on the table. From my new vantage, I could see Mr. Grant more clearly. He wore a flannel shirt, jeans and cowboy boots, presenting a striking contrast to his Washington business attire.

"Dotty didn't mention that you would be staying at this motel."

He just smiled. He placed one of coffee cups in front of me. "Do you like cheese danish?" I nodded. He took a danish out of the bag and set it in front of me on a napkin. He took a cherry danish for himself, and began to eat it. In the silent ritual of Mr. Grant sharing his food, I became relaxed as the feeling of heightened awareness came over me.

As Mr. Grant swallowed his first bite he said, "I like this time of morning. There is so much…potential in the promise of a new day about to dawn. It's so pregnant with hope, don't you think?" I became aware again of the surroundings. The motel was isolated on a secondary road. It was not part of a chain. Native American art adorned the single story peach stucco structure. There were sand paintings, feathered head dresses and dream catchers. The homey motel grounds featured wood carvings and rock sculptures, a fire pit and picnic tables. This was a place tourists would stay to soak up some of the local flavor, and it certainly didn't normally cater to business travelers.

We sat in silence eating the danish and drinking coffee for a while. A faint ribbon of light was forming on the horizon. The serenity was broken only by the sound of waking birds.

I finally broke the silence. "I spoke to Barbara Everheart, and Terry Li at the observatory. They told me about the Visionary and Protector Endowments."

"Good. And what did you learn from them?"

"Well...the Visionary is an evolved form of the Inventor. The Visionary is driven to comprehend the totality of future possibilities. And the Protector, evolved from the Builder, sees the future possibilities, but is fixated on mitigating the risks that might threaten life and society."

"That's a good nutshell description, I suppose." Dawn was breaking on the horizon. The sound of passing cars was more frequent. The motel manager said good morning on his way to some chore.

I continued, "The Visionary sees potential for human civilization beyond Earth. The Protector sees the many risks to our planet from natural and man-made threats—those that come from this planet or from space."

He nodded, and looked into the distance, squinting as if trying to better make out something of significance.

He finally responded. "The Visionary is the means by which we are informed what the future can and should be. The Visionary sees many possibilities that impact myriad aspects of life. They can be found in all walks of life, including politics, technology, health care, social services, and virtually every dimension of our human endeavor. It's important to understand that the future possibilities that all Visionaries are compelled to see, and driven to live into, collectively, are in fact guiding civilization into a particular direction. It feels good to embrace a vision and passionately pursue it, because it *has to* make us feel good. This point, by the way, is true for all the other Endowments. When we are truly in alignment wholeheartedly with an Endowment, and acting on it, the feeling is…*very good.*"

He stopped to take another bite of his danish. He chewed slowly and washed it down with a coffee. When he didn't immediately offer some further insight, I became impatient.

"So now what, Mr. Grant?" I blurted. "I mean I've spoken to all six representatives of the Endowments. I kind of see that these traits can be said to make up the human condition. I also see that they serve as motivators driving interest in space development, at least among some people. But, honestly, Mr. Grant, I don't see how this all relates to what was on the plaque in your office, or any notion of an Obligation to colonize space."

This last sentence came out sounding more desperate than I intended. When I stopped I could feel my face redden from embarrassment. Mr. Grant just chuckled and motioned to the half-eaten cheese Danish in front of me, "Go ahead. Finish it. It was made fresh this morning."

Obediently, I picked up the pastry and took another bite. He continued. "OK, John. Let's start with the Endowments themselves. It's important to understand that these represent the core capacities within the human psyche. These are not learned behaviors, and they are not personality traits. The Endowments, however, can and do influence personality, and can be used to describe what someone is like. But, personality is a genetic and developmental overlay on top of the Endowment traits.

"All humans are born with all of the Endowments. However, each person will more strongly express one or two Endowments more than the others. You see, in order for humanity to survive and develop as it has, we needed people expressing all six Endowments. If you think about it—and I do want you to take your time with this—civilization could not have possibly emerged without these six Endowments. If there are others, I can't think of any. Every time I think there might be another Endowment, I realize it's just a variation of one that's already been named."

I had thought of this as well. "For me, 'curiosity' comes to mind."

"Yes, that's good. Curiosity is a dimension that seems to permeate all of the Endowments, so it is more of a common characteristic, but not an Endowment on its own. At least not in the way we're discussing here."

"But…forgive me for asking, what is the 'here' that we are discussing. Is this all about some psychological theory of human behavior?" I couldn't help attempting to get to the context of what Mr. Grant was talking about.

"A theory, yes. But it encompasses much more than human psychology, or rather goes beyond psychology. Be patient. Hopefully this will all become clear. The Endowments all played a critical part in enabling humanity to ascend beyond the confines of the rest of the animal kingdom. They are all essential traits that helped us to flourish over the millennia to where we have arrived today. These Endowments are also related directly to why people, like those you've been speaking with, are so interested in space travel."

He paused for my reaction.

"Yes," I said, to acknowledge his point, though nothing about that seemed to enlighten me more than I had gotten from the others.

"Now, this is getting to the heart of the subject. The Endowments are the very traits that are *required* for our species to become space faring. If these traits hadn't emerged in our consciousness then there is no way we could have built a rocket to the moon, and be able to even contemplate the settlement of Mars."

I agreed with his conclusion, but still did not see any particular revelation in it.

Mr. Grant must have seen that I was having difficulty

grasping the implications of what he was saying, and decided to take an alternate logic tack.

"Let's back up for a moment. To fully understand the six Endowments we need to go back fourteen billion years or so, literally to the moment of the Big Bang. Whatever else we know about our evolving universe, we are certain of two constants since that epic moment. One, that the universe has been expanding outward since the instant of the Big Bang; and two, that it has been moving toward ever greater complexity. These two forces, we could say, are the opposing resonating forces between which all of creation and evolution unfolds: expansion and complexity. The ancient Chinese identified these forces as the Yin and Yang. The Yang, the masculine impulse, is aligned with expansion, and the Yin, the feminine impulse, is aligned with movement toward complexity. Many cultures have affirmed these forces in nature by other names and references. The man, the hunter, strikes outward into the unknown: expansion. The woman, the nurturer, seeks to create a protective environment for her children: complexity. I am speaking in archetypal language, of course, so don't interpret any of this as anti-feminist."

I interjected, "Ms. Everheart spoke of the masculine and feminine nature of the Endowments."

"Good. So you see, these forces are very much evident in the Endowments themselves. But that's getting ahead of myself. Back to the Big Bang. We see in moments after the Big Bang that the expanding cloud of undifferentiated particles coalesce first into simple particles, and then into simple atoms, which continue to expand outward and evolve into molecules. The great expanding gas clouds of molecules condense, forming the galaxies, stars and planets. Eventually complex molecules evolve to cellular life on Earth about four billion years ago, which began the steady biological expansion and increase in complexity that led to the remarkable human species we are today.

"What's remarkable about evolution is that it is not

exclusive to the physical dimensions of the universe. It also has taken place in the subtle realm of consciousness. We can easily understand, for example, that humans are more conscious, or are in a higher state of consciousness than, say, a dog or cat. And we can further understand that a dog or cat is more conscious than a tree, and so on.

"To take this further, the consciousness of humanity has itself evolved significantly from our earliest beginnings. Though humankind is far from any virtuous pinnacle of development, our consciousness has certainly advanced over the course of five thousand years of recorded history. We see this with social advancements of the last century in human rights, civil rights, womens' rights, and so on. While we still have a long way to go, we are a much more enlightened world, as a whole, than we were just a hundred and fifty years ago."

"So, how does this relate to the Endowments?"

He paused with raised eyebrows. "As you've been told, the Endowments represent specific stages in the evolution of human consciousness, with each stage transcending and including the one before. The evolutionary emergence of each of the Six Endowments can be visualized as an upward spiral. Here."

Mr. Grant produced a pen and pad. He drew a spiraling line that was wider at the top than at the bottom. On either side of the spiral he labeled the opposing forces of expansion and complexity.

"The Wanderer and the Settler endowments emerged first, though the Wanderer emerged slightly ahead of the Settler." He labeled his sheet with the Wanderer on the expansion side of the coil near the bottom, and the Settler at the same level on the complexity side. Similar he labeled the sheet in ascending order on the expansion side with the Inventor and the Visionary, and on the complexity side with the Builder and the Protector.

"All six emerged very early in the human brain, and are the core capacities that allowed us to accomplish everything we have achieved, the good and the bad. And, to stress again my earlier point, all of these Endowments are the essential capacities that make our species uniquely capable of constructing vessels that will take our species off this planet and be able to build new civilizations among the stars."

He waited for my response, "Yes, I see…," I said. But I was still confused.

"The point is," he leaned forward. "The fact that we can build spaceships *is no accident.*" He seemed to want that to spark a great realization in me, but my confusion would not give way.

He seemed frustrated with my lack of understanding, and again went in a new direction. "So, let's go back to the beginning. What is this all about? Why have you met those six amazing people?"

I thought for a moment before giving the answer. "The Obligation. It has to do with understanding of the Obligation. Right?"

"Yes, of course, the Obligation. That is what this is all about, isn't it? If almost any other word replaced Obligation on the plaque, we might not have gone through all this fuss." He laughed, but I didn't see the humor.

He paused here to gather his thoughts. "To discuss the Obligation, we have to appreciate that there are actually *three Obligations* that humankind, as a whole, must fulfill." He smiled at my surprised look.

"The Obligation referenced on the plaque is just one of the three. But before we get to that one, perhaps it would be helpful to explain the Primary Obligation first. The Primary Obligation is so basic that it's easy to overlook as a distinct obligation. The Primary Obligation is the obligation humanity has to itself—making sure that everyone has what they need, such as food, shelter, protection, access to education, opportunities, and so on. The members of the CRFS, for the most part, are motivated to fulfill this obligation. In one way or another, each of the CRFS member groups are concerned with the wellbeing of the citizen populations they represent.

"It is in response to the Primary Obligation that our value system was created. We see this obligation fulfilled in the Ten Commandments, the Golden Rule, the law of Karma, the Torah, the Koran, and the general rule of law that reminds everyone how they should treat one another and warns of consequences should we disobey those rules. Beyond setting rules of conduct, this obligation takes many forms in functioning society, such as maintaining a school system, health care, social welfare, police and fire departments and so-on. It's about people making sure that other people have as good a quality of life as they can have. For people living in developed countries, these systems work fairly well. Even though people like to complain, in reality we have very little to complain about in modern western cultures. Internationally, foreign aid and charitable contributions are increasingly filling humanitarian gaps in struggling nations and nations in crisis." I recalled a late night commercial with a celebrity imploring that for pennies a day the viewer could feed a child at risk of starvation in a famine stricken African nation.

"The Endowments, as we've said, enabled the development of every aspect of civilization, which certainly includes our capacity to ensure our mutual wellbeing. We call it the Primary Obligation because humanity must become very good at taking care of itself. Even though there have been grim periods where systems and technology were turned against the people with horrific results, these situations have proven to be anomalous and temporary. Nations function best when the people have freedom of action with minimal but meaningful government involvement. There is universal agreement that our institutions should foster health, growth, development, safety and general happiness. We are far from perfect, but there is much about human compassion to be proud of.

"The Primary Obligation was first sensed in the nuclear

family and tribal units. It expanded to feudal communities. Eventually we were able to sense an obligation at the national level. In the twentieth century we see the beginning of the Primary Obligation taking shape at the global scale. That's where human rights and the fight against world hunger and disease comes in. This is still very much a work in progress, as you know, but that is quite clearly the direction we are heading. The fulfillment point of the Primary Obligation is when all humans, or nearly all of humanity, value the life of every other human as precious, regardless of race, politics, religion or geography, and act accordingly.

"You see, it's important that we move to a new level of global unity. I'm not speaking about a centralized world government, but a place of coexistence where all-out war between nations becomes a thing of the past. This is the only way to stabilize all governments and systems. Many people maintain that such a thing is impossible, but our only hope for survival is universal mutual respect and active desire for the wellbeing of every other person on the planet." He stopped there and held my gaze, his eyes shining with the reflection of the rising sun over my shoulder.

Something was moving in my head and body, something I wasn't quite able to grasp. There was a truth in what Mr. Grant was saying that simultaneously was obvious, and yet signified some larger truth I could not understand. My feeling of expanded awareness seemed to magnify at that point.

After eyeing me for a few moments, Mr. Grant broke into a broad smile and patted me on the arm. "Okay, John. That will do for now. We'll talk more later. We've got to get ready to head out if we don't want to be late." He gave me one more smile and without warning stood up and headed to his room.

I sat there for a few minutes, still blanketed in expanded awareness. I still felt I had missed something, or more likely that something had intentionally not yet been stated.

"What about the other Obligations?" I whispered.

THE CONFERENCE

We drove in separate cars to the conference hotel. I suggested that we go together so we could continue our discussion. "No," he said, "Driving is not conducive to this kind of talking." Driving alone to the venue, my head rattled with everything Mr. Grant was trying to convey to me.

I also thought of Tara. But the prospects for that encounter faded in the light of the experiences of the past few days. I wanted to see her and still hoped to resume our relationship. It just wasn't a burning desire at that moment.

I got to the hotel a half hour before the planned rendezvous with Mr. Grant and easily found the conference registration area. The hotel was a mid-level business class high rise. The second floor was dedicated to a meeting space, with about a dozen rooms of varying seating capacities to accommodate a range of meeting and conference needs. The conference on climate change had attracted a little over three hundred attendees, which easily fit into the available space.

I scanned the hall for Tara, but she was nowhere in sight. I picked up the badges and conference packets for Mr. Grant and myself. I met up with him in the lobby. There was no time for us to talk, as he was already beset by a handful of conference attendees. He shook hands, chatted, and joked.

The flannel-shirted man I spoke with early that morning was replaced by the suit-and-tie politician I knew from Washington. He gave everyone his attention, but was particularly interested in those who might have held leadership positions.

I felt a jab in my arm and then heard a familiar voice. "Mr. Grant, how are you? I'll be escorting you to the plenary session." It was Tara who had entered the cluster, introducing herself to Mr. Grant. She looked amazing in a foam-green sleeveless linen dress. Her skin was tanner than when I last saw her, emphasizing her physical beauty. We shared a glance, but that was all the communication we had for the moment.

"Yes, Tara, I remember you. Good you could make it all the way out here. I hope John here has been helpful to you and your colleagues with CRFS?" She assured him that I had, and gave me a smile. Being in her presence evaporated any feeling of indifference about her I might have felt on the drive to the hotel.

Appearing out of the small crowd was Kyle McAllister. Almost invading Mr. Grant's personal space, he said, "Mr. Grant, it's good to see you again. Kyle McAllister of the Council for Responsible Federal Spending."

Without flinching Mr. Grant acknowledged him and shook his extended hand. "Yes, Kyle. Good to see you again, as well. With all the issues under the CRFS's umbrella, I wouldn't expect you to make it out to an event like this." He was already looking past Kyle to another attendee wanting a word with him.

Kyle was dressed in the same crisp seersucker suit he wore at the first meeting in Mr. Grant's office. I locked eyes with Tara briefly in a shared memory of my last encounter with Kyle that ended with him sitting in a puddle of beer, and Tara wanting nothing more to do with me.

"Uh, let's just say I wear many hats." He was eager to keep Mr. Grant engaged. "I'm looking forward to our discussion after the plenary session." I had almost forgotten about the meeting scheduled immediately after Mr. Grant's plenary session to discuss the Weinstein amendment. I would not have expected Kyle to be included. When Mr. Grant's attention shifted to another attendee, Kyle acknowledged me with a smile and a pat on the shoulder.

Mr. Grant's voice commanded over the group, "Tara, would you be kind enough to lead the way to the general session room?" Tara and the congressman walked the carpeted corridor with the rest of the clutch in their wake. Kyle made small talk on the way to the room. I felt uncomfortable with his chumminess, but appreciated that he acted as if the horrendous house party incident had never happened.

The three hundred attendees filled the ballroom where the plenary session was held. Seats were arranged classroom style—rows of chairs arranged behind eighteen-inch wide tables, providing just enough room for note taking and sipping coffee or other beverages provided by the hotel catering staff. The staging was a modest platform on two-foot risers with a pipe-and-drape backdrop. A large screen dominated the center of the arrangement. A logo placard was attached to the front of the hotel podium. Speakers sat at a long skirted table set to one side of the stage waiting for their turn to present. A few potted plants gave the stage its only color.

Mr. Grant was the third plenary speaker following impressive slide-show presentations by two of the top scientists in the field of climate change. Mr. Grant paid close attention to these talks, frequently jotting notes on a legal pad. You would not have known that within a few minutes he would be at the lectern himself.

At the designated time, Mr. Grant was introduced and recognized for his long-time support of environmental issues. As I might have expected, based on the Kiwanis Club experience, Mr. Grant didn't refer much to his prepared remarks. He was so steeped in these issues that my patchwork job of a speech seemed to be of little use. As he moved from point to point, he artfully referenced material from the previous two speakers. I noted how his speaking style and body language had adjusted to suit the audience. In contrast to his folksy "good ol' boy" delivery at the Kiwanis Club, for the environmentalists his delivery was earnest, projecting solid command of the issues and a comfort with its complicated vocabulary and jargon. He went out of his way to reinforce his commitment to help drive a planet-friendly agenda in Washington.

Then he began speaking about the importance of spaceflight. "Our ability to survive as a species," he told the audience, "will be increasingly linked to understanding the universe that surrounds us. And the better we are able to gain an extraterrestrial perspective with regard to this planet, the better able we will be to objectively understand what will be needed to restore and maintain ecological balance down here.

"After all, it is the image of Earth taken by the Apollo spacecraft that brought to our global consciousness the visceral realization that we share a very small and vulnerable home planet. This Overview Effect, as we now call this phenomenon, sparked the environmental movement that has produced many positive changes in the last twenty-five years." This was the first time I heard him refer specifically to the Overview Effect. I recalled how he spoke about the fragile planet on the day he told me to see Chip Johnson, that launched me on my improbable journey.

In the dim light of the ballroom I saw Tara hanging on Mr. Grant's words. As if sensing my stare, she turned her head and smiled her approval.

At the end of his talk, Mr. Grant invited questions. Immediately, as Tara had warned, the audience was on him about the Weinstein amendment. "Congressman Grant, I understand that you will be voting against the Weinstein amendment scheduled to come to a vote in the House within a week. If you truly believe all the wonderful things you've just said about the environment, how can you in good conscience vote to spend billions on an unnecessary project like the space station when that money could be better spent researching renewable energy technologies?"

Mr. Grant took a drink from a cup of water, and then slowly replied. "You make a very good point. It was hard for me to decide how to vote on the Weinstein amendment. And to be honest, I agree that the space station program has experienced some pretty expensive bumps in the road. I also agree that more funding is needed for environmental and renewal energy research. Now, I could talk about the valuable Earth science planned for the space station program, but then, you would argue that we could pay for ten times the amount of Earth science research with unmanned satellites. I will just say that there are many programs I would like to support with discretionary funds available. One of those areas is environmental sustainability. Another area is human spaceflight. We clearly have an obligation to do what we can to ensure that this world is in good condition for our children. We also have an obligation to make sure they have something exciting to reach for."

Obligation rang in my ears. Was that it then? Was that what the saying on the plaque meant: space colonization was an obligation we owed to future generations so they would have something to excite and motivate them? I thought hard on that, hoping perhaps that he had given me the answer I had spent so much energy exploring. I hoped it was.

Mr. Grant fielded a few more questions on the Weinstein amendment, handling them diplomatically and sincerely. In the end he received a respectful if not a rousing applause.

I waited for him as he came off the stage. Tara and Kyle were close by. There was a gaggle of questioners who had approached the stage. Before Mr. Grant had a chance to engage the group, Kyle leaned in holding the elbow of a bearded man in a jacket and open collar shirt. "Congressman

Grant, I'd like to introduce Dr. Beatty from the University of Southern Arizona. He'll be meeting with us."

Trying not to be rude to the others who wanted an extra word with him, Mr. Grant acknowledged the pre-arranged meeting. He shook hands with Dr. Beatty and told Kyle he'd be along in a moment.

Tara shrugged at me, saying, "Sorry, I told you in Washington. All they care about is Weinstein."

"I got your letter." A squeeze of my hand was her only reply.

While we waited for Mr. Grant to finish, I introduced myself to Dr. Beatty, and two other scientists who were to be part of the same meetings. When Mr. Grant was ready, we all adjourned to a small meeting room with a conference table and padded high-back swivel chairs. Tara and another senior staff person from the World Conservancy Alliance attended the meeting as well. The scientists were very gracious, but Mr. Grant was ready for their attempts at arm twisting.

Though Kyle tried to project an air of running the meeting, it was Dr. Beatty who set the agenda. "Mr. Grant," Dr. Beatty began, "climate change and global warming are emerging as two of the world's most pressing issues. You clearly agree with this assertion." Mr. Grant nodded his agreement. "As a top priority, we will need to see a substantial increase in research funding to understand this issue and what we can do to mitigate its effects. The Weinstein amendment will, among other things, put more money into this critical research area."

When Dr. Beatty was finished, the other scientists added their points of emphasis as well. Mr. Grant was a polite listener, but once the appeal began to drag on, he was clearly beginning to show his impatience.

Finally picking up on Mr. Grant's non-verbal cues, Dr. Beatty wrapped up his arguments. Mr. Grant thought for a moment and looked at me. "Well, John. What Dr. Beatty and his colleagues said is all very convincing. What do you think?"

I had half expected him to deflect a response into my lap, and was prepared.

"I agree these are all very important arguments. But as Mr. Grant said earlier, the space program represents an obligation we have to future generations." I thought the response was clever, and Mr. Grant smiled at it. The scientists, however, simultaneously burst into objections at the comment. For a few minutes, Mr. Grant watched me fumble through an awkward exchange with the scientists, who were clearly becoming irritated.

Mr. Grant finally rescued me. "Well, this has been very helpful. I will discuss this with John later and let you know what we'll do."

"Then you will consider changing your position?" Dr. Beatty asked, expectantly.

"Why yes. You've raised some very strong arguments. I'd be a fool not to take that into consideration for my vote...Now, Tara, didn't you say something about a reception?"

I was surprised that Mr. Grant held out hope that he might change his position. The scientists were clearly excited and in good spirits, though Kyle seemed unaffected by the positive energy. Perhaps he knew better than to make too much of a politician's words of encouragement. Mr. Grant entertained the group as it made its way to the reception in another of the hotel banquet rooms. Tara gave me an appreciative smile and squeezed my arm as we walked together.

The reception was packed. There was a modest hot-and-cold buffet with two bar stations serving wine and beer. I stayed close to Mr. Grant, which further delayed any private time with Tara. Occasionally he asked me to make a note to follow up on a promise he made to someone in the group. He did not stay long, however. After half a glass of wine he excused himself, and left without saying anything in particular to me. I watched him leave the room, only stopping briefly a couple times to converse with an attendee.

With Mr. Grant gone, I was finally able to turn my attention to Tara. I didn't know many people in the room. But Tara did, which made it hard to get her attention. It was all vaguely reminiscent of the fateful house party. Including the presence of Kyle McAllister, who sidled up to me without warning.

"He's not going to change his vote, is he?" There was something about Kyle's voice that grated on me, and I hated myself for feeling that way. He was talking down to me. It wasn't overt, and I tried to convince myself I was projecting more condescension on him than was actually there.

"You heard him. He will take your arguments into consideration." My mind filled with images of the beer-soaked party, and even convinced myself that he must have coerced Tara to leverage my affection for her to influence Mr. Grant's position.

As he began to talk again about the support that was building for the amendment, I was distracted by thoughts of my early morning picnic table session with Mr. Grant. There was an expansive view of the world to which he was drawing my attention. My irritation with Kyle seemed pointless by comparison. My animosity toward Kyle vanished. He looked needy to me. I couldn't help feeling a little sorry for him. We talked for a while longer, and I saw only his inner pain in his veiled insults toward me. Before long, he smirked to himself and rushed away to catch someone he'd been needing to speak with. A calmness had come over me as if I had been speaking with Mr. Grant or one of the six Endowment keepers. Kyle McAllister and his kind, I thought then, would have a harder time getting under my skin from that moment on.

I saw Tara and, when she caught my eye, she broke away

from her conversation and walked toward me. I looked at her. God, she was beautiful. I hoped what I saw in her eyes was a similar attraction for me. We met each other with a long hug.

"I can't believe you made it here. You were the last person I expected to see."

"It's a long story. I can't wait to tell you about it…But, more important, thank you for the note. It really meant a lot." I put my hand on her waist.

"You're a great guy, John," she said, touching my arm. "I felt you deserved a real apology."

"I behaved pretty badly myself…" Eager to put the whole matter behind us, I changed the subject. "Tara, so much has happened since I saw you last in Washington. Why don't we get a table in the hotel restaurant and catch up?"

Taking a glance over her shoulder she said, "Better yet, a bunch of us are going to a restaurant down the road. Why don't you come? We can talk more there." There was a group of people clearly waiting for Tara to join them.

I was not up for making small talk with a group of people I hardly knew. "I…I think I'll pass. I was actually hoping for a little one-on-one time with you."

She made an exaggerated frowning face. "Hmmm. Not tonight. But I have an idea," she said after a moment's thought. "Meet me tomorrow morning for breakfast. You'll have my undivided attention."

This wasn't exactly the compromise I was looking for, but I agreed. It would have been presumptuous to expect her to jump right back into my arms after all that had happened. She pulled me in for a solid kiss on the mouth, beamed another smile, and was off again to join *her* people.

Halfway to the group she turned and shouted back, "See you later, Billy Blastoff." She laughed as she turned away.

As satisfied as I was that things might be getting back on track with Tara, I found myself far more interested in the teachings of Mr. Grant. On the trip back to the hotel, along the dark highway, I wondered what more there was to say. Had he let slip the final piece that explained the full meaning of the Obligation? Part of me wanted that to be the end of it, yet it still didn't seem to be the full story. I had visited the six representatives of the Endowments and gleaned wonderful insights from those conversations. But the morning session over coffee and danish had stirred an uneasiness in me. Mr. Grant said there was more to discuss, but I was beginning to think I didn't really want to hear any more. This uneasiness was not intellectual, but something unconscious that I couldn't quite identify. Like a bad dream that I knew I'd had, but the details I couldn't remember.

THE OBLIGATION

I arrived at the motel after ten, eager to get as much sleep as I could and be back at the conference hotel to meet Tara by seven in the morning. As I pulled the car into the space in front of my room, I noticed a fire going in a pit at the far end of the make-shift recreation area. I could see Mr. Grant tending the fire. He had changed back into his flannel shirt and jeans.

I didn't want to join him. I was dead tired. That was a fact. What made me more hesitant, however, was seeing Mr. Grant move around the open fire like some aboriginal shaman. The sight heightened the apprehension I was feeling on the drive from the hotel. Our talk that morning had taken the Endowments to a deeper place than I had expected. I believed I wanted to know more, but the sense of discomfort about where further dialogue with the congressman might lead was more than I wanted to consider at that moment.

Just as I decided to pretend not to see him, Mr. Grant looked straight in my direction and called my name, leaving me no alternative except to join him. Walking over to the pit, I resolved not to engage in a lengthy conversation, and I would respectfully decline any offer to discuss the Obligations that evening.

"Nice night for a talk," he said as I stepped into the light of the fire. The warm flames imbued Mr. Grant and the whole setting with a strange quality. There was a split-log bench and a few lawn chairs around the pit. Mr. Grant sat in one of the chairs and said I should sit opposite him on the bench, with the fire crackling between us. The excuse to not linger, which I had mentally rehearsed only moments before, faded to nothing as I sat down. Immediately I fell into a state of light-headed receptivity. Mr. Grant smiled as if he saw the heightened awareness coming over me. He suggested that I drink some water, and pointed to a cluster of bottles resting on the opposite end of the bench. I opened one and took a drink.

He didn't say anything right away. The chair he sat in, of frayed nylon straps over a thin aluminum frame, strained under his bulk. He had a long stick that he used to coax and tend the fire. Watching his focused attention on the fire served to deepen my calm state of mind.

In time, he began.

"There are many people who understand the six Endowments and the Obligations. We are not well organized, but there are many of us. Exactly where this particular perspective of the universe and human motivation first came from, I don't know. Some think it might have started at the turn of the twentieth century and was refined as better science helped to fill in the details. Some think it goes back much further. It seems to have evolved itself through many people and conversations."

"The Obligation," I muttered. "You still have not explained the remaining Obligations. You said there were three."

"Yes, of course, the Twin Obligations. We still need clarity on that, don't we?" As I puzzled on his use of the word *twin* to characterize the remaining obligations, he continued, "You were very astute at picking up on how I used 'obligation' in my talk today. I was impressed that you brought it into the discussion with the scientists."

"So, is that it, then? When the plaque speaks about the Obligation to the Earth, it's talking about the future generations?" Something seemed off even as I mouthed the words.

"I can see how you could reach such a conclusion, but I'm afraid there is much more to the story. Actually, I am surprised, after coming this far, that you would settle for such a simple answer. Remember what we discussed this morning. There are three Obligations. I talked about the Primary Obligation: the obligation that humanity has to itself, or that we all have to each other. This obligation implicitly includes not only the wellbeing of the living population, but future generations as well. So, any sense that space migration fulfills an obligation to our children's children owes its source to the Primary Obligation."

I was thoroughly confused.

He placed another piece of wood on the fire, causing sparks to erupt and dance high above the pit. He adjusted the pile with his stick and settled back into his creaking chair. "Before discussing the Twin Obligations, I need to give you a larger context in which to consider them. To understand the Obligations is to understand evolution of the universe ... *and* the DNA of the universe." His delivery was casual but deliberate, and in my heightened state I was perfectly accepting of what he had to say. "We have to consider that the way in which the universe took shape existed as a potential prior to the Big Bang. The potential for stars, planets and galaxies were present billions of years before they were formed. That they formed the way they have was not happenstance. They emerged from the undifferentiated matter according to a predetermined pattern. Whether or not that was God's plan, or someone else's, is really not relevant to this discussion.

"In much the same way that the potential for what a living organism on Earth will become is contained in the egg or seed, so too was the universe, in all its complexity, contained in the essence of what it was just prior to the moment of its creation. If we embrace the multiverse theories, such an idea becomes easier to grasp. The multiverse, as the term implies, says that our known universe is just one of an infinite number of other universes beyond our ability to observe. Multiverse theories explain the birth, growth and decline of universes—not unlike the life-cycle of living organisms on Earth—or that of stars, planets and galaxies."

He reached for his bottle of water and took a long drink. "Therefore, since the universe and everything in it existed as a potential at the very beginning, then we have to accept that life, such as it has evolved on this planet, must have been an aspect of that potential at the moment of the Big Bang as well. Does that make sense?" He waited for my agreement before continuing. "Maybe life wasn't predestined to evolve precisely as ours did, but some kind of life forms with higher order cognitive abilities such as those we possess were very much part of the universe's DNA—provided that everything went according to plan under the right conditions."

"According to plan?" I asked.

"Well, yes. If we make the presumption that universes have the potential to create human life, there is always the possibility that that potential is not fulfilled for any one of a million reasons. As with all species, not every seedling or egg will yield new life, or grow and develop to its full potential.

"So, now we have an image of a universe that is intentional, and not a result of completely random occurrences that by sheer chance created the conditions that allowed life on this planet to emerge. We see that the universe's evolution or, we could say, development, followed a pattern we might call a cosmic DNA code."

I nodded, finding myself drawn in by the logic. The flickering glow of firelight on his face, distorted by the heated air and smoke, made it feel as if I was receiving a message from another dimension.

"In this way, fractal geometry can be applied to at all levels of magnitude in the universe. You're familiar with fractals?"

I had read about them. "Yes, I've seen the fractal images. They are computer generated designs of infinite complexity based on non-linear equations. As you zoom in on the images the basic patterns will repeat on an ever-infinitely small scale, or large scale if you zoom out."

"That's right. Though the science hasn't caught up yet, it seems that fractals help explain the chaos and order of the universe. Patterns are repeated over and over at the amazingly large scale and the infinitesimally small scale. As incredibly diverse as our universe is, we are beginning to glimpse the totality of the common threads that run throughout. In school you talked about electrons orbiting a nucleus being similar to the planets orbiting the sun, even though the analogy has some flaws. Now, we see similar patterns in the galaxies and even clusters of galaxies.

"We also see repeated the life-cycle pattern occurring on a cosmic scale, with stars being born out of super-hot nebulae. Stars live for billions of years. They go through phases from a proto-star to a yellow sun like ours to red giant to a white dwarf. Ultimately they die with either a bang or a whimper, many of them casting off their treasure troves of complex molecules that are the building blocks for life. You see, all systems in the universe have a life cycle just as we do. So to carry this reasoning to its highest order we see a universe that itself has a life cycle. It was born in a Big Bang, it has matured, and will in some fashion, billions of years from now, extinguish itself, and perhaps in its demise, or even now perhaps, feed the birth and development of other universes.

"This morning I spoke about the forces of expansion and complexity. We know that the universe is expanding and has been for fourteen billion years. The undifferentiated particles formed atoms. Atoms formed molecules. And molecules formed galaxies, stars and planets. This process can also be explained in the concept of *holons*. Do you know what that means?"

I shook my head no, and he explained, "A holon refers to a system or organism that is a whole in itself and, at the same time, is a part of larger whole. It's a system that is considered evolving and self-organizing. For example, the human cell is a complete unit and is also part of the human being. Similarly the molecules that make up the cell are also complete. Holons can also be used describe social hierarchies. You are a citizen that lives in a city that is part of a state that is part of a country that is part of the world.

"The process of cosmic evolution has been the process of holons combining to create higher order holons, which in turn combine to create still higher order holons and so on. Understanding holons helps us understand how the universe adds complexity to the structure of matter."

"I see that."

"And this is important to the Obligation, as I will explain. This pattern in which smaller less-complex units combine to form more-complex systems really got interesting on this planet, didn't it? The primordial soup produced the first single-cell organism four-and-a-half billion years ago, and it's been an explosion of life ever since. Some theorize that the emergence of life was an impossibly rare accident of chemicals randomly falling together in just the right combination. This is a fool's notion. As I said a few minutes ago, the potential that life would emerge is encoded in the cosmic DNA. In other words, the universe is programmed to produce life wherever the conditions are right.

"From that first spark of life on this planet there came the remarkable process of speciation. For hundreds of millions of years the natural world churned unabated to create and destroy species of plants and eventually animals all in the name of balance of our ecosystem. This process seemed chaotic and random. And yet, as Darwin so wonderfully showed us, out of the chaos of survival of the fittest and natural selection came a steady progression of species refinements. The system of life became more complex and balanced. Everything was perfect…That is, of course, until we showed up."

He laughed, looking at me across the fire. He let that sit with me while he adjusted the wood, exposing the bright embers.

"What I want you to consider is the apparent lunacy that the natural world would allow the ascendance of the homo sapiens. Think about it. Up until about ten thousand years ago there was a beautiful balance to the global ecology. Sure, there were volcanoes, earthquakes and asteroids, but in the long stretches in between catastrophic events, nature kept things fairly well balanced. Homo sapiens was just another species running around the plains and forests gathering, scavenging and occasionally hunting. Then, of course, as the story goes, humans were kicked out of the Garden because Adam and Eve ate the fruit from the Tree of Knowledge. This acquisition of knowledge, we could say, roughly equates to the emergence of the Endowments.

"In an astronomical split second the Endowments have enabled us to evolve to the point where we have completely thrown off the planetary equilibrium. We are polluting the water and air, killing ourselves and the world around us. We're deforesting the tropics, wiping out untold unknown species that may hold the key to treatment of disease, and we don't have enough clean water to serve the needs of the world's poorest. We're triggering global warming and climate change. And then to top it all off, we have created a nuclear arsenal poised with the firepower to destroy the world many times over. Why would God give our species any such gifts of consciousness when the risks to the environment, let alone to ourselves, are so great? On the face of it, the Endowment capacities in human consciousness seem to be in opposition to the grand DNA design of the universe. Don't they?"

He cocked his head, raising his eyebrows toward me.

"Now...for those who believe that all of evolution was just an accident in time and space, the prospect that humans emerged with all our risks and promise is no more or less significant because it's just part of the random nature of the universe. It was just a big crap shoot anyway, they say. So we might as well enjoy the ride as long as it lasts. Like a top spinning perfectly for billions of years, finally starting to wobble with the introduction of an unintended element, humankind has thrown us out of balance, and therefore, some will say, that's just how it goes sometimes.

"Cultural and religious traditions, on the other hand, have developed good stories about our origin, which usually places humans at the top of the natural order, with the understanding that we hold dominion over all we survey. In a religious context, God created us the way we are. He created this world for us to inhabit, and if we followed his laws, as interpreted by his prophets, we would receive heavenly rewards. So in this way, the world is a big Monopoly board, and we are all just playing the game to win or lose God's favor. The world itself, in a larger universal context, has little meaning. So, any search to understand the greater universe is little more than a curious exploit of intellectuals." He chuckled at his own irreverence.

"With the concept of a universal DNA and holons, I'm trying to suggest a third way of looking at the world and our place in it. Viewed from the perspective I am about to explain, you'll see that the emergence of the Endowments makes perfect sense. To understand what I'm getting at, let's take another look at how the balance of nature works. Systems and species interact with each other on the planet to keep order, right? We understand the classic food chain, of course. The gazelle eats the grass, and the lion eats the gazelle. Big fish each little fish, and so on. Mutual nourishment goes a long way to keep all species flourishing yet not overrunning each other. The balance of nature is also maintained by cooperation between species, as well as trying to feed on each other."

"You mean symbiosis?"

"Exactly! Right now, in your stomach there are billions of bacteria living off what you eat, helping you digest your food. Without them you would die. You are not aware of these bacteria and they are certainly not aware of you, but the relationship works very well, doesn't it?" He paused again to stir the flames.

"For our purposes, the symbiotic relationship between bees and flowers is perhaps most relevant. Look at the life of a bee. The bee is perfect in itself: its ability to fly so beautifully, hopping from flower to flower, constructing its hive with precision, helping to create a society that it and its fellows and the queen bee can share for their own benefit. In this activity the bee has created a wonderful society for itself. Right?" I nodded. "At the same time, however, in taking what it needs from flowers, the bee serves a critical function for the flowers from which it takes. You know what that is. What is it?"

"Pollination. Bees help to pollinate the flowers."

"That's right. Without being aware of what it is doing, the bee is fulfilling an essential reproductive role for the plants. By doing what it does naturally, the bee we could say is fulfilling *an obligation* to pollinate flowers.

"On some level every species plays some role in maintaining the balance of nature. All species except, of course, the modern human—gut bacteria notwithstanding. Prehistoric man was nicely part of that that natural system. We were food for large predators, and we pruned the landscape by scavenging, foraging and hunting. But, once the Endowments kicked in, we became a different kind of creature altogether. As I said a minute ago, all hell seemed to break loose once we were given these extraordinary gifts of consciousness. With the Endowments, our long history was as much paved with blood and destruction as it was with great

141

wonders and achievements.

This reminded me of Barbara Everheart's discussion of the dark side of the Visionary.

"But, and this is important, what if there was a very good reason for the Endowments arising in the consciousness of a relatively weak biped species?" Mr. Grant's voice became more energized as he drove home his message. "What if the risk created by the Endowments was a risk that *had to be taken* in order for that species to attain the abilities to fulfill a symbiotic purpose? What if that purpose wasn't just with respect to another species or group of species? What if that purpose, or obligation, was to the planet as a whole? While the Endowments put the planet at risk, it was a risk that had to be taken because the capabilities made possible by the Endowments were the only means by which our species could fulfill an ancient Obligation it owed to the planet that gave it life. Once the Endowments were granted, the clock started ticking. Would humanity develop the means to fulfill our Obligation, and do so, before it destroyed itself, and possibly the whole planet in the process?"

I heard myself asking, "But, why…how is space settlement a fulfillment of the Obligation?"

He let out a big laugh. "Why, don't you see? Isn't it clear?" His outburst startled me, and I could only respond with open mouthed silence. He leaned forward in exasperation, the light of the fire dancing in his eyes.

"Have you ever heard of the Gaia Hypothesis?" I told him that I was only generally aware of the concept. He explained.

"It's a theory that says the Earth, in its totality, can be viewed as a single living organism. Gaia is the Greek goddess of the Earth. The biosphere, the thin layer at the surface of the planet, which contains all life, itself is alive. All life and life systems, such as the atmosphere and the oceans, all species of plants and animals, are uniquely interconnected and comprise a single super organism.

"Essential to all life is the birthing or reproductive process whereby a species is able to survive through its progeny. This is true for all life on Earth. It's true at the level of the organism. And it's true for the world system as a whole. This is consistent with what we just discussed about fractal theory and the concept of holons.

Mr. Grant stirred the fire again. "You see, John, the living world, Gaia, must reproduce in just the same way that her constituent species and cellular life forms reproduce. Can you see that?"

"Well...maybe... I don't quite understand how that would be possible..."

I tried to imagine the planet, like some giant ameba, splitting itself in two. The thought was absurd.

"To explain it a different way, look at the oak tree. The oak tree doesn't produce a single acorn for at least twenty years—some will take fifty years. But at some point, for no apparent reason, in one season an oak will produce tens of thousands of acorns. A casual observer, ignorant of the oak tree horticulture, could live next to an oak tree for decades without seeing a single acorn. If someone were to suggest to that person that the tree will one day sprout nuts, it might seem a preposterous idea."

With that he cleared his throat, and leaned forward.

"Gaia is like that oak. After billions of years of growing and maturing, she is now ready to create her acorns and send them out into space in order for new life to take root. We find it strange to consider that Gaia might have a reproductive system, because we've never observed one, and for all we know she has not been pregnant before. We are not surprised when a woman becomes pregnant only because we know that such a condition is part of human biology. Yet to a child of a certain age, to learn about the birthing process comes as a shocking revelation. Similarly, in speaking of the whole planet system that has taken over four billion years to grow and mature, the idea that this system has the capacity to reproduce can be an equally astounding revelation."

He paused to tend the fire. Sparks rose from the embers. His face glowed orange through the smoke. He was in no rush to add anything to his last statement. Finally, I broke the silence. "I still don't see…" I stopped short. In that moment the implication of what Mr. Grant was suggesting began to dawn on me.

"We, all of humanity, are like the bees, John. And Gaia, we could say, is like the flower. We will carry the seeds from this planet to other worlds. This is the symbiotic relationship we have with the Earth, to assist in her reproduction."

"So that's our Obligation," I said, almost to myself.

Mr. Grant smiled broadly, and continued. "In order for Gaia to reproduce there had to emerge within her the means by which that process could take place. There had to come into being a biological agent capable of organizing her resources to create the seedpods and deliver her essential DNA to other parts of the solar system and beyond. That *agent*, of course, is us. The seedpods are the rocket ships we build. We will not only disperse ourselves, but all sorts of biological life, as well as all the informational content of our civilizations. This is the Obligation that humanity was destined to fulfill from the moment our species emerged on this planet."

He casually lifted a block of wood and threw it on the fire, sending sparks into the air. I stared blankly into the flames. My state of open consciousness seemed to deepen even further.

After more than a minute of silence, Mr. Grant told me to have another drink of water, which I did as he continued.

"Let's now return to the Six Endowments and our discussion this morning." It seemed a lifetime ago that we shared danishes on the picnic table just 15 feet away. "The Six Endowments are the means by which we are able to fulfill this Obligation. So let me summarize."

He leaned forward, counting off each Endowment with

his fingers, "The Visionary sees what life in space can be like and what it will mean to human development. The Protector understands that not diversifying our population beyond Earth puts our species, and all life, at risk of premature annihilation. The Inventor will respond to the challenges set down by the Visionary and Protector by creating the scientific, technological and institutional means that will enable us to move beyond this planet. The Builder will replicate what the Inventor creates over and over so that ever greater numbers of people on Earth can make that journey, as well as continually expanding the living capacity of our off-world homes to support a growing population. The Wanderer's nature will reawaken stronger than ever, enthralled by the opportunity to explore ever more distant reaches of space, never again having to endure the geographic limits of a single-world existence. And the Settler will follow in the path of the Wanderer to establish new and better homes for humankind and its decedents.

"Once the Endowments emerged in our psyche, humankind was set on a path that could only have led to space travel. In fact, space travel and the prospect for space colonization is so ingrained in our collective psychology that most people have already concluded that space colonization is inevitable. Popular culture is steeped in visions of people buzzing all over the galaxy and beyond. The only unanswered question is, *When?* When will we build space settlements?—not *if* such things will happen.

"John, I hope you're starting to see that space migration is much more than an interesting extension of human capability. It is quite literally the reason for our being. Everything that we've accomplished up to this point has been just a lead up to it."

He paused, and looked at me to make sure this point sank in.

In my heightened state I had no desire to reject anything. Nonetheless there was a growing sense of unease even as the full impact of the meaning of the Obligation was becoming clear to me. "I see. But it's very strange to think that humans might have come into being for the specific purpose of carrying life to other worlds."

"To say humanity exists only to serve the reproductive needs of the planet would be an oversimplification of the human experience. At each era of our development, we were certainly complete in ourselves, in the same way that a baby or child is complete in every way. We certainly serve our own needs and continuously strive toward collective development and betterment. The bee is very much involved with the fulfillment of its beehive community in every way, even as it fulfills the critical function of pollination. So we must not interpret anything that I am saying as suggesting that people are drones serving the dictates of some larger cosmic machine." He chuckled at the visual image he had just created.

"At the same time, it is no coincidence that the highest ideals of our civilization and species are completely consistent with the needs of the planet we live on, including her need to reproduce just as any living organism must do. Like the bee, by fulfilling our own purest desires, we are simply fulfilling the purpose of a larger whole of which we are a part.

"But, as I said earlier, the clock is ticking. In our ignorance we have created many risks and caused much damage. Our immature application of the Endowments was the price Gaia had to pay to nurture the technological capacities needed to fulfill the Obligation. We can look at the damage we have caused in the same way that pregnancy puts an expectant mother's life at risk. The new life that wants to be born is greedy and takes resources from the mother. And even after the baby is born, it demands the attention and nourishment from the mother who must be ever attentive. But eventually, the child grows and becomes independent of the mother, and the mother is able to heal herself, and find a balanced life to coexist with the child.

"The industrial age has ravaged the planet as we progressed toward space-faring capability. Perhaps on other planets around distant stars this birthing process has put less strain on the indigenous ecology than it has here. I imagine many worlds never make it at all. Of course, we can only speculate on how this process plays out elsewhere. But I believe we can conclude that some amount of ecological imbalance is to be expected during the development of the species presenting the Six Endowments. The question is: now that we are conscious of the long-term damage our technological evolution has had on the world, will we be able to adjust our behavior enough to restore some sense of balance—and at the same time keep moving in the direction of space migration?"

He leaned back, making a loud creaking noise that challenged the structural limits of his lawn chair. He took a drink and continued, "Of course, there is no guarantee that we are going to make it all the way. We may not be able to get beyond our collective stupidity long enough to fulfill this purpose. For as much as this impulse is burning inside many people, there are enormous inertial barriers that may in the end prove insurmountable."

He let that sit for a few moments. I didn't have any more questions, and he finally said, "Well, John, I think I've kept you up way past your bedtime. Why don't you get some rest?"

He had finally shared with me the full meaning of the Obligation, yet somehow the story seemed incomplete. "Is that all of it then? The Obligation is our responsibility to help Gaia reproduce itself?"

He smiled. "Yes, and no. You can take what I've said as a complete explanation if you wish, but there is more to the story. But, we can't go any further right now. You first need to hold in your mind the nature of the Obligation for a while, as I've described it, before we can continue. Next, we'll want to get further into the Twin Obligation. Now, get some rest."

"Twin Obligation?"

"Think on it for yourself, in the context of what I've said. Try to reason what the Twin Obligation could be. If you think about the events of today, the Twin Obligation will become obvious."

I remained seated and I tried to conceive an answer in that moment, hoping he'd offer more clues about the meaning of the Twin Obligation. He said nothing and eventually I got up to leave. He only gave me a faint smile and nodded as I headed back to my room, leaving him to stir and coax the flames.

THE TWIN OBLIGATION

Mr. Grant's challenge disturbed my sleep and still consumed my thoughts on the way to meet Tara the following morning. As much as I looked forward to seeing her and perhaps rekindle our relationship, it all seemed secondary to the Obligations. The final explanation of the Obligation to colonizing space was unsettling. It was still hard to accept that humankind was unconsciously on a ten-thousand-year mission to expand civilization out into space on behalf of a living planet. At the same time, it was what I already knew to be true in some place in my dreams.

And the dream did come again. The full Earth alive and whole. Silently communicating an imperative I couldn't quite understand. And it left me no clue as to what the Twin Obligation might be.

Tara told me to meet her at seven o'clock, so it was a nice surprise when I pulled up to the hotel ten minutes early to see her already waiting for me. She wore snug khaki shorts, hiking boots and sunglasses. She waved as she jogged over to the car, threw her day pack into the backseat, and climbed in.

"Hey you," she said, and gave me a kiss on the lips. I had almost forgotten how incredible that could be. "We're going to do a little hiking this morning. Sound okay?"

"Not exactly what I had in mind, but I'm game." I thought we'd have a meal in the hotel restaurant and maybe sit by the pool. But, I was perfectly happy to go anywhere with her.

"Great. Somebody told me about an awesome hike in the Saguaro National Monument a few miles west of here. We can stop for breakfast on the way. Take this road for a few miles west and head into those hills," she commanded, as I pulled away.

"God. I love this conference, but I just need to get out of those stuffy rooms, especially here. Look at this place." She craned her neck to get a better look at a passing red rock formation. The landscape was spectacular. Arizona was like no place else on Earth. It was so alien you could almost believe we were on another planet.

I stopped at an intersection and looked over at her. She was radiant. It was as if I had never quite seen her that way. It wasn't her clothes. She glowed from the inside.

"Tara, there is so much going on that I want to share with you." I needed to share my experiences with someone, and Tara was the only one I felt might understand.

"I feel the same way. This conference has really opened me up to so many possibilities. For you and me, yes, but for the whole world as well." There was a sense of elation in her voice. "Sitting in those sessions about the state of the global environment you really begin to understand that the situation is worse than ever. Then you have hundreds of people who are all committed to making a difference —all committed to turning this horrible situation around. Even you, John, and Mr. Grant. His talk was so stimulating it made people stop and consider an even bigger picture that included outer space.

"Just being there with that passionate vibe running through the building I felt that there was a chance, a real hope for the future. We're not going to sit back and simply *allow* the conditions to get worse if we can in any way stop it. We can no longer sit on the sideline, John, hoping that sanity will miraculously take hold of government and society."

Tara was clearly on a mind-expanding high. She talked about some of the speakers, the breakout session topics, and brainstorming workshops. She truly believed that the meeting represented a break-through for the environmental movement. And I didn't doubt she was right.

We stopped at a diner for a quick but full breakfast. I was determined to open up to Tara about everything that I was experiencing, but decided to restrain myself for just a while longer, and confined our talk to the conference.

There was only one other car in the flat patch by the side of the road that served as a parking area to the trail head. The trail we chose was marked by nothing more than a five-foot-high post tipped with faded blue paint. Though I didn't have hiking boots, I was glad to be wearing tennis shoes instead of my Docksiders, which would have provided no support. Tara was in good physical condition. I wasn't, but still insisted on carrying the day pack, and struggled to keep up almost from the start. Tara stood at least ten inches shorter than me, but her stride was nearly equal to mine. "It's about an hour and a half each way. We'll have to keep a steady pace if we want to get the top and back in a reasonable time."

Looming ahead was our goal: a mountain that jutted out of the desert floor like a rocky crystal. The first part of the hike was flat and easy. The desert scenery was spectacular. The diverse low lying scrub vegetation was punctuated by saguaro and other cactus plants of every size, some reaching well over ten feet. Tara pointed to the precious white saguaro flowers, which blossomed for only a few weeks each year.

After about a mile, the trail became more rugged and began to slope upward. We didn't speak much. Tara seemed focused on burning off her excess energy. I focused on getting enough oxygen into my lungs. We finally stopped for a rest, which I was glad for but longed for some shade as well. Tara had taken care of the provisions we would need for the hike, including plenty of water, apples and a large bag of trail mix containing nuts, raisins and carob chips.

"A little out of shape, huh?" she smirked.

"Well," I puffed, "if you had told me about this Ironman competition in advance, I'd have done some training."

We drank some water and put on sunscreen, which Tara insisted I apply. We sat for a few minutes in the quiet of the beautiful setting and I took the moment. "I want to share something with you. It's about these incredible conversations I've been having with Mr. Grant."

She gave me her full attention. "It's a bit outrageous and I didn't know exactly how to talk about it…It all started with a plaque in Mr. Grant's office…"

"Do you mean the one with that says something about space colonies?"

"Yes! Yes, that's the one." My heart quickened at the thought of her seeing the plaque as I had.

"I noticed it that day the CRFS delegates met with Mr. Grant. I thought it was an odd thing to show off," she said. "But…what about it?"

"Well, I thought it was odd as well. I became a little obsessed by the inscription that claimed space colonization to be an obligation humanity had to the Earth."

"Is that what it said?"

"Yes, in essence. When I asked Mr. Grant about it, his whole attitude toward me changed. He said if I wanted to understand what was meant by the Obligation on the plaque, that I needed to interview a series of specific people. I was so curious, I couldn't refuse. The first was astronaut Chip Johnson." By this point, Tara was completely drawn in.

"There was also a scientist at JPL, the space entrepreneur Evan Phillips, whom you may know, and Barbara Everheart, the famous science fiction author. There were six in all. I would find out these individuals each represented a particular basic human trait, and how that trait related to the human desire for space travel. It was as if each person was giving me a piece of some philosophical perspective on how human consciousness works."

Tara was intrigued. "Wow. That's wild...Well, let me hear it."

We started hiking again at a slower pace. "These traits are represented by six archetypes, the Wanderer, the Settler, the Inventor, the Builder, the Visionary and The Protector. They are generally referred to as *Endowments*. Chip Johnson, for example, represented the Wanderer." Tara licked her lips and, with furrowed brow in concentration so as not to misunderstand anything, urged me to continue.

"All of these Endowments share two dimensions. In one sense, each endowment has been essential in developing the human civilization from its earliest beginnings to where we are today. Yet, at the same time, each of these Endowments is essential to enable our civilization to expand beyond this planet. Take the Wanderer Endowment, for example." I knew I was being a bit pedantic, but earnestly wanted her to understand. So I explained, as succinctly as I could, how the Wanderer Endowment not only spurred humankind to populate the globe using only pre-historic technology, but that the same primal impulse was drawing us inevitably into space. I gave similar examples for other Endowments in response to Tara's questioning.

Tara's reaction was tentative. "Hmm...I admit this is a fascinating way to look at human consciousness—but I still don't get what it all means. You almost sound like you believe what the plaque says, that humanity has some intrinsic obligation to build space colonies." There was so much I wanted to say in response, but suddenly realized raising the topics at all with Tara might have been a huge mistake. After all, Mr. Grant had communicated the information in much greater detail over many days.

"For me," she continued while I hesitated, "listening to

your description of the Endowments, I was beginning to see how they fit as the critical traits we need to resolve the environmental crisis we've created down here. Not so we can run away to Mars. Especially the Inventor and Visionary and the Protector, as you call them. How can we restore balance to the Earth without these capabilities?"

"I...I see what you're saying. I don't doubt that's true." I realized how ridiculous it was to have this conversation with Tara. How could I possibly expect her to appreciate the ideas based on my brief and no doubt flawed summation?

I let the topic drop as we focused on the climb that had become more difficult. My muscles had loosened up and the going was easier, though I knew I would feel every mile the next day. The incline became very steep, requiring us at points to crawl up and over or around jutting rock formations.

We stopped two more times before reaching the summit, but I chose not to bring up the Obligation again. It was clear the topic had disturbed her. Instead we talked about the beauty of our surroundings, and compared notes on the wildlife and vegetation we had spotted along the trail.

The roughest bit of climbing came just before reaching the summit. We had to scale a ninety-foot rock face. Proper rock-climbing gear would have been required if not for the thinnest ribbon of a trail up along the wall. It wasn't so much a trail as it was a barely marked climb. If you followed the markings, there were just enough firm hand and foot holds to take you to the top.

It was worth it. We reached the summit just before nine o'clock. The view on all sides was spectacular. I even spotted Kitt Peak and its little white dot of an observatory off to the southeast.

Tara went up to the highest point she could reach. She spread her arms out and put her head back as if to soak in the glory of the place. She looked even more beautiful, almost angelic. I couldn't take my eyes off her.

"*This*, John. *This* is what it's all about," she said gesturing to everything and nothing in particular. As she began to speak, the feeling of lightheaded attentiveness began to come over me. I had not experienced that feeling before with Tara.

She began to talk about the conference again. "The world is waking up to the need to bring ecological balance or we will destroy ourselves."

"The sixth Endowment," I blurted out. "That's the *Sixth Endowment*—The Protector." It should have occurred to me while discussing the ecology with Mr. Grant at the fire pit. "You see how it fits? The Protector Endowment sees the macro threats, or threats to the whole, and takes actions to avoid, eliminate or mitigate those threats."

"Yes, self-preservation is no doubt part of the picture. But, what I'm speaking of is much more about harmony with the world we live in. It's much more about caring for other life forms we share the planet with. Yes, if we can restore ecological balance then we are likely to ensure our own survival as well." She paused, reaching for the best way to put what she had to add, "It's like this. We have been cared for and nurtured by this planet for millions of years while our species matured as a conscious organism. Now that we have matured, or at least some of us have, it is time for us to fulfill an *obligation* to serve as stewards to the planet to which we owe our very existence."

"Obligation..." Something was opening up inside me.

"Yes. It's an obligation," she continued, "that goes beyond merely our own self-interest—even as a species. It's a much larger realization that we are part of a whole living planet. The obligation isn't to build space colonies; it's to take care of the world we already have. Don't you see that?"

This was the Twin Obligation Mr. Grant spoke of. It had been staring me in the face all along. It all somehow made perfect sense. Rather than being in opposition to one another, space migration and planetary stewardship were linked as two halves of an undeniable Obligation that humanity had to the Earth.

The shift in my mind was felt as a physical sensation. My feeling of otherworldliness deepened in that moment. I seemed to be sinking into a kind of deep relaxation, though my awareness of Tara and my surroundings was as sharp as ever.

Tara spoke further, "Have you ever heard of the Gaia Hypothesis?"

"Yes...I have." I didn't mention that it was only the previous night that the concept was explained to me by Mr. Grant.

"Then you know that all life, humanity included, is interconnected with the Earth. We all live together in harmony or we all die together from stupidity on the part of the human race. It's that simple. We can't keep taking from the Earth without giving back in equal or greater measure. It is now time for us to transition from being the species that holds dominion over the Earth to a species that acts as its responsible steward. Like a child who, after years of being cared for by his mother, ultimately matures into adulthood. In a healthy family the roles reverse and it becomes time for the mother to be cared for by the sons and daughters. That's where we are now. Or at least that's where we should be now." With this she stared straight into my eyes intensely for a few beats, and then broke into the warmest most beautiful smile. "Think about it? It makes sense, doesn't it?" she said at last.

"The Twin Obligation," I whispered, but Tara didn't seem to hear me. I felt my body sink further still into a state of relaxation with each word Tara spoke.

"Come here." She guided me to a flat sandy patch in the shade of a boulder. She sat down cross-legged and signaled me to do the same sitting opposite her. As a gentle breeze kept us cool, Tara told me to close my eyes. I could not have been more receptive as she guided me into meditation as she did in the park next to the Rayburn building.

She told me to breathe normally, and focus all my

attention on my breath. In and out. In and out. She became quiet, and we sat with only natural sounds coming from the desert.

My initial relaxation only deepened in the quiet of my mind. Everything seemed to melt away with each breath. After a short time, the sensation of my physical body dissipated. I could identify myself only as a point in infinite emptiness. There was something supremely perfect in this no-place.

After a time my perception changed and I felt myself moving upward, high above the mountain we were sitting on, and the Arizona desert. Higher I went, seeing the ground as if from an airplane at thirty thousand feet. Then higher still. I saw the curvature of the Earth and the blackness of outer space above. This sensation was similar to my recurring dream of floating in orbit.

I became aware of points of light covering the landmasses below me. They were all interconnected like a web of neurons. I intuitively saw these as all life forms connected to each other as a single entity. Then the physical aspects of the planet disappeared, leaving only the network of lights. Seeing them more clearly, I saw that they varied in brightness. Some were blinding in radiance while others were barely visible.

At that point, I noticed that I was connected to the Earth by a thin cord of light. I followed the cord down and distinctly made out the light of Tara, which shone as brightly as any on the globe. I could clearly see that her light was seeping into the ground beneath her. The surface was translucent, with the connected point of light on the surface of a dull grayish subterranean mass.

Tara's light seeped into this mass, illuminating it until the entire globe glowed with her radiance. The other surface lights got brighter and many made light thread connections to the subsurface as well.

Then I became aware that my own light essence, which

had been viewing the Earth scene below, began to expand. My light expanded to engulf the moon. As this was occurring other light threads were extending out from the surface of Earth into space. At first there were a few, then dozens. They multiplied into thousands, then millions. My light continued to expand and merge with other light forms that were connected to the Earth as I was. Together we expanded outward to ultimately engulf the planets, the sun and the stars. There was a blinding radiance from above and from below. The scene was so moving my being ached at the grandeur of it all.

The radiance of everything increased in intensity until there was nothing but whiteness. Brilliant whiteness.

I felt Tara gently shake my shoulder. My awareness returned to my body and immediate surroundings. When I opened my eyes she said, "I didn't want to disturb you, but it's getting late and we should be heading back. It looked like you went pretty deep." Then she added playfully, "I could tell you were an easy one even on that the first day in the Capitol Hill park," she laughed.

Though the blissful lightheadedness was gone, I still felt extremely serene and was not interested in disturbing that state by engaging in conversation. I instantly recalled my vision in all its detail but was content to keep it to myself for the moment.

I said very little as we ate apples and trail mix. Several times I caught Tara staring at me. When our eyes met she would break off in a giggly laugh, shaking her head. There was something about me that Tara found very amusing. It wasn't long before we gathered our things in preparation for the hike down. As we began the precarious descent, the feeling of serenity stayed with me making my progress seem effortless.

We took our first break soon after the most difficult stretch was behind us. After a drink of water and a few minutes of soaking in the surroundings in silence, Tara said, "I think I'm beginning to understand what you said before about the Obligation to colonize outer space, even though the whole concept is very difficult for me. I'm still finding it hard to see beyond the wasteful expense and the limited value of the current space program."

This pronouncement was more than I was expecting. I had contented myself earlier that it was okay with me if Tara didn't accept space settlement ideas. I was still processing the information myself, and was a long way from fully comprehending the meaning and significance of it all.

She continued, "But, my change of heart is not from anything you said, but something that happened during my meditation. I've been debating whether to even tell you about it." She paused, and took a breath. "Well, I was very agitated all the way up the mountain by what you said about space colonies and the Endowments, and all that. I couldn't help feeling that people who wanted to colonize space were copping out, looking to abandon the Earth, just when perhaps she needs us most. I knew that was irrational, but that's how I felt.

"Anyway, I make it a practice to meditate on the things that bother me the most. In meditation you can actually get some distance between yourself and the thoughts that are causing distress. Meditation can create a space to silently watch the negative thought circulating in the mind, and usually helps you gain new perspective about them. I also visualize the showering of *love* around the thought, and intentionally release whatever the distressing thought might be." Seeing my questioning expression, she added, "Don't look at me like that. Believe me, this stuff really works.

"So, I gave myself over to the source of my agitation. At first my mind resisted and wanted to remain identified with the feelings. Gradually, however, I was able to step out of the thought loop and watch it from a distance. I began to shower my love on to the negative thought, but rather than feeling relief, I became even more distressed. I felt a deep anguish that I couldn't identify. I cried with tears running down my cheeks. I was surprised you didn't hear my whimpers. This cry was a purging or cleansing release even though the source or catalyst was unclear.

"Then, suddenly, my awareness shifted and I had the distinct sensation that I was pregnant with a child and feeling the first pangs of labor. I mean, I could really feel a baby in my belly. I felt panicked that I was not ready for this child to come out. The labor pains increased but still I wasn't ready, until I finally realized what every mother knows: If the child is not born, both the mother and child will die. With that thought and a final push, the child emerged from me with a massive *whooosh*. And—if you don't think I'm completely crazy already—I saw the baby floating in space among the stars. Like something straight out of *2001: A Space Odyssey!*" She laughed at her own recollection. I felt a rush of emotion at her words, and a deep identification with her story.

She went on, "In that moment, I knew I was Gaia, and I was giving birth to a child that would live out in space somewhere. You believe that? I was Gaia! This is what you were trying to tell me. Our species has to step out into space, even as we seek to protect the mother planet."

Tara and I looked into each other's eyes silently for a long moment. We shared a long embrace and kiss. Then, as best I could recall, I told her about my own vision.

Our experience on the mountain had renewed our bond more intensely than either of us expected. We stayed in each other's arms as long as we could back at her hotel room. She had a meeting and I had phone calls to make, but we filled every spare second with playful tender lovemaking.

Way behind schedule, I finally said goodbye to Tara around three that afternoon. I wanted to linger, but I was due in at the Riverside office at nine the next morning, which meant I was looking at a seven to eight hour ride. In the lobby, we hugged firmly and held each other's gaze, and without a word she was off again to catch a meeting for which she was already late. I watched her quick legs take her away, and I warmed at the thought of seeing her soon in DC.

Just as she disappeared from sight, I heard a familiar laugh just over my shoulder. I turned to see a grinning Mr. Grant.

"It looks like you've been having an *interesting* day." I should have felt embarrassed. Instead I was just glad to see him. The blissful feeling from the hike easily re-emerged with his presence.

Without hesitating, I asked, "The Twin Obligation is planetary stewardship, isn't it?"

He laughed softly. "Let's go find a seat. There's a nice garden in back of the hotel." We walked in silence out the back entrance. The urgency I felt a few moments earlier to get underway was gone. A discreet dirt path led to a semi-secluded area surrounding an exceptional cactus and flower garden. Taking in the serenity of the setting, we sat down on two of the chairs that were spaced around the perimeter of the garden.

After a few moments, Mr. Grant began, "I'm glad to see you have discovered the meaning of the Twin Obligation. I hoped you would. Tara is a special woman."

He paused. I could see his massive chest take in a big breath, hold it for a moment and release it very slowly. He finally continued, "Like the space migration Obligation, the Twin Obligation of planetary stewardship is also tied to human ascendance. These Twin Obligations have always existed, lying dormant until the time came when we would be mature enough to take responsibility for them. On rare occasions throughout history sensitive souls have been stirred by the primordial call of these Obligations. Most often they suffered ridicule, marginalization or worse by cultural conditions driven by basic need for survival through control and competition.

"Nevertheless, there has been a steady progression in the evolution of our capacity to fulfill these Obligations, as well as, of course, the Primary Obligation. With each generation of our technological and social development, we unconsciously inched toward the knowledge and capabilities necessary to take on these Obligations. And finally, in this generation, our collective consciousness is ready to accept these Twin Obligations. We finally have the technical know-how to consciously engage these efforts.

"By fulfilling these Obligations, it's relatively easy to see how it will ensure the survival of the human race. However, it is more important to understand that in fulfilling the Primary and Twin Obligations, we are preserving and extending the totality of life that emerged on this planet, as well as ensuring its future evolutionary potential. Do you see the distinction?" I nodded as he searched my features for confirmation that I did.

"Regarding the planetary stewardship Obligation in particular, we realize that humankind does not hold dominion over this planet. Rather it is our job to be the servant tenant ensuring that this planet remains healthy and viable for as long as possible."

I felt a need to ask, "As long as possible?"

"This world, like everything else in the universe, will one day come to an end. All we can hope to achieve is a degree of harmony with her as long as she lives. Reduce our footprint. Assist in restoring the ecology when necessary. Remove harmful toxins. And," with comic emphasis, "don't forget to recycle. Over time, we'll get better at taking care of the planet. But, it is essential that we continue to build on the small steps we've made. We have so much farther to go in bringing back balance to the global ecological system.

"For sure, the planetary stewardship Obligation has been fairly well defined in the past twenty years or so. If you ask anyone who is sufficiently conscious, they will likely agree that protecting the environment is our obligation. But, you will probably get the opposite reaction if you suggest that space migration is also an obligation, right?"

"Yes, I suppose so." I was reminded of my own skepticism toward that Obligation.

"Of course it's so," he snapped. "Now, let's look at these obligations in the broader context of universal constants I've already discussed with you. The universe exists or is sustained by the tension between the forces of expansion—all matter since the Big Bang has been expanding—and the tendency for matter to become ever more complex. These are the ultimate Yin and Yang forces governing space and time. These forces play out in infinitely different ways throughout the evolution and function of the universe. In everything I have been trying to relate to you, I am merely attempting to illustrate how these forces are manifesting in a particular way in the context of life that evolved on this particular planet.

"So once again, we have a pair. Like the pairs of Endowments, we have a pair of Obligations, with one associated with the Yin, complexity, planetary stewardship, and the other associated with the Yang, expansion, space migration. To keep this simple, let's agree that the Primary Obligation embodies both expansion and complexity. Once we as a species can fully embrace this trinity of purpose—to our collective well-being; to the well-being of the planet; and seeding of the stars—then, and only then, will we experience absolute harmony."

He paused, allowing me to absorb his words. He spoke more softly when he began again. "We are a species that is only now emerging from the throes of adolescence. In one way or another, many people are already committed to the trinity of Obligations, but there is still a long way to go. I believe we can we can look forward to a world in which understanding of the Obligations will be woven into the fabric of our global culture. To not act in accordance with these Obligations will be immediately recognized as counter to the purpose of human life."

There was an intensity in Mr. Grant I hadn't seen before. As if he desperately wanted me to grasp the full meaning of all he was conveying. My body was positively pulsating, feeling the words almost more than I was hearing them.

"Don't be mistaken. This process I'm describing is closer to a scientific theory than it is to a philosophical or spiritual way of thinking. These principles of the Endowments and the Obligations are grounded in an understanding of larger universal patterns that are already well understood. In our own limited way, humankind is expressing those patterns. The Endowments and the Obligations are not the only ways we express these patterns. There are infinite small and large examples in nature and culture where the creative tension between expansion and complexity plays out. The Endowments and the Obligations tells the specific story of the symbiotic relationship humanity has with its birth planet."

Leaning into my face, he emphasized, "Know these things. And let them guide your life."

His impassioned instructions suddenly stopped, and I was blissfully engulfed in silence, gazing into the cactus bed, sensing my body processing what Mr. Grant had said. And as my mind expanded beyond the confines of the garden patio, I spied some bees dancing around the few flowers among the cacti, dutifully fertilizing them and blissfully ignorant of it.

THE FLOOR

The seven-hour drive from Arizona was exhausting. Keeping me going were contemplations on the meaning of the Obligations, thoughts of my new intimacy with Tara, and no fewer than five coffee stops along the way.

After a less-than-adequate night's sleep, I arrived at the Riverside office the next morning to a polite but cool reception. By being away from the office so much, I had forfeited any chance of getting chummy with my West Coast coworkers. And, being booked on a red-eye flight back to Washington that evening left little opportunity to make up for lost bonding time. Dotty was the most annoyed. "Not sure you've gotten a whole lot out of this trip in terms of learning what we do out here, but nevertheless…" I tried to assure her I had learned quite a bit about the office operations and that it would make a difference back in Washington. She was not convinced.

Mr. Grant had already returned to Washington directly from Arizona. So at least there would be no risk of his pulling me away from the office on my final day. Yet, even in his absence, his voice in my head was a continuous low-level distraction.

While at my post at the front desk biding my few

remaining hours in California, Tom Rogers, Mr. Grant's legislative director, called in from DC wanting to speak with me. "The debate and vote on the Weinstein amendment is in three days and Mr. Grant wants to see a draft of his floor speech by noon day after tomorrow." When I explained that I had already prepared the draft, Tom explained, "He said he wants you to rewrite it. Start from scratch, he said, and that you'd know what to do. Does that make sense to you? Can you get it done in time?" I assured Tom that I knew what Mr. Grant meant and that I could complete the assignment in time. "If you need help, let me know."

I was certain of Mr. Grant's desire for the speech, and it seemed daunting. The anxiety of having to rewrite the floor speech was overwhelmed by the excitement of being asked to craft a message based on the insights of the Obligations and the Endowments. I admired Mr. Grant for his willingness to make such a broad philosophical statement to Congress— one that transcended the politics of budget debates. I had finally come to appreciate Mr. Grant's motives and felt a sense of pride in my role in bringing these ideas to light.

I began making an outline at the reception desk, between answering the phone, completing busy work for Dotty, and sincerely doing my best to make a favorable last impression with the staff.

I finished the bulk of the speech in long hand on the overnight flight back to Washington. I was too wound up to sleep. This assignment gave me a reason to put down on paper what Mr. Grant had shared with me while it was still relatively fresh in my memory. Once back at my desk on Capitol Hill, I typed the speech. It was too long, as I knew it would be. Before trimming it, I saved a copy of the long version, which amounted to a bare-bones summary of the Six Endowments and the Obligations.

My internal clock was shot from the jet lag, so I slept when I needed to, night or day. The demands of those two days were intense, with preparing the speech and catching up with all the other duties that had piled up while I was away. But the speech was my top priority. Fortunately, Tara was not due back in town until the night before the vote. I let nothing get in the way of giving it my best effort.

I crafted an argument that began by explaining the various reasons why people are motivated to support space projects: the thrill of exploration (the Wanderer), the desire to make new homes (the Settler), to expand our knowledge and capabilities (the Inventor), to promote private industry and markets (the Builder), to have a place to direct our dreams (the Visionary), and to guard against global catastrophe (the Protector). I then showed how the space station program fulfilled each of these basic human desires. In the summation, I wrote:

> "In many ways, the space station is the culmination of a thousand-year vision toward which humankind has always been moving. In this way, we must view the space station and human expansion into space as a profound obligation to future generations of Americans and the world they will inhabit."

I also included near-term benefits, such as global competitiveness and international security, as I had with the previous draft, but confined them to a few short paragraphs. The bulk of the text focused on the Endowment and Obligation message. I felt confident that I was able to maintain the essence of the insights without straying too far from norms of political debate.

I continued to polish the text right up until the last minute. On the day before the floor debate, I gave the speech to Tom Rogers for his review and sign-off before showing it to Mr. Grant. After reading it, Tom came over to my desk scratching his head. He didn't know what to make of it. "Are you sure this is what he asked for?" I assured him it was, so he shrugged and handed me the draft with minor edits.

Within a half hour I was in Mr. Grant's empty office with the finished speech. I placed the document on his desk for him to see when he returned. My head turned mechanically to the wall behind his desk, and I paused to consider once again the inconspicuous plaque hanging there. It seemed an eon had passed since the first day I had asked Mr. Grant about its meaning. Since that time, the plaque's inscription had transformed from a simple aphorism into a profound new way of looking at the world.

With the speech out of my hands, I was able to put my attention to my beautiful Tara. She had gotten back to Washington that afternoon and I was eager to see her. I woke her up when I arrived at her basement apartment at seven PM bearing Chinese carry out. She was sleepy-happy to see me. I was exhausted too, so we just lounged on her bed intermittently eating, talking, dozing and making love.

Lying on her back looking at the ceiling, she said, "I think I agree with this whole concept of Obligations. I like the idea that humanity is playing a part in the evolution and development of the planet—*Gaia.*" She widened her eyes when she said Gaia and laughed at how she overemphasized the word. "I can see that this world wasn't just created for our amusement. Yet, when I think about the vote on the floor tomorrow, I'm kind of brought back to the realities of fiscal limitations. I still believe that the amount of money we want to spend on the space station can be spent more effectively in so many other areas. The Obligation to planetary stewardship must come first. We have to clean up our act here first, and then once we've straightened everything out, then we can make plans to create space colonies."

"But your vision?" I reminded her. "You were Gaia, you said, giving birth to new life into the cosmos. Hasn't that changed you?"

"I know... *I know*. I felt...I feel this transformation happening, that it is inevitable. But I just don't know if it needs to happen *right now*. I'm having trouble reconciling the vision I had in Arizona with the political realities of our space program as it is—one that serves as a revenue stream for shareholders of the military-industrial complex."

How could I argue with her? She had a point. The way NASA's procurement system worked, aerospace contractors were incentivized to go over schedule and over budget. This is not a criticism of these corporations. It's merely a statement of their primary purpose –to maximize profits. At the same time, the NASA bureaucracy is often wasteful. Like Tara, I found it hard to bridge the gap between the evolutionary perspective of space migration and present political realities.

"What if," she continued, "we canceled the space station? Shut it down altogether. Would that mean the end of the space program? Would we no longer be able to meet our Obligation to colonize space?"

"Well, I wouldn't think so…"

"I would hope not. If this *Obligation* is as real as Mr. Grant says it is, it will find another way to achieve its end. Isn't that the idea?"

"You must be right. Perhaps the Chinese or some other country or group of countries would find a way to meet the Obligation. Or, maybe the private sector can figure out how to lower the cost of space travel and lead the way…"

"So there, you see! Why do we have to keep *this* particular space project going?"

"Hmm. I don't know if I have a good answer. I suppose it comes down to doing what you can, when you can—if you are someone who has some level of passion about mankind's future in space."

She sat up and looked at me for moment before

continuing. She seemed about to add something, but changed her mind, and concluded, "Well, anyway, I'm sure, thanks to you, Mr. Grant will make a very compelling case tomorrow in support of the space station."

There was something else she wanted to say, but there seemed no point to press her on it. I fed her some lo mein. She stretched and fell back on her pillow, curling up for another nap. I lay down close to her playing with her hair and watching her, before falling asleep myself.

The Floor debate was scheduled to begin about two PM. The time leading up to it was nerve racking as I waited to get feedback on the speech. I finally cornered Mr. Grant late in the morning returning from a meeting. This was the first time I had seen him since our patio chat in front of the cactus garden at the Tucson Marriott. Though he had been in the office for days, he was so tied up with meetings and hearings I had not even seen him.

I intercepted Mr. Grant without warning, which elicited a startled and irritated response. He growled, "What?!" I knew this reaction well. His impatient cranky-boss personality was startling, after all that had happened out West.

Though flustered, I pressed him about the remarks, and asked if he had a chance to review them, and were they okay. No doubt my anxiety showed. The impatient looks of the other staff nearby only made this worse.

Mr. Grant's temper softened only slightly. He said, "It's fine, John. Just fine," and without looking at me, disappeared into his office with his senior staff in tow. Rationally, I knew Mr. Grant's reaction was due to his preoccupation with other pressing matters, but that rationalization wasn't enough to blunt the rush of embarrassment I felt.

I was clearly off the high I had been on since Arizona.

The debate had already begun when I found a seat in the gallery above the House floor where the action was taking place. Coming to the gallery to watch the debate was a luxury of time, for sure. I could have watched it on C-SPAN from the office, but after all that had gone on, I felt a need to witness the action in person. I spotted Tara three sections away with her companions. We had agreed in advance that it would be best not to sit together during the debate to avoid rumors that either of us was "fraternizing with the enemy." Kyle McAllister sat next to Tara and seemed to be very conscious of my frequent glances in her direction.

The action on the floor was heated, but organized. Unlike many amendments that come up for a vote, the space station amendment did not split strictly along partisan lines. What determined a representative's position on the measure was whether or not any portion of the space station funding would be spent in his or her congressional district. The Coalition for Responsible Federal Spending, however, had organized a formidable voting bloc, many of whom actually had some connection to the space station. At the start of the debate, there were enough undecided representatives to make the final outcome anyone's guess.

One congressperson after another was recognized by the Chair to rise in favor of, or in opposition to, the proposed Weinstein amendment to cancel the space station program. As with the original draft, I provided Mr. Grant a long and short version of his remarks. The short one fit the brief time allotted under the rules of the debate, and the longer version was to be included in the permanent record.

I didn't think much of the fact that Mr. Grant was not on the floor when I arrived. And I was sure he had not given his remarks before I arrived. But as the time for the debate was winding down, I became vexed by the thought that he might miss his chance to give the speech at all.

Just as it was clear the debate was about to conclude, and feeling a knot of panic growing in my chest, I spotted the large figure of Mr. Grant lumber from the cloakroom and make its way to the podium. The congressman managing the floor debate recognized the gentleman from California, Mr. Grant, for five minutes.

"Mr. Chairman, I ask unanimous consent to revise and extend my remarks." With approval from the chairman, he continued, "I rise in strong opposition to the amendment offered by the gentlemen from New York, Mr. Weinstein, which proposes to cancel the space station program. First, let me say emphatically, I respect the views and position of my colleagues who support this measure. However, I must state without hesitation that now is not the time to turn our back on human spaceflight capability. Since the first flight of Alan Shepard, the first American to pierce the atmospheric veil and touch the heavens, human spaceflight has been part of the fabric of our democracy, and a capability that has been and continues to be the awe and envy of every other nation on the planet."

This is not right. The words had been changed.

"In my humble opinion, there are three paramount reasons why we cannot afford as a nation to turn away from the space station: technological competitiveness, national defense and international prestige…"

What is he reading? It took a minute or so to register that Mr. Grant was not delivering the speech I had prepared for him on the Endowments and the Obligations. Instead, he was reading the words from the original draft I had written before my west-coast trip. I had difficulty accepting this reality, but with each sentence he read the truth of it became ever more evident. My amazement and confusion turned to frustration and anger.

Tara no doubt could see the mood I had gotten into, and kept looking my way with a questioning expression. But I wouldn't respond. I watched the remainder of the debate in numb silence. Mr. Grant only once briefly looked up at me without expression, and left the floor immediately after casting his vote. The amendment had failed by a narrow margin, but the outcome of the vote was no longer important to me.

I left the Capitol building without waiting for Tara and did not return to my office in the Rayburn building. I spent the next few hours in a fit trying to figure out what had just happened. I whipped my mind into a froth of anger I couldn't shake. Everything that had happened since the day I saw that plaque, the meetings about the Endowments, and Zen master talks with Mr. Grant, all unraveled into meaningless nonsense, whose purpose all along must have been to make me look like a fool.

It wasn't that he gave a different speech. That can happen anytime on any subject. Anyone on the Hill can tell stories about how hours of work went unused without explanation. Mr. Grant's slight cut to the bone because I thought he was going for something deeper in his message, and it drove me crazy that he would cast aside the opportunity the way he did. Worse, my blissful connection with the material had eroded into dark cynicism.

By evening, I found myself walking aimlessly on the National Mall. The clear warm night under a full moon did nothing to calm my agitation.

Ahead of me I noticed a large man sitting alone on one of the benches under a lamp post that lined the wide path of the Mall.

THE EVOLUTIONARY IMPULSE

Even from a distance I could tell who it was, though I tried to reject the reality of it. With clenched fists I stopped a few feet from where he sat. He was relaxed, his tie loosened. "Sit down, John," he said in a matter-of-fact way, as if he had been expecting me, and perhaps he was.

My pent-up frustration was too much to contain.

"What the hell kind of game are you playing?" The torrent began, and once the valve was open it was impossible to shut off. "What makes you think you can jerk people around like that? I worked my ass off writing that speech. At least you could have told me it was crap before making a jackass out of me. I thought you wanted to share all of these insights with Congress, and by extension the entire world. Did you chicken out or something? And decided to read that piece-of-shit speech I wrote weeks ago. Why did you bother to tell me all that stuff about Obligations and Endowments? Do you like fucking with people?" Mr. Grant listened impassively.

The outburst felt good. And then it felt awful. I stood silently for a while, breathing heavily, and red faced. Finally, I slumped down on the bench next to him with tears coming from my eyes. I swiped a sleeve across my face like some eight-year-old kid whose bike had been stolen.

"Anything else you would like to add?"

When I didn't reply, he continued, "You first need to know, John, that whatever happened in there today," gesturing to the Capitol dome, "is of minor importance compared to the knowledge you have acquired in the past few weeks. The insights we discussed go beyond the world of politics, and therefore, cannot be appreciated at the political level—at least not yet. This knowledge we now share may well influence the future, but in the back and forth of political horse trading, this kind of insight has little relevance. That's neither bad nor good. It's simply the way it is. To share these ideas with my colleagues would be like trying to explain the inner workings of a Boeing 747 turbofan engine to someone who just wants to know if his flight to Chicago will leave on time. They are just not going to care enough even if they could somehow comprehend the message.

"As long as we have to work within the current political system, arguments for space development, like everything else, will always have to be couched in parochial and nationalistic terms. The occasional reference to broad long-term implications is little more than creative flourish. I knew this crowd was not ready for the kind of speech you so admirably prepared. Nothing would have given me greater pleasure than to read your words and know they were falling on receptive ears. The truth is that most people, and especially Congress people, are not evolved enough to truly hear that message."

He moved closer, and his voice softened further, "I had you write that speech for your sake, John. It was a way for you to capture the essence of what you have learned, and to some degree internalize it. There is no book I can give you that contains all of it, at least not one that integrates the various theories in the principles of the Obligation. You now have it in your head, and in your heart." Mr. Grant's soothing words calmed my agitation. My anger was replaced by shame for my disrespectful tirade a moment earlier.

Having regained my composure, I asked, "If it's pointless to discuss these ideas with your colleagues, then how will this future of space migration ever happen? What's the use of some truth about an Obligation if no one knows about it?"

"Those are good questions. Just because Congress may not be ready for this message right now doesn't mean it won't be at some point in the future. This kind of language needs to percolate up from individuals who embrace this perspective. Eventually, fulfilling the Obligation will take the form of legislative proposals, and Congress will debate those proposals on their local, national and global merits. If a large enough constituency for such ideas can effectively demand that government take action, new policies and programs will be adopted—we'll build those colonies in space. This is, of course, how the legislative process has always worked. The only things that ever change are the interests and demands of the people. A more evolved constituency will insist on more evolved action from its government. The emerging perspective of the Obligation will represent a new collective priority that Congress, and other government bodies in other countries, will eventually be forced to address and contend with. You see?" He paused for my reaction and laughed, "Sorry if all this sounds a bit wonky."

The wonkiness of it was more than fine with me. Putting the Obligation in a congressional context was a comfort zone that I could get my head around. As Mr. Grant continued, however, my mind eased once again into familiar feeling relaxed attentiveness.

"But when will this all take place? You talk about this being an imperative, yet there is little evidence that Congress or NASA are anywhere near taking steps to make the vision a reality."

This made him laugh, "You're absolutely right, of course. That's why it's important to be clear that it will not necessarily be NASA and the U.S. Congress who will be leading the way toward space settlement. I suppose it's possible they will, but there is simply too much institutional inertia at NASA for it to be the right vehicle to lead our full transition to a multi-planetary existence. It may be Evan Phillips and his kind who will lead the way. The entrepreneur, unfettered by bureaucratic baggage, and driven by passion and high ideals, will solve the riddle of space colonization. Or perhaps there is some yet-to-be-created economic mechanism that will need to be invented in order for such a future to come into being.

"The good news is that our collective consciousness is being propelled to take action in the direction of space migration whether anyone wants it to or not."

"Propelled?...By what?"

"Ah, now that gets us to one of the most important topics of all. We are *propelled* toward space migration by the Evolutionary Impulse."

"Evolutionary Impulse?" He took a moment to smile at the question, locking my gaze.

"We haven't discussed this concept yet, at least not in specific detail. The Evolutionary Impulse is integral to everything you have learned so far. First, let's review." He picked up a stick and in the dirt and gravel in front of the bench he drew two vertical lines side by side. The lines were about two feet long, spaced a foot apart at the base, flaring apart to about two feet at the top. I recognized the diagram as the one he had drawn for me in Arizona, sitting at the picnic table while we ate danish and coffee.

"We've discussed the universal forces of expansion and complexity, which correspond to the male/female and Yin/Yang dimensions of life." With the stick he pointed to the left line as representing the expansion force and the right line as representing complexity. "What I haven't mentioned is that these two opposing forces create evolutionary tension, which precedes and gives rise to creation in all its forms.

"We also discussed how these forces are expressed through human consciousness in the form of three pairs of Endowments: the Wanderer and the Settler; the Inventor and the Builder; and the Visionary and the Protector." As he named each of the Endowments, he made a dot with the stick in the space outside the two lines. He arranged the dots in three pairs, with the Wanderer and the Settler dots situated in parallel positions near the base of each line. The subsequent pairs held ascending parallel positions above the first two. The dots along the left line represented the Endowments associated with the expansion line: the Wanderer, the Inventor and the Visionary. And the dots along the right line coincided with the complexity: the Settler, the Builder and the Protector.

"The Endowments evolved within our consciousness over some period of time in our early development. We illustrate the emergence of the Endowments as a spiral, a process of oscillation between the opposing forces." With his stick he drew a spiral up from the base of the lines and between them. "And we said that each pair is an evolved form of the one before it."

He paused to make sure I was following him. "The Evolutionary Impulse is the force that drives the whole train." With that he carved a deep line right up through the middle of the spiral. "The Evolutionary Impulse is that urge to create on all levels in the universe. It is the urge for a star to come into being, and it is the urge for a piece of art to emerge on a canvas. It is the engine that gives power to the Endowments. It was the driving force to create the Endowments, and will impel our action until the Obligation is fulfilled. And it will sustain us into the next evolutionary stage, whatever that might be."

Down the Mall path came two evening runners, both women. One had large breasts which were hard not to notice as they bounced freely under the tight spandex top. As they passed, Mr. Grant chuckled. "The human sex drive is perhaps the best example of the Evolutionary Impulse at play. The species must propagate or die. It's very important that men and women are sexually attracted to one another. By responding to that basic urge, you are responding to the Evolutionary Impulse to reproduce.

"In the most basic sense, it was the Evolutionary Impulse that started the whole universe in motion from the Big Bang on. In this context, Darwinian evolution comprises just a small subset of an infinitely larger picture. When something emerges from nothing we call it an act of creation. While the act of creation describes the moment something is made manifest in the physical world, the Evolutionary Impulse is the guiding force behind just what that "something" will be and how it will emerge into form. In other words, the Evolutionary Impulse is the intelligent energy that nudges creation into specific directions."

He paused. By this point, I had thoroughly slipped into heightened attentiveness. There was a question forming in my mind, but he did not wait for me to ask it.

"Each evolutionary advancement—the emergence of new species of animal, plant, or other life forms—occurs in response to the Evolutionary Impulse. Prior to the moment of creation, the Evolutionary Impulse generates a certain tension or pressure on the physical world that prepares the way for a particular act of creation. This process is occurring in every moment in every square centimeter of the universe. It certainly occurs with the emergence of a new species, but actually is the intelligent energy that literally sustains everything. We see its work with each birth of a child. We see it in the formation of stars. We also see it in the advance of civilization, technology, culture and, as we've been discussing, in the development of consciousness.

"The tension that the Evolutionary Impulse imposes on human consciousness has helped guide our development out of the caves and into skyscrapers. The pull toward space migration is just one expression of this evolutionary tension. We see it is clearly present in the consciousness of the six individuals you interviewed. It is nothing less than a primordial demand to move off this planet and become a multi-planetary species.

"Someone might say that they're interested in space travel and would like to work for NASA. If that person is talented enough he might live his dream and become an astronaut. If he lacks the requisite talent and skills, he might otherwise seek to build a career somewhere in the aerospace field. At a minimum, that individual will follow each launch with great interest, and perhaps join groups and write his congressman to keep NASA well funded. The important thing is that the Evolutionary Impulse coursing through the astronaut and the amateur lobbyist are no different. Although space advocates may feel that their passion is self-generated, it is actually a response to an encoded stimulus that is part of their being, which they are not even aware of.

"When Armstrong stepped on the moon the world was united in awe and wonder. It wasn't merely a Cold War victory as some historians have concluded. Something momentous happened. A milestone had been reached. And the reaction of billions of people went much deeper than could be understood in technical rational terms. That global moment of euphoria was an expression of our movement toward fulfilling the Obligation."

Now he paused long enough for me to react. "But that excitement about the moon missions didn't last. The public got bored after Apollo 11, and the launches were no longer headline news."

"Is that really so surprising?" At that moment, the sound of a child's yelp drew our attention. About a hundred feet down the path a mother firmly held the hand of a pre-school boy. She pulled him along while he resisted, whimpering that he did not want to go home. She was clearly angry and fed up with the uncooperative child. It was getting late and the boy was no doubt tired and cranky. Mr. Grant chuckled at the scene. "I've certainly been there," he whispered to himself, recollecting his own parental frustration.

"When there is a new birth, everyone is excited and drawn to the wonder of a new life joining our family. After the initial event of the birth, however, the child eventually becomes just another kid. There are diapers to change. You have to child-proof everything. They throw tantrums on the Mall. The first moon landing was a lot like a newborn. When we first saw it, it was wonderful, incredible, a miracle. After that it was still nice. You still believed in the mission, of course. But, what about the football game or the 'I Love Lucy' rerun you wanted to watch? How can you blame the networks or the public for Apollo's drop in viewership? But the lack of newsworthiness never made the missions any less worthy. Just as being in the world for a while doesn't diminish the value of any of God's children, even when they get to be a pain in the ass." The mother and uncooperative child were some distance down the Mall, the boy's outcries still audible.

"God's children," I repeated, sparking a question. I hesitated, but I needed to know. "The Evolutionary Impulse sounds like the guiding hand of *God*. You used the term "intelligent energy" and said that the Evolutionary Impulse guides the creation of things in the universe. Are you saying there is a God?"

Mr. Grant leaned back, drew a deep breath raising his eyebrows. "Now, that's a loaded question. To say there is an intelligent directionality to the evolution of the universe is not to say that that force is the essence of what traditional religions accept as God. Remember we spoke earlier about the universe unfolding according to a DNA blueprint. The potential for human existence preceded our arrival. We have free will, but at the same time we are guided by the Evolutionary Impulse to accomplish certain things, including being stewards of the planet as well as migrating beyond it.

You see, no one, or any god, is forcing us to be interested in space travel; therefore we have free will to deny it—and certainly many do. However, it is part of our collective DNA to be very interested in such things.

"As for the existence of God, I believe the mystery that the prophets and sages have been speaking about for millennia is still very much intact. As significant as the revelations of the Obligation may be, it is nothing more than peeling back one more layer of the onion. There will always be greater depths to fathom. And the fact that humanity may have a particular symbiotic relationship to its host planet does not imply that there is not yet some additional divine or genetic purpose for our existence. There may well be. But, on the question of our divinity and of God in general, I am afraid to say, I am completely unqualified to speak. On the other hand, could anything be more divine than serving in a role similar to that of the bumble bees?"

He shifted his body on the bench, turning it to face me. "What's important to emphasize here is that the Evolutionary Impulse is driving us to find the way into space. There are differences of opinion on how that will best be achieved, and by whom. But these debates, and even the space race itself, are moving civilization as a whole in the same direction. We may not have made all the right decisions so far. Certainly, had we maintained focus and funding after Apollo, it's perfectly conceivable that by today astronauts would be exploring the far reaches of the solar system, and we would be well on our way toward building self-sustaining human settlements. But, we were distracted by other priorities and global challenges—issues we could say relate to the Primary Obligation. It's not that the interest in space development had diminished. We simply couldn't get past other roadblocks of the last few decades. In fact, it's amazing how successful NASA has been considering the political challenges and modest public interest.

"This impulse to expand into space is like water rolling

downhill; the water will trickle in many directions before it finds the right groove, which becomes the brook and eventually the mighty river. The U.S./Soviet space race of the sixties is a good example of this point. Historians will say it was Cold War tensions that provided the impetus for the moon race. While it's true, without the Cold War we might not have had Apollo, it is also important to remember that the desire for space travel was a fire in the minds of many people long before tension with the Soviet Union created a rationale for demonstrating mastery in missile technology. The original rocket scientists like Goddard and von Braun dreamt of space travel for the benefit of all mankind, not so one nation could show technological superiority over another. The first space visionaries were expressing the ideas that trickled down the mountainside, finding the niches and cracks, gathering and pooling. The Cold War merely provided a wide channel through which the current of the Evolutionary Impulse could surge in the direction of the Obligation."

When he finished, a prolonged silence helped to anchor his words in my mind. I looked down at the diagram Mr. Grant had scratched in the dirt. There was an elegant simplicity about it that made perfect sense.

"So is that it? Is that all of the philosophy of the Obligation?" Once again, I reached for closure. It all seemed complete.

"Yes…and no. But it's getting late, my friend. And I am late for a fundraiser at the Willard Hotel."

And without further comment, he stood, smiled at me and walked down the Mall path. I wanted to ask him something else and keep the discussion going, but nothing came out of me as I watched his hulking figure get smaller and disappear.

My anger over the floor speech was a distant memory.

I drifted back to my apartment, my head filled with the Evolutionary Impulse. Once again, Mr. Grant had forced me to look beyond the veil of what I knew.

When I arrived at my brownstone, I found Tara sitting on my front steps. "Where have you been? The way you looked in the Capitol…I was worried." I fell gratefully into her arms.

"Thank you for being here," I whispered.

As we pulled apart, she asked, "What happened? I called your office. They said you never came back."

"It's okay," I said. "I behaved like an idiot. You shouldn't have paid any attention." I became aware of how calm I felt, in contrast to Tara's agitation. All the vitriol of just a few hours ago had completely drained from my body.

Tara looked exceptionally beautiful, with the street lamps and moonlight artfully competing to illuminate her features. I could have looked at her forever.

"What?" She smiled and then laughed. "What are you looking at?" When I didn't respond right away, wanting only to linger on her features, she said, "Come on. Let's take a walk." We strolled to East Capitol Street and turned toward the Hill. I had just covered the distance across the Capitol grounds on my way from the Mall to my brownstone, but was satisfied to walk in any direction Tara wished.

I told her about why I was so upset during floor debate, and how Mr. Grant seemed to appear out of nowhere on Mall. I told her about the Evolutionary Impulse, and how it wasn't just another term for God. I told her about the boy and his mother and the girl with bouncing boobs, which made her giggle an "oh, my god." In describing the events, there was no separation between what Mr. Grant said and my own views. Somehow I had arrived at a place where I fully accepted all that he said as truth.

Tara was an impeccable listener. I didn't want to give her any more information than I sensed she was interested in hearing about. But she was intrigued, and at several points when I felt I had said enough, she prodded for more details.

"And do you, John? Do you feel the 'Evolution Impulse' to expand life into space? Because, I can tell you without hesitation, I feel the Evolutionary Impulse, if that's what you to call it, for planetary stewardship... So, do you, *Billy Blastoff?*"

Through our laughter, I answered. "Yes, of course I do. I have always known or felt this pull. It's only now, spending this time with Mr. Grant, that I can fully understand the source of these feelings. I do sense the Evolutionary Impulse for space migration, and...I think I always have. Though I have rarely acted on it, I have always been drawn to space travel activities, particular human spaceflight. Certainly, I was turned on by *Star Trek* and *Star Wars*, and certain space toys not to be mentioned." She laughed, wrapping both her arms around mine in an affectionate squeeze.

"I wasn't just fine with being assigned space issues for Mr. Grant. I lobbied for it, and was jazzed when I was given the chance to work on space policy." The perception of my own motives was shifting even as I spoke. "In my head I've always seen the space program as absolutely essential to our civilization. Now I know it's so much more important than I ever imagined." My personal feelings came out in an unexpected gush. "The truth of the Obligation has always been there, just beyond my conscious mind, like something you catch out of the corner of your eye. It's only now that I can tell that space travel was always a part of my aspiration."

Tara listened, flat footed and open mouthed. "Wow, that's a little intense."

I grabbed the top of a wrought-iron garden fence feeling a need to steady myself. "It's like I'm just starting to understand what I've always wanted in life. On the one hand I know it's always been there, but on the other hand it's like something I've never paid any attention to before. Does that make any sense?"

She said nothing and put her arms around my neck. We

embraced and kissed again.

We had wandered over to Independence Avenue and we unconsciously began to head back east along Pennsylvania Avenue. After a block or two of silence, Tara said, "There's something I still can't reconcile in all of this. If space colonization is truly the Obligation of humanity, then why isn't the way forward much clearer?" While I considered this question, she elaborated, "I mean, why is there so much confusion and ambivalence and outright hostility with regard to humanity fulfilling this purpose? If we are pre-programed, as Mr. Grant says, to take this giant leap for mankind, why isn't everyone on board with it already? The fact that you won the vote today for the space station—congratulations by the way—doesn't mean the space program we have now will lead to the kind of colonization you see in the sci-fi movies. In fact it's hard to imagine when, if ever, we'll gather the political will to get back to the moon to visit, never mind colonize it."

"Mr. Grant said that we had to be ready for this transition. He said it would come from the bottom up, and Congress will pass related legislation once enough of a constituency insisted that they do so. He also said this was not something that could be stopped either... but still, you bring up a good point that I'm not sure if I'm clear on either. Why all the struggle?"

She responded, "I agree with everything that you've said, but the simple reality is that space colonization is a minor interest in the global scheme of things. I suspect more people think about alien invasions than the prospects of putting a settlement on Mars."

Tara had hit on a puzzling and obvious issue that I knew I would have to raise with Mr. Grant. Did this contradiction point to a flaw in the philosophy of the Obligation?

As we walked, I slid my arm around Tara's waist and gently pulled her closer. She responded by putting her arm around me as well.

THE SEVENTH
ENDOWMENT

I slept more soundly that night than I had in weeks. Tara stayed with me for a while, but left to sleep at her place. In the morning the world looked different. There was a shine to everything, similar to what I experienced on the Arizona mountaintop after my meditation session with Tara. I felt a deep serenity. I drank my coffee with the world around me shimmering with clarity as if I were somehow seeing it all for the first time.

Even as I enjoyed the blissful sensation of that quiet morning, my thoughts went to Tara's point, the lingering question I feared might unravel everything that Mr. Grant had shown me.

It was mid-morning that day when I caught up with Mr. Grant in the hall of the Rayburn Building not far from our office.

Sensing my intentions, he said, "Come, walk with me. I can't miss this vote." The bells summoning Members to the floor for a vote had just started ringing.

He smiled as we entered the elevator down to the basement.

"So, John. Are you feeling better today?"

"Yes, sir. I feel great in fact. But there was something else that I'm not clear on..."

"Well, you've gotten a lot to chew on." The doors of the elevator opened, and two other Members came on. Mr. Grant bantered with them about the pending vote.

From the elevator we walked to the Capitol subway cars. Other Members of Congress flowed out from adjacent elevators making the same route.

"Go ahead, John, what's on your mind?"

I felt awkward bringing up the topic in such a public place, but nonetheless followed Mr. Grant's opening.

"If it's as you say, that space migration and planetary stewardship are part of the natural order of things, why does it seem as if we're not getting anywhere in these areas? With so much opposition to space development, like the battle we just faced over the space station, for example, it seems the whole future of the space program is in doubt. And if space migration and environmental protection is such a sacred pair of the Obligations, why are people so divided over these issues?" I put the questions as straight as I could.

Mr. Grant was amused, "Well you get a gold star. You've asked one of the most important questions." I made a mental note to pass the gold star to Tara. We climbed aboard one of the cars. Though we sat shoulder-to-shoulder with other Members, they paid no attention to our conversation.

Once seated, Mr. Grant continued, "The answer to that question lies with the Seventh Endowment."

"The seventh...?"

"Did you think our evolution was complete?" He laughed, and I made no attempt to respond. "This is the supreme arrogance of our species. We believe we are as good as it gets—an attitude that may yet do us in."

I was amazed that there was not a flicker of interest from any of the other riders as the car glided the short distance to the Capitol Building.

"I've told you that the six Endowments emerged consecutively in human consciousness over a long period of time. The reason some of us are becoming conscious of the nature of the Twin Obligations at this time is due to the emergence of the Seventh Endowment."

"But, what...?" The car came to a stop before I could finish my question. I held my thought as we bustled from the car.

"Let's pick this up later. I'm sure my colleagues are not as interested in this topic as we are." There was eye contact and chuckles between Mr. Grant and other Members as they disappeared behind the doors of the Capitol elevator.

At about half past seven that night I was still at my desk. Everyone else had gone for the day. Tara told me to come by her place as soon as I could. I had not spoken to Mr. Grant since our ride on the Capitol subway, and was eager to find out more about the Seventh Endowment. The blissful feeling I woke up with stayed with me all day. It felt strongest in the quiet moments. It was a knowing that everything was the way it should be.

The office phone rang. Normally I let the answering machine pick up the call at that time of night, but I felt an urge to answer it myself. "Hello. Congressman Harrison Grant's office?"

"John?" I knew the voice instantly. It was Mr. Grant. "I was hoping you'd still be there. Why don't you come over to the Capitol and meet me at the top of the steps on west side of the building."

I left the Rayburn building and walked toward the Capitol. The sun was low in the sky but still bright. The slight humidity in the air was a refreshing change from the controlled environment of the office. I made my way to the west side of the building. I took off my jacket and loosened my tie. I didn't see Mr. Grant at all until I nearly reached the top of the long set of stairs on the House side of the building. Mr. Grant was seated on the top-most step and invited me to sit next to him.

"I like this time of year in Washington. It's warm and comfortable. A nice period before the summer heat."

"The Seventh Endowment? What did you mean by that?" I was eager to get the conversation going.

"Just hold that thought for a bit, son. Let's just take in the view for a while, shall we?"

The view was spectacular. The Mall stretched out in front of us to the Washington Monument. Beyond that I could clearly see the reflecting pool and Lincoln Memorial. The sun was just touching the horizon giving the entire scene an otherworldly glow. The inner serenity easily came back to me.

In his own time, Mr. Grant began. "The Seventh Endowment is a difficult Endowment to understand. There is not yet a descriptive archetype we can associate with this Endowment as there are with the Visionary, the Inventor and the others. It has not fully matured as a distinct characteristic in our collective psyche. Yet, it is the emergence of this trait that is essential to the fulfillment of all three Obligations, and resolving all the world's biggest problems."

"All of the world's problems…?"

"Yes. As grandiose as that may sound." He looked at me. "The Seventh Endowment is about wholeness in all aspects of the collective human and planetary existence. With the Seventh Endowment it becomes possible to solve even the nastiest of problems such as extreme poverty, war, energy scarcity, environmental imbalance, man's inhumanity to man, and so on. The Seventh Endowment is essential for the fulfillment of all three Obligations; the Primary and Twin.

"But, before I discuss the Seventh Endowment further, let's start with your question. If space migration, as I've suggested, is encoded somehow in the planet's DNA, then we might conclude that there is nothing to worry about. Sooner or later we'll get there. But, of course, there *is* something to worry about, as you recognized. The progress into space is happening in fits and starts. Space migration seems even more remote a possibility today than it was when *Eagle* landed on the moon decades ago.

"As long as we are focused on the incremental advancement in space development, and do not *consciously* understand that those advancements, or some of them at least, are stepping stones toward attaining the capacity for human migration into space, there is no guarantee that we will fulfill that Obligation. The main culprit in stopping our progression is *Planetary Inertia*." He paused here and leaned back, placing the palms of his hands on the stone patio behind him.

"Planetary inertia has to do with our bond to this planet. We've never known any home other than this pretty blue marble. The idea that we could actually make a home beyond the atmosphere is simply beyond what most people can visualize. For those who can conceive such a future, most see space settlement as a remote future possibility with no relevance in today's world. Most people say space exploration is fine, but permanent settlement? *Give me a break.*

"Planetary inertia was perhaps foreshadowed in mythical and biblical stories of Icarus and the Tower of Babel. Be careful, these stories warn. Don't try to reach the heavens or you'll get burned. If you try to build a tower to reach the heavens, where humans don't belong, God will put you in your place. These stories actually illustrate the primordial struggle between the Evolution Impulse to expand beyond this planet, and planetary inertia that wants no part of it. But interestingly, these stories have never stopped the ruling class of nearly every age to build their soaring cathedrals and temples in symbolic gestures to get closer to God.

"Planetary inertia acts as a cultural and psychological brick wall, with space settlement most definitely on the other side. Unless humanity begins to *consciously* engage in the evolutionary process—of which it is already a part—it simply may not be able to overcome this inertia. People must learn to see space migration as a desirable end in its own right, and not simply for the immediate benefits that we might derive from it."

He paused, giving me an opportunity to ask, "I see. But what does this have to do with the Seventh Endowment?"

"Why, everything! As I just said, humanity must begin to consciously engage in the evolutionary process if it is to overcome planetary inertia. That's the Seventh Endowment, the capacity for Conscious Evolution."

He stopped again to let that sink in. "Let me explain. We know the Endowments emerged in human consciousness one after the other as a progression in an evolutionary process, beginning with the Wanderer all the way through to the Protector. We've also said that these traits are all integrally associated with the flourishing of human civilization, and are essential for creating the means for space migration.

"The human race has come an amazing distance through the application of these traits." Looking over the sparkling city that stretched below, I had an odd sensation that I was seeing the city as the culmination of all past history. "We say quite often that human civilization has evolved through time in a manner that is not dissimilar to Darwin's process of natural selection—from grass huts to the Sears Tower. This evolutionary process, as miraculous as it has been, has also been an *unconscious* process, only fully appreciated looking back in retrospect. There was nothing deliberate or intentional about how we transitioned from one age to another. From the Bronze Age to the Iron Age. From the Industrial Age to the Information Age. Inventors simply came up with ideas and inventions and the Builders copied the new stuff they liked. Populations adopted technologies that made sense to them. Gradually society changed with each new age to become something different that no one had intended it to become. Sometimes these changes were good for people and sometimes they weren't. But over the long haul, technological progress was made and the standard of living for people improved. True, the Industrial Age came with horrors, and most of the world's population still lives life at the economic margins. We can't disregard these truths. Nevertheless, our quality of life is remarkable compared to what it was even a hundred years ago, particularly in western developed countries, and certainly with the rest of the world trying to catch up.

"To stress my point again, the remarkable series of events that brought us to where we are in history have occurred without our *conscious* intent."

I was puzzled by this and it must have shown on my face. He shifted his position and considered his next statement.

"Let's look at unconscious evolution in terms of chaos theory. What seems to be chaotic disorderly process of trial and error, actually proved, in hindsight, to be quite an orderly progression of events that led to all of this...perfection." He gestured to the panorama before us. "Throughout history, there was a lot of *stuff* going on in many different directions. Some ideas achieved mass adoption, while other ideas, regardless of their worthiness, were discarded. You can picture this cloud of activity that includes all the archetypes; the Wanderers, the Settlers, the Inventors, and so on, all doing the things they like to do. Sometimes things went terribly wrong, but a lot of the time things went very right. Out of this cloud of chaos emerged an order. Things somehow all fell into place. We call it modern civilization. We have agriculture, writing systems, mathematics, music and art, electric lighting and indoor plumbing. And it all feels good.

"But, it all came about unconsciously over the millennia,

with the players merely acting in accordance with their Endowments, and unsuspectingly in alignment with the Evolutionary Impulse. People acted according to free will, yet were motivated by an unconscious urge that propelled their action toward a particular future. And this was all well and good. Past generations didn't need to be conscious of the evolutionary process they were a part of.

"But this veil of ignorance is now in the process of being lifted. In order for the human family to go any further, and indeed manage the advances that are taking place, we will need to embrace the Seventh Endowment and become Conscious Evolvers."

"Conscious Evolvers?"

Mr. Grant rocked his head from side to side, "Conscious Evolution...Conscious Evolver. I suppose eventually we'll come up with a better archetype to properly capture this Endowment. Or, perhaps the term Conscious Evolver will make enough of an imprint on our culture to survive as a suitable label. Who knows?"

We sat in silence for a few moments, our attention on the scene before us. "Look at the Washington Monument." The landmark obelisk gleamed as the dominant object in our view. "It almost looks like a rocket, doesn't it? You know that D.C. building codes prohibit construction of any building taller than the Washington Monument." He paused briefly but did not look at me for a response. "I mentioned earlier that the ruling classes throughout the ages have all had the great central construction projects—the towering structures that dominate the culture and serve as a focal point of communal activity. The pyramids, temples, castles, cathedrals, the Eiffel Tower, the Twin Towers, and the Sears Tower. It didn't really matter whether they were built for religious, political or commercial purposes. They were our unconscious attempts to reach the heavens. With rocket technology, we finally have the means to literally lift those monoliths toward heaven.

"One way to grasp the evolutionary progression is to imagine a slide show of all large structures throughout history, flipped through rapidly, it would almost look like an organism growing, becoming more refined and complex with each generation, culminating with the Saturn V rocket ready for takeoff—like a spore that grows on the surface of a dung heap and is ejected to carry the seeds of the organism in the hope of finding fertile ground to sprout anew. In serving what we believed to be a selfish purpose of erecting monuments to ourselves, we were all along, methodically and unconsciously, developing the capacity to carry the Earth seed to other planetary shores."

With that he said nothing for a few minutes. I felt a crack in my being, like something was breaking away.

"Another way to look at planetary inertia and the Seventh Endowment is to compare it to the transformation of a caterpillar to a butterfly. Once in the chrysalis, the caterpillar goes through a metamorphosis. What takes place inside the body of the caterpillar is a war between the caterpillar's old cells and the new butterfly cells, or what are called the *imaginal cells*. At first the new cells are rejected, and many die in the battle, but eventually the imaginal cells overwhelm the old order and a new creature is born.

"Right now the old caterpillar cells still dominate the planet, and they are doing their best to squash the imaginal cells that dare to show themselves."

I impulsively asked, "Then, there have been people in the world who are...Conscience Evolvers?"

"Yes, of course. Martin Luther King, Jr. and Mahatma Gandhi would be obvious examples, but there are and have been many in all walks of life throughout history. They are among the prophets, scientists and enlightened thinkers of history. In our time the numbers are increasing dramatically. So much so that individually today's Conscious Evolvers don't necessarily stand out the way King or Gandhi did in their day.

"The Conscious Evolver helps us to see beyond the parochial interests. She sees things in evolutionary terms and is willing to act according to that larger context. Eventually, when the Seventh Endowment takes firm hold in our collective consciousness, there will be little tolerance for actions that are taken for short-term, selfish gains. In this way we also recognize the Seventh Endowment as the Endowment of the 'we' and not of the 'I.'"

We paused on this note. I used the break to asked a question that had been on my mind since Mr. Grant first mentioned the Seventh Endowment. "If I have it right, the Conscious Evolver is an evolved version of the Visionary?"

"Yes, the Conscious Evolver is a masculine Endowment, an evolved version of the Visionary in that he is able to see vast possibilities for the future. The difference is two parts: first, the Conscious Evolver feels a strong sense of the holistic order that already exists in the yet unlived future, so it's not so much the feeling of being a kid in a candy store, which is how the Visionary can sometimes feel. The Conscious Evolver has a clear sense of how things should be in the future, and possesses a profound desire to bring that future into being. Second, the Conscious Evolver is interested in outcomes that benefit the whole. So we could say that Henry Ford was a visionary, but in the end his vision really had to do with selling lots of cars so that he could become rich and famous.

"Why do you think Martin Luther King and Mahatma Gandhi were so revered? It is that level of human being who embody the Seventh Endowment. But, to make all of this work, we need not just one or a few like King or Gandhi to break the inertia. We will need thousands, millions of people to walk in the same shoes as these men to truly transform the world and clear the way to our extended home in space, as well as bring humanity together in a new level of unity.

"Again, in order to fulfill the Obligation, we must become conscious of it. Clues of this truth can be found in nature. For example, it is the fetus in the mother's womb that chooses the time of its own birth. It is the baby that sends the signal to the mother's body that the time has come and she's ready to come out. It is not the mother's body that says it's time. Another example is the chick breaking out of its shell. Any kid growing up on a farm knows that you don't help chicks break out of the shell. When the chick is ready, it begins the process on its own. If you break the shell for the chick, its leg muscles will not develop as they would in the process of breaking out on their own.

"Humanity, like the baby and chick, must decide on its own that it will birth itself into the heavens. This has to be a conscious decision that we make collectively. Once we can come to the decision as a human family, then there will be very little that will stand in our way, and nothing can stop us. Planetary inertia becomes simply a hurdle to overcome.

"The Seventh Endowment is the process of consciously evolving ourselves and our collective civilization: to heal and connect the global human community—the Primary Obligation; to heal and achieve balance with the planet that gave us life—the Twin Obligation for Planetary Stewardship; and to send life out into the waiting Cosmos—the Twin Obligation for Space Migration.

"This capacity for conscious evolution is a unifying principle of all humanity. With it we will not only build colonies in space, we will also end war, crime, poverty, and every malady that has plagued humanity. Conscious Evolution allows us to see without reservation that we are all part of one living system. And with that perspective we could no more allow a child in Africa to go hungry than we could one of our own."

Mr. Grant stopped speaking. I realized I had been immersed in focused reverie. His words and voice had carried me off to another place. In the absence of his voice, the silence engulfed me. He sat up straight on the step, rested his hands on his lap, and closed his eyes. Night had fallen and artificial light bathed the scene before us. I was in a meditative state. I focused my attention on the Washington Monument. It seemed to shimmer. A shaft of light rose up from its column and extended into the infinite reaches of the sky. The shaft glowed brilliantly, and a fine web of light overlay the entire scene, similar to my vision on the Arizona mountaintop. One of the threads came from my chest and Mr. Grant's. I was overcome with bliss.

I lost consciousness for what could only have been a minute or so. I looked over at Mr. Grant who was smiling at me. I looked at the Washington Monument and the light vision was gone.

"To embody the Seventh Endowment is to consciously take responsibility for the future of humanity—all of it. That means you, personally, have to accept the responsibility that if the world is to survive, it is completely up to you. You must act in accordance with how the Evolutionary Impulse in moving within you, whether it's to build a space colony or to be a damn good first-grade teacher. Only a small percent of the population is needed to take action in response to the Evolutionary Impulse to expand into space. But, a big enough percent of the population will have to become awake enough to say 'Yeah. I get it,' in order for us to overcome the inertia."

He searched for my reaction. His call to take responsibility for all humanity unsettled me. Did he mean *me*, personally? Seeing the disquiet on my face, he let out a long hard laugh. "Don't sweat it, John. It's not all up to you." But, just as suddenly his mood became somber again, "Or is it? …That's something you'll have to chew on for a while to know what this all means for you. But, for certain, there are many people who are accepting that level of responsibility and choosing to be Conscious Evolvers in the world. We see these individuals most urgently in environmental activism, civil and human rights, anti-poverty efforts, and so on. The Conscious Evolvers in fields relating to space migration are here as well. Because of our planetary inertia, many Conscious

Evolvers in the space arena lack the confidence of their own conviction. At times they will even question the very passion that is pounding in their chest, and too easily accept the delays and inefficiencies in moving our society toward space migration. They'll too quickly admit that even though they hold that vision as central to their personality, the prospects for such a future are too distant for us to meaningfully advance in this era.

"You see, by denying the immediacy of the Evolutionary Impulse that we feel inside is the very act of giving in to the planetary inertia. But if we can attain the perspective of the Conscious Evolver we create much greater clarity around our intentions. The Conscious Evolver becomes conscious of the Evolutionary Impulse itself. For those who can achieve this state of being, much of the internal struggle, insecurity and uncertainty fades into the background, and they are able to take decisive action to fulfill that calling that the Evolutionary Impulse is pointing to.

"Therefore, the full emergence of the Seventh Endowment is the key to our fulfillment of the Obligations. While this emergence is happening spontaneously to some degree, complete success will only come when those who feel the pull of the Obligation decide for themselves, beyond a shadow of a doubt, that space migration is essential to human existence, and with that knowledge are willing to put themselves on the line in pursuit of that goal."

His words were spoken with intensity that frightened me. My body was awash with vibrating tension. "But,…why tell me all this?" My voice was shallow and weak compared to his deeply graveled tones. As the full weight of the Obligation came crashing down on me, I felt woefully inadequate to the call that Mr. Grant was making.

As my head reeled, Mr. Grant studied me, then responded compassionately, "Why that's simple, John. You asked. You said you *had* to know the meaning of the plaque. That told me that you possessed the capacity to express the

Seventh Endowment. Unconsciously, you said you were ready to evolve."

The floor of my being fell out from under me. I sat next to Mr. Grant on the steps of the Capitol Building, but I was also adrift in empty space. There was nothing for me to hold onto. My moorings to reality had been severed.

After what seemed an eternity, Mr. Grant continued in as gentle a voice as I had ever heard him use, "John, this is only an invitation. You don't have to accept or do anything about it. If you do accept this challenge, it will be unbelievably difficult and exhilarating. If you do not accept it, you will be forced to block the Evolutionary Impulse from your thoughts. Unfortunately, attempting to ignore this truth now that you have come this far will be particularly difficult."

He laughed again at my blank response. He did not seek an absolute answer from me on that night, but my heart was full of wonder and peril of what the Seventh Endowment represented. Through Mr. Grant I saw the world from that higher perspective. Things that once seemed important no longer were. The distant future was as palpable as the present moment.

THE INTENTION

The euphoria I felt in the wake of my experience on the Capitol steps, as powerful as it was, would soon subside. That's when the real work began. It would be a long road to internalize the knowledge of the Obligations. At first I was hyped. I was impatient about space settlement. I wanted Mr. Grant to sponsor legislation. I organized congressional briefings. I joined the advocacy groups that embraced space settlement as a long-term goal.

There were times when I didn't feel my efforts were making progress quickly enough, and frustration would creep in. At those times I began to doubt myself and by extension I doubted the veracity of the Obligation and even Mr. Grant's sincerity. I questioned the whole premise of the Obligation the way I did on the Mall after the Weinstein vote. Sometimes I wished I had never asked about the plaque in the first place. I didn't want it to be *all up to me*, as Mr. Grant put it. And then, the feelings of doubt passed. I would wake up the next day with renewed resolve to give myself to the call of the Obligations.

All this personal drama only amused Mr. Grant, both the lows and the highs. It took me a while to understand that the Obligation and being a Conscious Evolver was less about any particular actions I took and more about stabilizing an internal position that was in alignment with them. "Your actions matter, of course," Mr. Grant said. "But, you can't get to the top of the tree with a single bound. You must be content climbing to the first branch first. It should be enough to know that you are climbing the right tree whether or not you reach the top."

If my waffling entertained Mr. Grant, it was an annoyance to Tara who was already well aligned with the Obligation for planetary stewardship. She loved it when I was at ease with the new perspective. But she was less patient with my manic depressive mood swings.

About a month after the Arizona trip, I confronted Mr. Grant on my feelings of doubt about the Obligations, and my part in it. The office was quiet one evening and I took the opportunity to interrupt Mr. Grant who was catching up on personal correspondence to campaign contributors.

We had settled into an ease with each other that no longer required much preamble with regard to the Obligations. At any time when we were alone I could ask him a question and he'd answer. After making me wait a minute while he finished a hand-written note, he explained, "Emerging into the Conscious Evolver for most people is a process. There can be leaps forward, but those are usually preceded by long spells of little changes. Holding the view of the Obligations allows us to make, if we are paying attention, the right small decisions that will eventually lead to the great leaps forward we need to make. But, unfortunately, you can never be a hundred percent sure you've made the right decision. So all you can do is be sincere in your *intentions*. Hopefully, if you live long enough, you will look back with hindsight and see whether or not the decisions you made were right.

"By simply being exposed to the knowledge of the Obligations you are already changed. There isn't anything in particular you need to do. Like Columbus' discovery of the

New World or Darwin's Theory of Evolution, the Obligations perspective will force people to reconsider the the nature of human life and our relationship to the world that supports us. Yes, there are actionable imperatives inherent in the Obligations, but paradoxically, what we do with the knowledge is not as important as simply embracing it intellectually and emotionally. The actions will be taken. People will step up, and many already have, to fulfill the Obligations. You've started to take action yourself. Whether or not you personally succeed is of no particular consequence.

"People who feel the Evolutionary Impulse toward the space migration Obligation have always been in our midst, though their desires have most often been choked to death before they could do their work. At best they were considered ahead of their time. More often they were labeled crackpots. Either way, they were marginalized for the obvious reason that although they may have felt the Evolutionary Impulse to expand life into space, they simply had no means to do so. That is all changed now and we are in the end game of fulfilling the Obligation. It's not going to happen tomorrow. We know that. But the light at the end of the tunnel can be seen. It may take us fifty years, or a hundred or more, but the wheels are in motion. Sometimes they'll stick and sometimes it may look as if no progress is being made at all. How quickly we reach that goal will depend on how much those who care about such matters keep their Intention on the goal. A sizable portion of the population, and ultimately all of us, will eventually embrace these Obligations as unquestionable. The sooner people can embrace these truths, the sooner the barriers will come down, the more the inertia will be overcome, and the sooner the actions you and others take collectively will lead to the fulfillment of the space-migration Obligation."

His countenance was so emphatic, I was hesitant to pursue my query further. "I see what you're saying and it makes sense to me. But I feel frustrated. I'm finding it hard to determine what I am supposed to do, personally, in response to the space migration Obligation."

He first laughed at my confusion. "Well, I already said that you don't *have* to do anything. If you feel compelled to take action, and clearly you do, you'll want to be patient. Listen. Watch. Be attentive to what is going on around you. You should adopt a *mindfulness* in your actions. Stop creating judgments about everything you see. Stop worrying about the past and the future so much. Mindfulness will help you to be present to what is right in front of you now. This will lead to increased sensitivity to knowing the right action to take in the present moment. Which is really the only time you can do anything anyway."

"Excuse me, Mr. Grant, but I'm not sure I'm following you."

"Yes, it's a little hard to explain. But, you've already made some progress toward mindfulness. You've mentioned that Tara has been showing you how to meditate. Meditation is a wonderful way to settle the mind, and bring it into the present moment, to eliminate bothersome distractions and gain attentiveness to what is important. Don't be so impatient about what you should do. But don't be timid about taking action, either, even though it may not feel like you're making progress. I've already said that there is no guarantee you're taking the right action, but with mindfulness you have a better shot at getting it right. So, if you're not sure what to do, sit in meditation for a while and listen and let the answers come to you instead of chasing after them."

It was true that during periods when I meditated with Tara I felt more at ease. Problems didn't agitate me as much and were easier to resolve. And my confidence in my commitment to the Obligations perspective was firm. But, when I let my meditation routine lapse, the old doubts and worries quickly took over my thoughts.

"You see, the most important part you've already achieved. You've arrived, I believe, at a place where there is no question in your mind that humanity must in the quickest time frame possible begin to migrate some of its population into space. That is the right position to take. What you do to help fulfill that mandate is still an open question."

I still wasn't satisfied. "It all just seems too big for anyone to take on as a serious goal. What would it take to build a space colony? What technology do we need? What laws need to be passed? What international partnerships would have to be formed? How would it be financed, governed, maintained? There are just too many pieces to even begin to get a handle on what to do that would be effective."

There was a slight tone of impatience in his voice. "Here's where we need to clear something up. The Seventh Endowment, the capacity for conscious evolution, is not only about realizing that we are all One. In a practical sense, it illuminates a way to engage in the world and *with each other*. The Seventh Endowment is emerging now because it is only with this capacity that we will be able to address the most challenging remaining problems the human race is facing— including and especially the amazingly complex task of building off-world cities. This Endowment makes it all possible because of its two main qualities: first, the ability to create unshakable *intention* for a particular outcome that is for the good of the whole; and second, a trust in collective intelligence and abilities of all participants drawn to a given project. In other words, you alone can't know all the answers. No individual could. It will take the combined commitment of many individuals to contribute in their own unique way to pull this project off. What you really want to focus on is holding the clarity of the shared Intention to achieve the goal.

"If you can approach this challenge from the perspective of the Seventh Endowment, you'll find that traditional ways of doing things will quite often not be good enough. The only thing that will matter is going with the best way. Methods will be easily adopted or abandoned according to their effectiveness. The notion of working with any particular 'system' will become anachronistic. There will be no 'system' other than those that fit the needs of the moment.

"There will be no Master Builder. No Werner von Braun or Sergei Korolev. There will be dozens or hundreds or thousands of such men and women spontaneously taking charge of myriad aspects of the project."

"I'm sorry, Mr. Grant. But, I still don't see the structural framework for how this will all come about. Are you talking about a U.N. entity, an International Consortium, maybe?"

Shaking his head, he exclaimed, "No. No. You're missing the point. The most important thing again is the *Intention* of those who are passionate about fulfilling the Obligation. They will be the ones, together, who will determine *how* the project will be realized and managed."

I was still puzzled. I couldn't see a workable blueprint for action in anything he was saying.

He sighed and his voice dropped, "John, all they need is a place to gather so they can engage in the process together. Do what you can to fan the flames of their commitment and sense of urgency. They need a place where the Evolutionary Impulse can run free in pursuit of the Obligation. If such places can be created and nurtured, it just may be that in a very short time the space migration Obligation will be fulfilled. As you step into this field of action, others who feel the Evolutionary Impulse in the same way will automatically respond in equal measure. So, it is not you at all, but the Evolutionary Impulse itself that is moving and you are merely someone who is willingly caught in its field of influence."

I pondered this for a few moments. I understood what he was saying, but still struggled to understand what such an engagement would look like.

Seeing my confused look, he offered, "Again, for now don't worry about just how this will all come about. Simply stay with the essence of your Intention. And be mindful."

That was the end of our conversation, but I used the opportunity to ask a question that had been on my mind since the evening on the Capitol steps. "The Seventh Endowment, the capacity for conscious evolution, you explained thoroughly. But, what about the Eighth Endowment? The Seventh Endowment's feminine counterpart. You made so much of the pairing of Endowments. Isn't the same true for the Seventh Endowment?"

"It's about time you asked me that." He let out a big laugh. "We're still evolving, aren't we, John? I think you see that. Of course there's an Eighth Endowment. And probably more beyond that! But you don't need to worry about that now. We'll get to that another day. For now, just focus on the Obligation using the Seventh Endowment."

EPILOGUE

The night before I received the news of Mr. Grant's death I had a dream about seeing him in his Capitol Hill office. It had been nearly ten years since I had worked for him. In the dream, the office was as I remembered it, with the dark mahogany desk, leather chairs and mementos. He greeted me standing in front of his desk. His smile was open and inviting. This was not the sort of welcome I had ever received from him. Yet in this dream nothing could have been more appropriate.

All of his warmth and love washed through me. He was silently welcoming me back. He stepped forward and clasped my hand with both of his, shaking firmly, gleefully, smiling broadly. His face, in full frame, glowed with compassion and friendship. After several long wonderful moments of just being there together, he stepped back, smiled in my direction once more, turned and left the room through the side entrance that led directly into the corridor. I was left standing alone in his office and the dream ended.

A few days later I received a package from Mr. Grant's estate. The cover letter from the lawyer said that he had given instructions that the enclosed item be forwarded to me.

I knew what it was. I retreated with the package to the

quiet of my bedroom, away from the bustle of kids, spouse and dogs. I removed the brown-paper wrapping, and held the wooden object in my hand. I ran my hand over the familiar engraving.

"The colonization of space will be the fulfillment of humankind's obligation to the Earth."

I stared at the plaque for a long while and, without warning, the old familiar feeling of heightened awareness came over me. I had not experienced the sensation in a very long time, and never so intensely since those weeks I first learned the meaning of the Obligation.

All of the teaching that Mr. Grant imparted to me years before came rushing back to my consciousness in a torrent. Like a wind blowing through me. I became emotional. Tears welled in my eyes. Once again, I viscerally felt the sense of urgency that he conveyed to me that night on the Capitol steps.

In the years since leaving Mr. Grant's employment I had drifted far away from the truth I learned about the Obligation. The deep sleep began about the time Tara left DC for a job in Seattle. Though we had professed eternal love for one another, we were on different paths. So when the job offer came, we both knew it was time to end the relationship. Once she was gone, I stopped meditating, and made only sporadic attempts to resume the practice. Mindfulness became an occasional fleeting whisper, a momentary reminder that there was something important I was missing. I stayed involved in space-advocacy causes and took some satisfaction in that. But with each year, I had less and less time to devote to such activities. Not long after Tara moved to the West Coast, I fell in love with the woman who would become my wife. We built a happy family together. Life was just fine for a while.

Sitting with plaque in hand, the ancient feelings were rushing through me again. The room was dim with the late afternoon light coming through the sheer curtains. It was all different in that moment. The feeling was overwhelming.

There was no excuse sufficient to deny the truth of this urgency I had learned about so many years earlier.

It was a sensation of having just awoken from a long sleep. I looked down at my hands. They were unfamiliar somehow, as was the whole room. I wiped the wetness from my face and looked at myself in the mirror. I was startled by how old I looked. The last time I looked at myself while in a state of heightened awareness I had been ten years younger. I had been asleep for all that time. In the quiet of my suburban bedroom, something had shifted, leaving me no longer able to ignore the responsibility of the Obligation.

Over the next few days, the sensation stayed with me. I relived the time with Mr. Grant discussing the Endowments and the Obligation. I reconnected with the memory of each of incredible six individuals he had selected to represent the Endowments. And, of course, I recalled the mountain hike with Tara Bingham. It was at that time that I chose to put down in writing as much about those weeks as I could recall. I found buried in a drawer the long version of the floor speech I had written for him, which served as a perfect outline and great resource. That seemed to be a good place to start, at least.

It was less than three weeks after I received the plaque in the mail that I found myself in southern Arizona on a business trip. I decided to take the opportunity to retrace the hike I had shared with Tara many years earlier. I thought the climb might help inform how I should respond to the old feelings that were now rekindled inside of me.

I found the trail head. The wooden pole with faded blue paint had been replaced by a more durable plastic and metal marker. It was about the same time of year. The flowers of cactus plants were blooming. I was glad to be better outfitted with proper hiking shoes, wide brimmed hat, a day pack of water and snacks. A steady breeze lessened the oppressive heat of the rising sun. If I was out of shape the first time I made the climb, I was certainly worse-off the second. I stopped frequently along the trail and took my time on the steepest parts. More than once I questioned the wisdom of ascending to the peak, and considered turning around before I hurt myself.

With a sweat-soaked t-shirt clinging to my torso I made a final fitful climb onto the plateau of the peak. A young couple was there, about the same age as Tara and I had been when we first made the trip together. They were friendly and expressed concern for my wellbeing. I assured them that I would be fine as soon as I caught my breath. Breathing through my mouth, I surveyed the view. It was as I remembered. It was still majestic despite the noticeable increase in housing developments in the distance. The young couple said goodbye, satisfied that I would survive, and made their way back down the mountain, leaving me alone with the silence.

I found the shaded spot and sat cross-legged once again. I took the plaque from my backpack and placed it on the ground in front of me. Staring at the object, and recalling Tara's instructions, I guided myself into meditation. I easily sank into a deep state of relaxation.

I sat still. I could have lingered there indefinitely as my bodily sensations melted away. But the absolute stillness was not to last. It started as a sensation at the base of my spine. I felt a tingling that moved up my back. When the feeling reached my mid-section I began to feel my body vibrating, almost imperceptible at first, but as this energy rose higher, the vibration became more pronounced. I was shaking. The energy accelerated up through my chest, through my throat and up to the top of my head. And then, with a whoosh, I felt myself ascending at a rapid speed into the sky. I was shot into the void of space. I passed the moon, and like some *Star Trek* special effect, I watched stars whiz passed me. I could see my destination. The center of the Galaxy. The mass of concentrated hot gases. I merged with the center and saw again the connecting threads. They crisscrossed every part of the galaxy, making connection between planets and stars. I was aware of the many races of sentient beings on other worlds that were also connected to these fibers. Then I saw the fibers extend outward from this galaxy, reaching neighboring and distant galaxies. And they all too were connected in this web. I became aware of the collective consciousness of all that I witnessed, as well as the consciousness of the individuals. There was an absolute collective Oneness in all of it. The vision of the universe connected by strings of light increased in intensity until I lost consciousness.

I came back into my body with a slurp of saliva. I opened my eyes. Everything had a shimmering quality. My body was blissfully tingling. I wasn't sure if I had gotten the answer I was looking for, but the experience did immerse me in a powerful experience of transcendence. What was clear to me was that I could no longer do nothing in the face of what I knew about the Obligation. That much was certain.

I sat alone among the boulders and brush with the sun sinking toward the horizon. I could almost hear the voice of Mr. Grant encouraging me forward. Urging me to get into the mix and push the space settlement agenda again. Or was it the voice of the Evolutionary Impulse itself? I suspected the two are the same.

I lifted the plaque from the ground, returned it to my backpack and carefully began my descent from the mountaintop.

Afterword

I wrote this book as a vehicle to express my philosophical view on the evolution of the universe and humankind's part in it. I could have presented the material in non-fiction prose, as some had suggested, but I felt the allegorical teacher/seeker plot structure would help to make the ideas more accessible to readers. I hope I have succeeded. If sufficient interest is piqued by this work, I will be more than eager to attempt a more scholarly treatment of the principles put forth in these pages.

With one exception, the characters in the book are all fictional and are not intended to resemble actual people. That one exception is Mr. Grant, whose personage in part is drawn from the late Congressman George E. Brown, Jr. In developing the story, I followed the writer's maxim to "write what you know." Early in my career, I worked on Capitol Hill for Congressman Brown, whose brawny stature is every bit Mr. Grant's. I was a young aide who worked on space policy issues, so this was a familiar and appropriate setting in which to craft my story. Many of Cong. Brown's devoted staffers and supporters actually did in fact consider him a "guru" in many ways. He had a richly curious intellect. He saw things in a larger context and was inclined to quote philosophical and spiritual writings. One of his favorite quotes, "Where there is no vision, the people perish" (Proverb 29:18), was permanently inscribed on the wall in the House Science and Technology Committee hearing room during his tenure as the committee's chairman. It was Congressman Brown who introduced the Space Settlement Act of 1988, a bill I wrote for him. He championed the measure for its inclusion into the NASA Authorization bill, which was signed into law by President Ronald Reagan. Though I never engaged in a conversation with Congressman Brown that in any way resembled those between the story's characters John and Mr. Grant, I like to think that he would have appreciated the philosophical inquiry presented in their dialogue.

Many of the philosophical and scientific concepts in this book were liberally drawn from the works of extraordinary thinkers. At the risk of leaving out key individuals, the following are those who have most influenced my thinking:

Dr. Gerard K. O'Neill (1927-1992): He was the genius who started my journey of wonderment of the possibilities in space. Dr. O'Neill convinced the world that human settlement of space was a real possibility with his 1976 book *The High Frontier.*

Frank White: Frank is an old friend and closest kindred spirit, who first opened my eyes wide to the evolutionary nature of human expansion into space. In his pivotal book *The Overview Effect: Space Exploration and Human Evolution,* he wrote, "The purpose of human space exploration cannot be found in human desires and ambitions alone, but must be viewed as a phenomenon actively encouraged by universal forces." Therein lays the kernel of the Obligation perspective.

Barbara Marx Hubbard: Barbara is an amazing soul whose path I was privileged to walk in for a short time. She is an author, futurist, the leading visionary in the Conscious Evolution discourse, and a space evolutionary to the core. She was an early and generous supporter of Dr. O'Neill and the story of her epic attempt to purchase a Saturn V rocket to send a commercial mission to the moon in the early seventies is a tale worthy of major motion picture.

Andrew Cohen: Andrew is an important contemporary spiritual teacher who is also an unflinching champion of evolutionary spirituality, and speaks forcefully about the Evolutionary Impulse. As I describe later, it was in his presence that the insight of the Obligation first crystallized in my mind.

Teilhard de Chardin (1881-1955): This Jesuit priest-theologian and a distinguished geologist-paleontologist first suggested, in *The Phenomenon of Man,* that humankind was evolving to higher and higher states of consciousness.

Howard Bloom: Howard is the prolific genius whose exhaustive study of the history of the universe, human civilization, and science has drawn stunning conclusions explaining why we are the way we are. His books, including *Global Brain* and *The God Problem,* are masterpieces of finding the underlying relationships of all things.

Krafft Ehricke (1917-1984): This German rocket scientist wrote forcefully of the Extraterrestrial Imperative, the idea that humanity can no more remain Earth-bound than a baby can remain in the mother's womb.

Ken Wilbur: Ken is great contemporary American philosopher, whose expansive work on Integral Consciousness helped me to see all life processes as interconnected.

Eric Chaisson: Eric is a cosmologist whose work on Cosmic Evolution has truly expanded Darwinian Theory to encompass all there is in the universe.

In addition, Don Beck's work on the theory of Spiral Dynamics is a theory of the evolution of social consciousness from earliest human culture to modern civilization.

I have provided a bibliography of books and articles by these and others that I recommend for further reading on concepts relating to the Obligation perspective.

I would like to also applaud the many space advocates who are already responding to the pull of the Obligation toward space migration. They are the Conscious Evolvers of the Seventh Endowment in our midst—those hard at work in today's space movement. Rick Tumlinson and Robert Zubrin are a couple of names that come immediately to mind. Tumlinson is Co-Founder of the Space Frontier Foundation and Chairman of Deep Space Industries. Zubrin is President of the Mars Society and author of *The Case for Mars*. Zubrin and Tumlinson are the "bad boys" of the space movement. Their irreverent approach to space advocacy has made them the bane of many in the aerospace establishment. Their influence, however, has literally turned the tide of history, and has set us on a course toward space settlement.

Equally effective, and perhaps more mainstream, are other space champions such as Peter Diamandis, Founder of the X PRIZE Foundation and the Singularity Institute, Elon Musk, Founder and CEO of SpaceX and Tesla Motors, Jeff Greason, Founder and CEO of XCOR Aerospace, Robert Bigelow, Founder and CEO of Bigelow Aerospace and George Whitesides, CEO of Sir Richard Branson's Virgin Galactic. These are among the most visible of a significant cadre of Conscious Evolvers who have unabashedly proclaimed their desire to help create a future that includes human settlements of space.

I particularly want to recognize my colleagues from the Alliance to Rescue Civilization, an organization that promoted *backing up civilization's hard drive* by building human-occupied arks on the moon and elsewhere as insurance against extinction level events on Earth. I was privileged to work on this effort with William E. Burrows, New York Times journalist and award-winning author of *This New Ocean* and *The Survival Imperative*, and the late Dr. Robert Shapiro, noted origins-of-life researcher and author of *Planetary Dreams*. These men exhibited the Protector Endowment in its purest form.

The list is long of those who are hard at work attempting to create a new civilization in space, and my apologies for many omissions worthy of mention. All of these individuals are carrying the banner. If they have their way, and I believe they will, life will spring anew on other worlds before this century is out.

All the great minds mentioned above inspired and helped me shape the full scope of the Obligation perspective. However, the distinctive element of the Obligation worldview I present in this book, to my knowledge, has not previously been articulated. You may, therefore, find it interesting to hear the story of my moment of revelation.

It was May 2002 and I was attending a five-day retreat in Lenox, Massachusetts. For those who have not participated in a spiritual retreat, the experience is a profound opportunity to let all of your preconceptions fall away in order to create an opening to receive new insights. It was on the third day. The morning meditation session had ended and nearly every other attendee had left the hall. I remained fixed in a deep meditative state with no desire to end the session. While it is difficult to articulate, it was in that state that I had for the first time what is called the experience of "the One without the second." In that moment I knew myself as the Absolute. It was truly a revelatory moment. There were no fireworks or grand visions like those John experienced. It was simply a supreme moment of stillness, an experience of being the Witness.

In my hotel room that evening, lying awake in bed, my thoughts turned to my passion for space settlement. I played with the old question that had teased my mind from a young age. *Why were people so interested in space exploration and settlement? Why was space settlement something that I felt we, as a civilization, had to do?* Then without warning there finally came an answer to my lifelong query. In an instant, as I stared at the ceiling, it became absolutely clear to me. From the very dawn of humankind's existence, we were fixed with the responsibility of one day carrying the seeds of life out into the universe. Space travel is not something we do for any other reason than that it is our *raison d'être*. It is encoded in our DNA. Life on Earth needed a way to spread beyond this planet, and it created the means to achieve that end: humankind. From the earliest tribal culture I saw the evolution of civilization rapidly progress, generation after generation. Incremental advance after incremental advance. It was a roiling cauldron of activity when taken as a whole, all of which landing civilization where it is today at the very threshold of space, poised to make the final push to fulfill that most ancient of primordial demands.

It was during this rush of recognition in a dark hotel room that I had an experience similar to that of the character John in this book where his body tingled. I got out of bed and looked in the mirror, and like John I barely recognized my own reflection. I felt that sense of looking out with eyes that had not looked out that way in a long time. For me it was a moment of awakening. From this kernel of insight, and many hours and years of contemplation on it, I developed broader concepts presented in the previous pages.

I am perfectly aware that there are non-spiritual explanations for my epiphany. The last thing I wish to do here is spark a discussion over whether I was touched by God, or just had a cool moment of insight. And from a practical standpoint, I don't think it matters either way. I share my story of awakening only to emphasize that these notions came spontaneously to me, whether divinely or neurologically induced.

So, where do we go from here? I suspect the challenges for the space movement going forward will be even greater than they have been to date, and will not ease up until we finally reach the essential milestone, when a community of people is living independently in a part of the solar system beyond Earth. Expansion after that point should be easier. I encourage you, if you are motivated by this challenge, to steel yourself for the difficulty ahead and not be distracted by naysayers, politics, economics and all the rest. It is my belief that you are engaged in a sacred struggle and must not let anything stand in your way. The space movement has been thriving since Dr. Gerard O'Neill inspired the formation of the L-5 Society in the mid-1970's. Many of those early activists joined the ranks of the budding, and now maturing, commercial space community. Their successes are inspiring new generations of activists who feel the urge to be part of this evolutionary process. We have reached an incredible threshold thanks to the efforts of the folks mentioned above and many others. But the going will get even tougher as we move steadily toward the end game.

So, if you're in this for the ride, buckle up. Things are going to get very bumpy. Your personal resolve and intention will be the only thing between success and failure. This is where a Conscious Evolver perspective is extremely useful. Granted, it may sound a bit esoteric. But, anyone seriously involved in helping to advance civilization toward space migration already is feeling the Evolutionary Impulse, and is likely already exhibiting the qualities of the Conscious Evolver Endowment.

If the perspective I've expressed in these pages resonates with you, I encourage you to explore more deeply the implications, and what it might mean in your life and the world around you. Dive into the writings of the authors mentioned above and others in related fields. I've included a limited bibliography for your consideration. You can also be part of the Obligation community at www.theobligationbook.com.

BIBLIOGRAPHY

Beck, Don and Cowan, Christopher. *Spiral Dynamics: Mastering Values, Leadership, and Change.* Malden, MA: Blackwell Publishing, 1996.

Bloom, Howard. *Global Brain: The Evolution of Mass Mind from the Big Bang to the 21st Century.* New York, NY: John Wiler & Sons, 2000.

Bloom, Howard. *The God Problem: How a Godless Cosmos Creates.* Amherst, NY: Prometheus Books, 2012.

Burrows, William E. *This New Ocean.* New York, NY: Random House, 1999.

Burrows, William E. *The Survival Imperative.* New York, NY: Forge Books, 2006.

Chaisson, Eric. *Epic of Evolution: Seven Ages of the Cosmos,* New York, NY: Columbia Univ. Press, 2006.

Chaisson, Eric. *Cosmic Evolution: Rise of Complexity in Nature,* Cambridge, MA: Harvard Univ. Press, 2001.

Cohen, Andrew. *Evolutionary Enlightenment: A New Path to Spiritual Awakening.* New York, NY: SelectBooks, 2011.

de Chardin, Pierre Teilhard. *The Phenomenon of Man* (1959). New York, NY: Harper Perennial, 1976.

Freeman, Marsha. *Krafft Ehricke Extraterrestrial Imperative.* Burlington, Ontario: Apogee Books, 2009.

Hubbard, Barbara Marx. *Birth 2012 & Beyond: Humanity's Great Shift to the Age of Conscious Evolution.* Shift Books, 2012.

Hubbard, Barbara Marx. *Conscious Evolution: Awakening the Power of Our Social Potential.* Novato, CA: New World Library, 1998.

Lovelock, James E. *Gaia: A New Look at Life on Earth.* Oxford. MA: Oxford University Press, 1979.

O'Neill, Gerard K. *The High Frontier: Human Colonies in Space.* New York, NY: William Morrow & Company, 1977.

Tumlinson, Rick & Medlicott, Erin. *Return to the Moon.* Burlington, Ontario: Apogee Books, 2005.

White, Frank. *The Overview Effect: Space Exploration and Human Evolution.* Reston, VA: American Institute of Aeronautics and Astronautics, 1st ed. 1987; 2nd ed. 1998.

White, Frank. *The New Camelot: Volume One: Camelot and the Overview Effect.* Kindle Books, 2012.

White, Frank. "The Overview Effect, the Cosma Hypothesis, and Living in Space," Chapter 1 in *Living in Space: Cultural and Social Dynamics, Opportunities, and Challenges in Permanent Space Habitats,* edited by Sherry Bell, PhD, and Langdon Morris, an Aerospace Technology Working Group Book, (2009).

Wilber, Ken. *A Brief History of Everything.* Boston, MA: Shambhala Publications, 1st ed. 1996, 2nd ed. 2001.

Zubrin, Robert. *Entering Space: Creating a Spacefaring Civilization.* New York, NY: Jeremy P Tarcher/Putnam, 1999.

Zubrin, Robert and Wagner, Richard. *The Case for Mars: The Plan to Settle the Red Planet and Why We Must.* New York, NY: Free Press, 1st ed.1996, 2nd ed. 2011.

ABOUT THE AUTHOR

Steven Wolfe has been a writer, speaker and advocate for the advancement of the space settlement concepts and related ideas for more than a quarter of a century. In the 1980s, Steve worked on Capitol Hill as a legislative aide to the late Honorable George E. Brown, Jr. (D-CA). He was the executive director of the Congressional Space Caucus, served on the board of directors of the National Space Society, was president of the New York Space Frontier Society, and an Advocate of the Space Frontier Foundation. He serves on the Board of Editors of the Journal of Space Philosophy. He is Program Director for SpaceCom, an international space commerce conference and exposition held in Houston, TX annually.

Contact Steven Wolfe at www.theobligationbook.com.

41649463R00141

Made in the USA
San Bernardino, CA
04 July 2019